Valley of Shadows

Heir to the Firstborn, Volume 7

Elizabeth Schechter

Published by Elizabeth Schechter, 2024.

Published by Raven's Wing Books

Editor: Michael Schechter

Cover design by GetCovers

Raven's Wing Books

ravens-wing-books.com

ISBN: 978-1-952598-53-1

Table of Contents

Dedication

To Corey, who was there when the journey through Adavar began,
but never got to see the end.
You are loved. You are missed.

Chapter One

T he sea was calling her. It always did — it was part of her, as much as the sky was part of her. Aeris leaned on the wall of the Water Walk and looked down at the canoes on the shore. The day after tomorrow, she'd answer the sea's call. She'd leave the Palace behind and go out on the Deep for a season with her father. Maybe this time, the part of her that was missing would be where they were supposed to be. She stood, stretching her wings wide, then folded them back against her back and leaned on the wall once more. One more day....

"You look like you're ready to leave already," a familiar voice said from behind her. An older man joined her at the wall, leaning next to her. He was solidly built, his skin perhaps a shade or two darker than her own, and he wore his long hair in twists, which were currently pulled back and tied at the nape of his neck. He leaned close enough to nudge her shoulder with his own. "Which, you can't. We still have the party tomorrow. The cutter should be here this morning, and everyone will want to see you. So no leaving early."

She nudged him back. "I know, Owyn. I just... maybe they're out there this time."

"Maybe," Owyn drawled. "All we've seen is that they weren't in the right place. So maybe they're back on the deep by now?" He shrugged and looked at her. "I know it bothers you. Truth be told, it bothers all of us. Nothing like this has ever happened before."

Aeris nodded. "All the lore says I'm supposed to find my Water first. I have everyone else and it's been nearly two years."

Owyn snorted. "And I here I thought we were done living in unprecedented times. I want some precedented times. Really. Any time now would be good."

Aeris giggled and straightened. "I'll find them. I know I will. It's just... where *are* they?"

"The last place you'll look." Owyn murmured. "That's what Fisher said. You'll find them in the last place you'll look." Then he shook his head. "Which... yeah, that makes sense. It's always the last place you look because once you have it, you stop looking."

Aeris took a deep breath, let it out, then looked at the sky. "I have my shift in the healing center soon," she said. "I should go in."

"I'll walk with you." Owyn straightened and fell in next to her as they walked to the stairs. "Did you eat this morning?"

"Tiras wouldn't let me leave the suite without eating," Aeris admitted. "They actually stood in front of the door and wouldn't let me open it until I ate my entire breakfast, including the porridge."

Owyn laughed out loud. "That's my Tiras. You have your hands full with that one. Your Fire got their stubborn from both parents."

"And has Gannet to back them up." Aeris smiled. "Tiras actually told me that they were going to have Gannet sit on me if I didn't eat."

"And Gannet would do it in a heartbeat. And not just because he's your Air and he adores you."

"He does," Aeris agreed. "But sometimes I think he loves my Fire more than he loves me. He'd fly to the moon for Tiras."

"And all it took was a broken nose." Owyn stopped at the bottom of the stairs and looked up at her. "You know, your bond with the three you already have is as strong as the bond we have with your mother. Don't worry about your Water. Once you find them, you'll be fine."

Aeris nodded, taking his hand as they walked toward the Palace. "We just need to find them."

THIS EARLY IN THE MORNING, the Palace healing center was cool and quiet. The only person Aeris was expecting to find there was Dyna, her Earth. No one had been surprised when Aeris had given the Earth gem to Dyna — they were as close as a pair could be already. They'd grown up together, then trained together as healers. Neither of them were interested in taking the other as a lover — there didn't seem to be a point. They already loved each other, and sharing a bed wouldn't make that love any deeper. So their relationship hadn't changed at all once Dyna wore the Earth gem, and the quiet, early morning shifts were their time to talk and share the way they had all their lives.

To Aeris' surprise, she heard voices when she opened the door to the healing center. She walked in, and smiled when a large wolf with a muzzle gone completely gray looked up at her, his tail swishing over the floor.

"Good morning, Howl," she said, going to kneel on the floor next to him. He rolled onto his back, and she scratched his belly as the voices came closer. She heard the squeaking before she looked up, but it wasn't a surprise. If Howl was here, then Karse wasn't going to be far away. And if Karse was here...

"Aeri girl!"

Aeris gave Howl a final pat and got up, going over to the wheeled chair to kiss Trey's scarred cheek. "Good morning, Uncle," she said. He smiled up at her.

"Hug?"

"Of course!" Aeris laughed and hugged him. "How are you feeling today?"

Trey shrugged slightly and waved one ruined hand. "Good. Feel good." He paused, looked up at Karse, smiled, then slowly and clearly said, "My man worries too much."

Karse burst out laughing. "Well, if my worrying means you'll say more than two words in a row, I'm going to keep doing it." He leaned down to kiss his husband. "Just a regular check," he added as he straightened. "Figured, it was quiet. There wasn't likely to be anyone here, so it gives Trey the time he needs, and it lets Aven do his work without rushing."

"My father is here?" Aeris looked back toward the examination rooms. "I didn't expect him to be. He's usually not on morning shifts."

"Benefit of being the senior healer on site," Aven said as he came out of an examination room. Dyna followed him, smiling when she saw Aeris. "I can sleep in and let my dawn bird daughter take the early shifts."

Aeris laughed and went to share breath with her father, going on her toes to kiss his cheek. He hugged her to his side, and she sighed and relaxed against her father's warmth.

"You ready to sail?" he asked.

"Looking forward to it, Fa," she answered. "Fa Owyn said he thought I was going to leave by myself this morning."

"Was he out on the Water Walk?' Aven asked. "I thought he'd gone to the kitchens." He paused, then laughed. "Oh, of course. Alanar and Vir are overdue on the cutter. He's watching the tide."

"Hard for him," Trey said, waving one hand. "Him here and them there. S'hard."

"Well, you are feeling good," Karse murmured. "Good enough to come watch the guards drill? Meri is out there. You haven't seen her for a while. She's gotten better."

Trey grimaced. "Not... no."

Karse sighed. "I thought that might be your answer. Come on. We'll go find Fancy, then I'll go make sure Meri isn't running roughshod over her brother."

"Tacen is sticking with practice?" Aven asked. "Even though he's decided not to go into the guard?"

"Yeah, he says it's good for him," Karse answered. "And I can't disagree. He'll follow his mother into service, but he'll also be able to break heads if he needs to. Can't see how that's a bad thing." He put his hand on Trey's shoulder. "So, shall I take you to help Fancy and Danir with the accounting?"

Trey sniffed. "Good for something, at least."

"Hey, none of that," Karse chided. He leaned down and kissed Trey. "You're good at a lot of things. And you're an expert at others."

Trey tipped his head back. "Really? What?"

"Being my man," Karse answered. "Being Fancy's man. Being Meri and Tacen's fa. Loving all of us. Do I need to keep going?"

Trey made a face. "Fine. You win. Fancy?"

"Let's go. She should be in her office." He moved to the back of the chair and started pushing. "Howl."

The wolf got to his feet, shaking himself all over. He turned toward them, then raised his head and growled. A moment later, they heard the deep tolling of a bell.

"What's that?" Dyna asked. "Wait... that's the Council bell!"

Aeris looked up at the ceiling. The last time the Council bell had rung, it had been the day her grandfather had died. "Fa?"

"I don't know, little bird." Aven looked up, frowning. "Get your Companions and go to the little Council room. Now."

AERIS AND DYNA WERE halfway to the Heir's suite when they met Tiras and Gannet coming the other direction. Her Air and her Fire were a study in opposites — Gannet was both unusually pale and unusually big for an Airborn — his long hair was almost white, as were his feathers, and he was nearly as tall as Aeris' uncle Othi. His wingspan was twice Aeris' own, and she didn't think he was finished growing. Tiras, on the other hand, was outwither — presenting as neither male nor female — and they could only be described as delicate. They were a month older than Aeris, as dark as Gannet was pale, and stunningly pretty. Tiras was so slightly built that it seemed as though they would blow away in a strong wind. But looks were deceptive — Tiras knew more about fighting than the rest of them put together, and had proved it by breaking Gannet's nose less than a month after the Heir's Progress had returned to the Palace. To be fair, Gannet admitted that he'd deserved it — his flock was one of the more old-fashioned ones, and he'd grown up believing that wingless Air only existed to be looked down on. He'd bristled at the idea of learning anything from Del until Owyn called him on his behavior, and explained just why Del had no wings. Gannet had been horrified and mortified in equal measure, but instead of learning his lesson, he'd found another target in Dyna. Once he learned that Dyna was part-Air and wingless, he'd started treating her like a servant. Patient Dyna had ignored him, and urged the others to do the same. He'd learn, in time.

Then Gannet said... something. Aeris wasn't certain exactly what — no one would tell her. But Tiras had lost their temper, lured Gannet out to the practice yards, and beat the big Air bloody. When called before the Firstborn, Tiras admitted to everything, and offered only the defense that some people needed their heads broken open so that sense could get in, a sentiment that caused two of Aria's Companions to burst out laughing. Once he'd stopped, Owyn promised to make sure that Gannet learned his lesson. Then he and Del had taken Gannet into a meeting room and locked the door.

An hour later, a chagrined and red-faced Gannet apologized to the Firstborn and her Companions, then to the Heir and her other two Companions. When Tiras attempted to apologize, Gannet refused to accept, and he insisted that there be no penalty against them, on the grounds that Tiras was right.

Aeris wasn't entirely certain, but she suspected that the pair had been lovers ever since.

"Aeris, what was that?" Tiras asked, spinning one of their wooden smoke blades. Gannet handed Aeris her belt quiver of javelins, and she noticed that he was also armed.

"It sounded important," Gannet added. "We weren't sure what it was, and I thought it was better to go armed than not."

"It's the Council bell," Aeris answered. "We were coming to get you. Fa says we're to go to the Little Council room." She strapped the belt of her quiver around her waist and looked at Dyna. "Being armed is a good idea. Dyna?"

"I have my blowpipe."

Aeris nodded. "I thought you might. Let's go." They started walking. "The last time the bell rang, it was the day my grandfather died," she said as they made their way through the halls. "I don't know why it's ringing now."

Tiras whistled softly. "Someone important died?"

"Or something important happened," Dyna said. "Hopefully, it's not a death." She looked at Aeris, then reached for her hand.

They filed into the Little Council chamber and found Danir waiting for them. The assistant Steward looked harried, but not upset, and Aeris felt her shoulders relaxing.

"Come through to the Hall," he said. "Your mother and her Companions are already seated."

"Uncle, what is it?" Aeris asked.

"News from the Temple," Danir said, and returned to the Hall. Aeris heard him announce them, but didn't move.

"Uncle Steward?" she whispered, and Dyna took her hand again. Tiras rested their hand on her shoulder, and Gannet moved to her other side.

"Let's go see," Gannet said softly. "Maybe it's... maybe it's nothing." He frowned. "An important nothing."

"Your counseling skills suck rocks, Gan," Tiras muttered. Dyna giggled, and Aeris smiled.

"Thank you," she said. "Let's go."

She led the way through the door to the Hall and toward the two daises. The higher dais bore five chairs, and all but two were occupied. At the center, in the seat marked by a circle of golden glass, was the Firstborn Aria, Aeris' mother. She had Aeris' youngest sister in her lap, which did much to calm Aeris' worries. If things were truly bad, Yana wouldn't be here.

Aeris led her Companions to the center of the hall, and they all bowed to Aria before making their way to the second, smaller dais to the left of center. Tiras stepped forward, whispering, "My turn!" as they offered their hand to Aeris, leading her to her seat. She bit down on a laugh — her Companions had devised their own schedule of who would be her primary escort on any given day, and refused to tell her how it worked. She suspected Tiras was the ringleader — they usually were. She took her place, with Gannet and Dyna on her right. On her left, just past the empty seat where her Water should be, Tiras took their own place. The smaller dais was angled slightly, so Aeris could see her mother, Owyn and Del. Her father and Treesi were nowhere to be seen.

"Mother? What's happened?" She rested her hands on the arms of the chair. "Word from the Temple, Danir said. Is Uncle Steward all right?"

Aria nodded. "Yes. He sent a message. And apparently, it's important enough that the messenger was waylaid on his way to the Palace. That's where Aven and Treesi are."

"Waylaid?" Gannet leaned forward in his chair. "Who would waylay a priest?"

"We don't know yet," Aria answered. "Once the messenger is in a better state, we'll see about some answers."

The doors to the hall opened, and Afansa came in, followed by Copper. Behind them were Aven and Treesi, walking on either side of a man wearing tattered and stained Temple livery. The stranger looked pale, and there were fading bruises visible on his face and neck.

"My Water?" Aria said as they approached.

"He'll be fine," Aven replied. "Worst of it was two broken ribs." He smiled at the stranger. "Lorn here will be sore for a day or two, but otherwise he's fine."

Lorn bowed. "Thank you, Waterborn."

"What happened?" Owyn asked. "Let's get that out of the way first."

Lorn turned to him. "I was sent with messages for the Firstborn and for Terraces. There's nothing unusual about that, so we didn't take any precautions and I traveled alone. I made camp a few nights ago, and... I don't know who they were, but they attacked at night. I never really saw them. They tried to kill me, and I barely got away. Lost my horse to them, so I just... kept on moving. It was closer to come here than go back, so I traveled by night, hid during the day, in case they were still looking for me."

Aria nodded. "And the message you have for us. You've told me already, but will you repeat it so that the Heir and her Companions can hear?"

Lorn turned slightly, pausing when he saw the empty chair. "Should I wait?" he asked. "For the Water?"

"They're not in residence at the moment," Aeris answered. "Please, go on."

Lorn nodded. "I was sent by the High Priest to tell the Firstborn and her Heir that Frayim has had a vision, and that it is imperative that the Firstborn and the Heir go to the Temple at once."

Tiras whistled softly. "Frayim... that's the one my fa calls the Seer, isn't it? Tall, thin enough to disappear if he turns sideways?" They looked at Aeris. "We met him, didn't we?"

Aeris nodded. "When we went to the Temple, after we found Gannet. He hasn't had a vision since before I was born." She frowned. "Mother, if we need to be on the road, I don't have to have a party. We can leave tomorrow."

Aria nodded, shifting a drowsing Yana on her lap, then laughing as Del came and picked her up, carrying her back to his own chair. "It will take longer than that to prepare the court to move, my dove. But we will not tarry, either. Afansa, is the day after tomorrow feasible for us to leave?"

"For how long?" Afansa asked.

Aria looked thoughtful. "I'm... not certain," she said slowly. "Plan for a month, I think."

"Feasible to leave in two days for a month?" Afansa frowned slightly, then looked at Danir. "Well?"

He closed his eyes, then nodded slowly. "It will be rushed, but I think so," he said.

"You are coming along very nicely," Afansa said, just loud enough that Aeris heard.

"Oh, was that another test?" Danir groaned.

"And you passed. Yes, Firstborn, we can have you on the road by the day after tomorrow. Now, what arrangements should I make for our visitor?"

"Lorn, you said you had messages to take on to Terraces," Aven said. "We could send you on your way on the cutter. It's due in today, and will sail back out tomorrow. Or we can take a canoe out today. In either case, you'll be there in a few hours."

"Ah... thank you, Waterborn, but... I don't..." Lorn looked down. "No boats."

"Sounds like he's like I used to be," Owyn said. "Lorn, you don't have to apologize. We'll just get you set up with a horse. Right?"

Aria nodded. "Danir, if you would arrange that? Supplies for the road, and a horse."

"And in the meantime, a change of clothes and a rest," Afansa added. "Come with us, Lorn, and we'll take care of you."

Lorn bowed toward Aria, then turned to the lower dais. "You're the one, aren't you?" he said. "The child of all four tribes."

Aeris sat up a little straighter in her chair. "I... I'm my parents' daughter. That's all I can say for certain."

Lorn smiled. "That's all any of us can say, isn't it?" He bowed, and followed Afansa and Danir from the Hall.

"Well, that was weird," Tiras murmured. "He's from the Temple. Is he one of those... what are they called? The sorry ones?"

"Penitents," Owyn answered. "And maybe? There were a lot of them who stayed as priests back when the Temple was rebuilt." He sighed. "Right. Time to get ready to get on the road again?"

"A short trip, I hope," Aria said. "It's been some time." She paused. "I regret that it will mean putting off your season with the family canoe, my Water."

"We'll take our season when we come back," Aven said. "The family will understand."

"What will the family understand?"

Aven whipped around, his jaw dropping. "Fa?"

Standing in the open door were Aeris' grandparents, Jehan and Aleia. Behind them...

"Allie!" Owyn crowed. "Where have you been?"

Alanar smiled, stepping into the hall, followed by his son Vir. Alanar stopped, cocked his head to the side. Then he frowned. "What's happened? Why is everyone in the Hall?"

"It's a good thing you got here when you did," Aven said. "We have a lot to tell you."

Chapter Two

Go to the Salon, Aria told Aeris and her Companions. Wait for us there.

Somewhat early in Milon's reign as Firstborn, he'd realized that there was no single room in the Palace where his entire personal circle, and his daughter's entire personal circle, and the increasing number of children could all be at the same time. So several rooms had been renovated and combined to create the Salon — a space that was large enough for everyone to be comfortable, where the children could play, and the adults could gather to talk. There were fireplaces on two walls, and cozy chairs for sitting and reading or napping. One corner of the room was entirely soft toys for the smallest children. Most of Aeris' childhood memories involved things that happened in the Salon, and it was usually her favorite place in the entire Palace.

Usually. Today, it felt more like she was being sent to her room.

"Is it just me, or were we just told to run off and play?" Gannet asked as he walked over to a quartet of chairs arranged in a small group. He sat down in one of the two low-backed chairs.

"It's not just you," Tiras agreed, dropping down to sit on the floor at his feet, setting their blades on the ground next to them. "They always include us in the talks and discussions and negotiations. Always. Owyn says it's important for us to learn, so we're not playing catch up the way they had to. This... this doesn't make sense."

Aeris took the other low-backed chair and frowned slightly, trying to put her thoughts in order.

"Aeri?" Dyna perched on the arm of the chair, putting her arm around Aeris' shoulders. "What are you thinking?"

Aeris leaned into her side and sighed. "That it's something to do with the people out in the hills who think I'm Axia come again," she answered. "The ones who hurt my father and Uncle Trey, and who kidnapped me when I was a baby."

"I thought they were all gone, though," Tiras said. "I mean... we all learned about it. The woman who did it was executed."

"She was, but we don't know if there were others. There are reports from the troops that went out into the hills. They didn't find anyone, but that doesn't mean much," Aeris said. "I don't know very much other than what's in the reports and the history texts. Mother doesn't like to talk about it, and the rest of her Companions take their lead from her."

"Which explains why we got sent out, I suppose," Gannet said. He leaned forward and started combing his fingers through Tiras' hair. Tiras sighed and leaned back, closing their eyes as Gannet started braiding. "So what do we do now?"

"Wait?" Dyna suggested.

Aeris chuckled, then straightened as Dyna tensed. They both turned toward the door, which opened to reveal a handsome young man in guard livery. He looked around, saw them and stepped inside, smiling. Aeris felt Dyna shiver as he came toward them.

"I thought the Salon was empty," he said. "I'm surprised you're not in the Hall. The Captain just went in."

"The Firstborn wanted to speak in confidence," Aeris answered. "I didn't think your rounds took you through the Salon, Lancir."

He laughed. "They usually don't. I was going past and I thought I heard voices. I wanted to be sure no one was in here that shouldn't be." He grinned. "We caught two maids and a footman in here one night. Told them to find a more private spot."

Aeris laughed. "Really?"

Lancir nodded. He shifted from one foot to the other, his dark hair falling over his forehead as he coughed. His cheeks colored slightly as he bit his lip, then asked, "Healer Dyna? I... I've been wanting to ask... if we might meet on the Water Walk after my shift?"

"Oh," Dyna breathed. Aeris looked up to see that her face was pink. "Oh, I... I'd like that. If I can."

Lancir smiled and bowed, then straightened and winked, his bright blue eyes merry. "Healers are busy. I know. I'll come find you when I'm off-shift and we'll see if you're free." He saluted. "My Heir." He turned and walked away, whistling. Dyna shifted on the arm of the chair, and Aeris moved over to let her share the seat.

"How long have you been hoping he'd ask?" Gannet asked.

"And why didn't you ask him first?" Tiras added.

Dyna's face turned even more pink. "I... didn't want him to feel any pressure... because I'm a Healer and a Companion, and he... well, have you heard his history?"

Aeris shook her head. "No. Captain Karse doesn't gossip about his men."

"Meri does," Tiras murmured. Their eyes were still closed. "But I haven't heard this. Tell, Dyna."

Dyna glanced at the door, then lowered her voice. "Meri told me that his village in the foothills was wiped out by raiders when he was young. The people who found him and took him in treated him like a slave. He ran away when he was old enough, and he's been on his own ever since. He entered the guard in Terraces three years ago, and they sent him here. He doesn't have anyone or anywhere else to go, and I don't want him to feel like he has to spend time with me to keep his place."

"How did Meri get all of that out of him?" Gannet asked. "She been spending time with him?

"Not like that," Dyna answered. "You know Meri. She prefers girls. She's been helping him with reading, and they're friends."

"And you're about as subtle as a thrown brick," Tiras teased. "I think the entire Palace knows you like him."

"Tiras, that isn't nice," Aeris chided. "Don't tease."

Tiras winced. "Yeah, that was a bit too far. Sorry, Dyna." They smiled. "You know I still love you, right?"

Dyna laughed. "I know. I—" She stopped and turned as the door opened and a pair children ran into the Salon. One of them laughed and shouted, "Dyna!"

"Mannit?" Dyna got to her feet. "I... Lachin? What are you... Mama!"

Three adults followed the children into the Salon, and Aeris stood up as Dyna ran across to hug her mother. Aeris followed, hearing Gannet and Tiras behind her. The two red-haired men with Trista both grinned, and one of them gave an exaggerated bow. Aeris laughed. "Uncle Astur, Uncle Elaias, it's good to see you. I didn't think we were going to. I thought you had... something? A project?"

Elaias elbowed Astur gently, then stepped forward and hugged Aeris. "We do, and this is the next step of it." He looked past Aeris. "Tiras, Gannet. Good to see you both." He frowned slightly. "Still not yet?"

Aeris shook her head. "Hopefully once I get back from my season I'll have someone to introduce to you."

"Well, it'll be a trip," Astur said. "We're not going back to Terraces for a bit."

"What?" Dyna asked. "Fa?"

Elaias smiled and held his arms open for Dyna. "I've been missing the mountains, lammie," he answered as he hugged her.

"And you can tell, because the hill folk accent is getting stronger," Astur teased.

Elaias snorted, "I always had more of it than you or Treesi or Minna ever did. Fa never could beat it entirely out of me," he said. "And yes, I'm missing it. Missing the height, and the sky."

"And not getting sick," Trista murmured.

Elaias laughed. "Yes. I'm missing not getting waterlung every winter because of how wet it is in Terraces. So, with the Senior Healer's permission, we're going back to open a healing center near to where Astur and I were born. That's the project we've been working on."

"You're... you're moving to the mountains?" Dyna repeated, her eyes wide. "I... where?"

"Not entirely to the mountains. Just to the crossroads where the Western Road meets the Mountain Road," Elaias answered. "There's already a settlement there, so we won't be starting from scratch. And once we're established, we can send healers on circuit to the Solstice village and the Temple, and to the little villages in the hills." He put one arm around Trista. "We've been working on these plans for a few years, and the main healing center is finally staffed enough that Senior Healer says they can afford to lose a level five and a level four, and a half-dozen trainees."

"But... Uncle Arjin and Aunts Pal and Sel and Jes?" Dyna asked. "Are they here?"

Astur grimaced. "They're... not coming," he admitted. "Not yet. Jes and Sel both say that the boys are still too young, and it'll be rough until we get settled. I'll be making the trip back to see them regularly, and once the center is running, then they'll come join us."

"Come in and sit," Aeris said. "I'll send for food."

"Might want to wait on that for a bit. The Firstborn said that she'll be joining us shortly," Elaias said as Aeris led them to couches underneath the window. "I wasn't expecting the Palace to be quite this... on its ear. Something to do with your naming day, Aeri?"

Aeris shook her head. "No. But I'll let my mother explain," she said.

"They're coming," Tiras added.

Astur blinked. "You're really that sensitive?" he asked, glancing back toward the closed door. "You can tell?"

Tiras shrugged one shoulder. "Owyn says I'm at least as sensitive as he is, and he expects me to start hearing the rest of the circle any day now."

"You're going to hear Gannet first, and we all know it," Aeris said. She held her hand out, and Tiras smiled and let her pull them to her side. She kissed their cheek, then turned back to the others. "Will Aunt Minna and Uncle Versi be going, too?"

"Ah... no," Elaias answered. Astur laughed.

"I don't think we could get Minna back to the mountains with a team of horses," he said. "She and Versi are happy, and she wants to stay with Mam. She's promised to help with the boys while I'm gone."

The door opened, and Aria and her Companions came inside first. Aeris looked at her father and straightened, letting go of Tiras. Aven was clearly trying to hide how angry he was, and wasn't doing a good job of it.

"*Fa?*" she signed.

He shook his head and turned toward the people who followed him — her grandparents. But it was the pair behind them that made her gasp.

"Fisher! Grandfa Mem!" She ran across to them and hugged her brother tightly. "What are you doing here? I thought you were in New Forge!"

"We needed to be here," Fisher answered. He glanced back at his grandfather. "We both saw it."

"The same vision?" Tiras came up next to Aeris. "Or just similar?"

"The same," Memfis answered. "How are you, Tiras?"

Tiras smiled. "I'm doing very well, thank you. And hoping we'll have a chance to talk while you're here?"

Memfis laughed. "Of course. Now, why did you ask?" He paused. "You didn't have the vision, too, did you?"

"No. This is the first time I'm hearing about it. But I'm here, so why would I have a vision to come here?" Tiras glanced at Aeris. "Owyn didn't have it either, or he'd have told me. You both had the same vision, but maybe it was just you two? I mean... your proximity to each other, and the relationship to you and this place... wouldn't that answer why you had the same vision?"

Memfis looked around. "Owyn, what are you teaching this child?"

"Depends," Owyn answered. "What did they say?" He came over to join them. "Tiras?"

Tiras repeated themselves, and added, "I know that Smoke Dancers aren't supposed to have the same vision unless it's really important, but aren't there other factors that might explain why only two had the same vision?"

Owyn looked thoughtful. "I... yeah, I think so. I mean... the only Smoke Dancers who had the vision that we had to leave Terraces back on Aria's Progress were the ones that were in Terraces. And that whole Protector of Now thing when Karse wanted to go after Trey? That was just us. So... maybe?"

"Interesting," Memfis murmured. "And not what I was taught. But you changed a lot of the rules of Smoke Dancing, Mouse. It shouldn't surprise me that you're changing the teaching, or that your student is changing the theories, too. We'll discuss this later."

"I'd like to be part of that discussion," Aria said. "But we need to discuss something else, first."

Everyone took a seat, and Aria waited until they were all seated and quiet before saying, "Frayim has had another vision. We will be leaving for the Temple the day after tomorrow."

"And the messenger was waylaid on the way here," Aven added. "I don't like the coincidence."

Jehan leaned forward, resting his elbows on his knees. "Have there been any other reports of attacks on the Western Road? Raiders? Bandits? We haven't heard anything from the traders who come to Terraces."

"Nothing that we've heard," Aven answered. He leaned back in his chair, frowning slightly. "Othi has taken over the guard patrols on the Palace roads. He hasn't said anything. Trees?"

"No. As a matter of fact, he was just saying how quiet it was, and that he might take the girls out with you and Aeris, and visit the family canoes."

"That's not good," Owyn said from his place next to Alanar. "If we don't know about it, we can't do anything about it. But why don't we know?"

"They...don get here?" Del offered. He growled slightly and tugged one hand free from Alanar's. "*If there are bandits out of range of our patrols, they might not be letting anyone past them to reach us.*"

"I don't like the sound of that," Aria said. "We have to see what we find out as we go east."

"Traders have been reaching us, so if there are raiders, they're not hitting everyone," Alanar said. "Which might make it harder to find out what's going on." He shrugged and stretched, putting his arms around Owyn and Del. "We're leaving when?"

"We?" Memfis repeated. "You're going with them?"

Alanar turned toward him. "I barely have any time with my husband. Of course I'm going!"

"Alanar—"

"Don't tell me no, Jehan," Alanar interrupted. "You can spare me for a month or two. Especially with Dyneh, Gisa and Minna handling things."

Jehan sighed. "They're all very good, but none of them are level five." He turned to Aria. "And I'm assuming you're going to ask us to stay and hold the Palace while you're gone?"

"The thought had occurred," Aria admitted. "We can discuss it over a meal. I don't think anyone has eaten yet."

"We did, before everything started," Tiras said. "Should I ring for Lexi?"

"If you would?" Aria studied Aeris for a moment, her brow furrowed. "Aeris, since you've eaten, you needn't stay. Will you take your Companions out?"

Aeris blinked. "I... Mama, may I ask why?" She got to her feet. "You always tell us that we're to learn by watching you, by seeing how things are done. And you've never closed us out before. But you sent us out already this morning, and now you're sending us out again? How are we to learn?"

Aria frowned, just enough at Aeris noticed. "Aeris, you don't need to be here. This doesn't concern you."

Aeris swallowed, trying to keep her wings still, her voice from shaking. "With respect, Firstborn, I disagree," she said. The room went still. "This involves Frayim, who has not seen a vision since I was born. His visions before that all revolved around me, or at least around who people think that I am. I think that him having a vision again concerns me very much."

Aven snorted. "I told you," he said. "Aria, she's yours to the tips of her feathers. If you push, she's going to push back. And she's right. This does concern her." He took a deep breath. "She's an adult tomorrow, Aria. And she's the Heir. She needs to know what we know, and what we think. We shouldn't be keeping things from her."

"There's more?" Aeris asked.

Aria folded her hands in her lap. "You may be an adult tomorrow, my dove, but you will be my little girl always." She paused. "Yes, there's more." She looked up. "Owyn, will you seal the room?"

Owyn looked unusually serious as he stood and went to the doors, closing them, turning the key in the lock, then leaning against them. Without a word, Alanar went to stand with him.

Aria took a deep breath and nodded. "There is more, but nothing of substance. Nothing we can point to and say '*this is what's happening.*' The roads have been clear, as far as we know. But over the past year, the mountains have not. We've had reports from the Solstice village that there has been fighting in the Eastern mountains. The flocks have been flying patrols and monitoring, and so far it has all been well away from the trade roads and foothills. The foot patrols we've sent into the mountains have found the remains of battles, but we haven't yet been able to find out who is fighting or why."

"But you think it's to do with Aeris?" Aleia asked.

"We think it's a possibility," Aven answered. "But we have no way to be sure. Only now... if Frayim is seeing again, there might be an answer waiting for us at the Temple."

"Is it safe?" Tiras asked. "I mean... should we be going to the Temple if there's fighting out there?"

Del snapped his fingers, then signed, "*Fa wouldn't send for us if it wasn't safe. He'd have come to us.*"

Aeris nodded. "The vision may involve me," she said slowly. "Do you think the fighting does, too? Are they connected?"

"We don't know. But maybe we can find out." Owyn straightened and unlocked the door. "Tiras, let's see what we can see."

Chapter Three

One thing that amused Aeris constantly was that when Tiras was excited about something, they *bounced*. There was no other way to describe it — a happy, excited Tiras was a bouncy Tiras. Standing by the bench just outside the low fence surrounding the Dancing Floor, Tiras bounced in place on the balls of their bare feet, talking animatedly with Owyn. Del stood next to them, carrying a basket.

"You said we were going to see what we could see," they said. "We. Not just you. That means I get to really dance for a vision? Not just practice?"

"Owyn, you haven't had him dancing for visions?" Memfis asked.

"Yes and no. It's complicated," Owyn answered. "Tiras is very open to visions. More than I was even before. Tiras, tell Mem when you had your waking vision."

Tiras smiled. "I was six."

"Six?" Memfis looked appalled. "That's too young!"

"Entirely too young," Owyn agreed. "But Tiras makes their own rules." He turned to Tiras. "And how many visions have you had without dancing for them?"

"In total? Or just in the year before Aeris claimed me?" Tiras asked. "And before you started teaching me?"

"Let's go with that year," Owyn answered.

"Fourteen? I think?" Tiras frowned slightly and stopped bouncing. "I... I wrote them down, but I think I forgot to pack some of my journals. Mama said that when I was little, I would see so many things that weren't there that I'd walk into walls that were." They shrugged. "Mama did her best, but as a Smoke Dancing teacher, she's a good cook. And Fa never knew what to do with me. I didn't have a lot in the way of proper lessons until I got here."

Owyn nodded. "And since they've gotten here, our lessons haven't been so much teaching them how to see as they have been on teaching them when to see. We've been working on channeling that... openness into more structured vision seeking, and working on trying not to see when they're not meaning to." He reached up and scratched the back of his neck. "It's been a lot of '*Try this. Nope, that don't work. Try that.*' And not much to go on in the records. I've been meaning to take them to the Temple to talk to Frayim, so we'd have made this trip anyway." He shrugged. "Right. Tiras, you have your boots off? You ready?"

Tiras started bouncing again. "Yes!" They hopped over the low fence, bounded out to the middle of the mossy floor, then turned to face Owyn. They paused, looking down at the wooden smoke blades, and Aeris watched all the bounce bleed out of them. "Owyn? I... am I ready?"

"You tell me," Owyn answered. "Are you ready?"

Aeris saw movement from the corner of her eye, and turned to see Gannet nodding.

"Gannet, stop that," Owyn called. "I know you think they're ready. But I need to know if they know it. And they have to know it here." He thumped Tiras' chest with one knuckle, then stepped back. "So?"

Tiras glanced at Gannet and Aeris, then smiled. "I'm ready."

Owyn nodded and walked off the Dancing Floor. Once he was on the other side of the fence, Tiras lowered their head and took a deep breath. A second. A third, and they started moving, flowing into the dance. Aeris knew the forms — Owyn had taught her, even though she'd never had the waking vision that marked a Smoke Dancer. So she saw where Tiras faltered as the vision took them. Owyn clearly saw it, too — he moved closer to the fence, watching intently, then jumped over the fence when Tiras took a sharp breath and dropped to their knees. Owyn knelt next to them, taking their smoke blades and putting them aside. Del followed, and handed Tiras an apple.

"Looked like a good one," Owyn said, sitting down on the mossy floor. Tiras nodded and took a big bite of the apple. As they chewed, Del set the basket down. Owyn rummaged through it, coming out with a journal and a silverpoint stylus.

Tiras finished the apple, then said, "I have no idea who he was, but he was right there!" They pointed to a spot on the mossy floor. "Real as you are!" They took the journal and silverpoint, rested it on one knee, and started scribbling as Owyn handed them a piece of bread.

"He was tall. Taller than me, maybe as tall as Gannet," Tiras said as they wrote. They took a bite of bread, swallowed it, and kept talking. "Dark hair. And... I've never seen eyes like his before. Two different colors. Right was blue, left was green." They frowned slightly. "Rough. He was rough. Clothes had hard wear. His hands... scars. Scars and callouses. He's a fighter. And... and he has a scar, here." They traced a line down their own left cheekbone with the silverpoint.

Owyn nodded. "Did he say anything? Or do anything?"

Tiras shook their head. "No. They were watching. Waiting. Waiting for something. At least, that's what it felt like."

"Any sense of when? Or where?" Memfis asked.

Tiras closed their eyes. "It's fading. I... where... shadows. All I see is shadows. And... soon. It's soon."

Owyn nodded. He took a piece of cheese out of the basket, handed it to Tiras, then reached out and ruffled their hair. "Well done," he said, and Tiras flushed with the praise. "You did very well. Keep on like this, and you might be ready to start forging a proper set of blades before Turning."

"Really?" Tiras squeaked.

"Really. Now go sit on the bench and eat that."

Tiras got to their feet and started toward the fence, weaving like a drunkard. Gannet laughed and stepped over the fence, picking Tiras up and carrying them over the bench, then sitting down with Tiras in his lap. Tiras sighed happily and leaned into him, starting to nibble the cheese. Aeris sat down next to them, leaning her shoulder against Tiras' back. Dyna reached between them and rested her hand on Tiras' shoulder.

"Dyna, I'm fine," Tiras said around a mouthful. "I just need to eat." They took another piece of bread that Del offered them, then sat up straight. "Owyn is going to dance? I want to see!"

Aeris turned and saw Owyn on the Dancing Floor, his own smoke blades in his hands. He looked at them, then pointed one blade at Tiras. "You can see me just fine from there!" he called. "Gannet, don't let them up."

"Yes, sir!" Gannet called, and wrapped his arms around Tiras. "You're staying here."

Owyn grinned and nodded, then lowered his head and started the three breaths. Aeris felt warmth at her back, and looked up to see her father was standing next to Dyna, with her mother on his arm. Neither of them were looking at her — they were both watching Owyn, who had started moving into the forms.

And who almost immediately fell to his knees, dropping both blades and catching himself on his hands before he fell face-first into the moss.

"Wyn!" Del leapt over the fence and dropped to his knees next to Owyn. He didn't touch Owyn — they all knew better than that.

"I'm... I'm fine," Owyn muttered. He took a deep breath. "I'm fine. That's... that's the strongest one I've had in a long time." He held his hand out, and Del put a battered blue book into it. Owyn smiled and sat down, taking the vine charcoal that Del handed him and starting to draw.

"What did you see?" Alanar asked.

"Pretty sure I saw the same person Tiras did," Owyn answered. "Just a moment." He frowned down at the picture, then tipped the book so that Del could see. Del took the book from him and handed him an apple. Owyn grinned and took a bite.

"Go show them. Show Tiras."

Del nodded and got up, bringing the book to them. The image was very much as Tiras had described — he was young, his face scarred. His clothing was clearly much mended, and the scarf he wore around his neck was fraying at the ends. He had a knife in one hand, and Aeris could see scars on his wrist. Aeris felt every hair stand on end, and she almost missed what her father said.

"Those are from manacles," Aven murmured. "He's seen a world of hurt, that boy."

"Who is he?" Aria asked.

"Someone important," Aeris answered. "I... he's important." She looked up to see her parents looking at her with matching shocked expressions.

"Important how?" Aria asked.

Aeris shook her head. "I don't know. I just... feel that he's important."

Aria hummed softly, and murmured, "Interesting..."

Aven glanced at Aria. "Don't jump to conclusions. You didn't recognize Del from the picture. You had to see him in person."

Aeris turned around on the bench to better face her parents. "Are you saying that you think that he's my Water?"

"No. We can't say that," Aria answered. "All we know is that he's important enough to occupy the visions of two of the strongest Smoke Dancers we know. When we find him, then we will know what else he is and why he is important." She looked up at Aven. "What are you thinking?"

"Wondering what the scarf hides," Aven answered. "And thinking of the other visions. The ones that say that Aeris' Water is in the wrong place." He frowned. "And... remembering Othi's hunts, and his theory on the missing ones."

"Oh!" Aria gasped. "How did we never consider that?"

Aven shook his head. "Wishful thinking?" He took a deep breath and let it out slowly. "Aeris, feel like taking a sail?"

"Now, Fa?" Aeris looked over her shoulder at the Dancing Floor. Owyn was still sitting on the ground, with Del on one side and Alanar on the other. Memfis stood with them, and they were discussing something in low voices. "And... just me?"

"No, all of you," Aven said.

"Aven, what are you doing?" Aria asked. Aven smiled, leaned down to share breath with Aria, then kissed her.

"Not listening," he answered.

AERIS WAS AT HOME ON the canoe, and since taking her Companions, Aven had introduced them to the canoe as well — teaching Gannet and Tiras how to swim, and teaching all of them to sail. He took them out past the harbor wall, then took in the sails and strapped them down.

"All right. Now we'll talk." He lowered himself slowly to the deck, wincing slightly. Aeris sat down next to him, and her Companions clustered around her.

"Fa, why did we need to come out on the canoe to talk?" Aeris asked.

"Because your mother won't like what I have to say, and you need to hear it."

"Oh, is that what not listening means?" Gannet asked. "You're not listening to her? Are you going to get in trouble?"

Aven chuckled. "I may sleep alone for a day or two. But I've never liked her keeping your history from you, Aeris. She thinks it's protecting you. I think it's clipping your wings. And I'm not doing that anymore." He looked up at the sky and frowned. "It'll rain, and soon. We can't stay out here too long. All right." He took a deep breath. "You know what happened, Aeris. You all know about what happened when Aeris was born. We know there were others out there that followed Risha. Aria has been terrified in her bones ever since that something like that would happen again, that someone else would try to take Aeris from us."

"But she's a Smoke Dancer," Tiras protested. "She couldn't... she couldn't look?"

"She tried, but she never saw anything. Memfis and Milon both thought it was because the answer scared her. She couldn't see past the fear to find the truth. But it's been quiet for years. The Penitents told us again and again that there was nothing happening in the hills. Othi took men out to the mountains four years running after he came back from his apprenticeship, and they only found abandoned camps. So Aria calmed down. But now..."

"There's fighting in the mountains, you said," Tiras said. "It's not quiet anymore."

"It's not," Aven agreed. "Something had changed out there. Something happened, and we don't know what. And now Frayim is having visions again, and he wants to see you." He shook his head. "And there were those camps. Othi's hunts? Were to try and find the lost Water. He had a theory that some of the Water girls who couldn't be accounted for were taken to the mountains... as breeding stock."

"Oh, that's vile," Gannet breathed. "That... that's horrible!"

Aeris stared at her father. "And my Water is in the wrong place," she whispered. "Fa, why didn't anyone tell me that? It's been two years! We could have gone to the mountains and found him–"

"Unlikely," Aven interrupted. "Othi never found any signs of Water prisoners or survivors out there. No signs of children. Nothing. Not even identifiable bodies." Aven sighed. "That's why he stopped looking."

"You said identifiable," Tiras said slowly. "That implies... unidentifiable?"

Aven grimaced. "There were pyres in every abandoned camp he found."

Aeris shifted uncomfortably. "Fa? Should I not go?" Aeris asked. "I can stay at the Palace with Granna and Grandfa."

"It's tempting to say yes, and leave you here, where it's safe. But if Frayim has seen something that makes him want to see you, it's important."

"Why didn't he come here, then?" Gannet asked. "If it's that important? It would have been faster."

"He and Steward haven't been here since Yana was born, and the Temple... well, from what Uncle Steward's letter after said, things got strange while they were gone," Aeris answered. "Three of the Penitents decided independently of the others that Steward wasn't coming back, and they all of them declared themselves High Priest."

Gannet's eyes widened. "You're joking."

"She isn't, and I'm not surprised you didn't hear about it, as far out as your flock is," Aven said with a laugh. "The funny thing is that none of them actually did anything against the others. There was no fighting. There were no factions, for all that each of them convinced a part of the Penitents and priests to follow them. They all picked a separate project off the list of things that needed to be rebuilt, and had their followers start work on it. By the time Steward and Frayim got back to the Temple, two of the projects were done, and the third was nearly finished. Steward called it a very civilized uprising, and all three of them were very apologetic when he got back."

Gannet whistled. "That... if he left now, he might go back and find they moved the whole Temple."

"Or started worshiping someone else," Tiras suggested.

"Thank you, no." Dyna shook her head for emphasis. "We've had enough of that." She gestured to Aeris. "There were people out there who wanted to worship Aeris!"

Aven snorted. "True. As much as I love you, best oldest daughter of mine, I'm not intending to worship you."

"Best oldest daughter?" Aeris grinned. "Fa, how many oldest daughters do you have?"

"Just one." Aven smiled and got to his feet. "One superlative oldest daughter. Who is going to help me with the lines so we get in ahead of that storm on the horizon."

The rain was just starting to fall as they reached the shore, and they walked up the beach together. Tiras poked Dyna in the arm. "There goes your walk."

"We can walk tomorrow," Dyna answered. "Or we can go and spend time in the library."

"Who is we?" Aven asked. "Dyna?"

"Lancir," Dyna answered. "He's one of the guards, and he asked me if I'd join him on the Water Walk once his shift was over. He's nice, Fa Aven."

"Lancir," Aven said slowly. "Young fellow? Dark hair? Came here from Terraces about a year ago?"

"Yes, Fa Aven," Dyna answered, her cheeks turning pink.

Aven smiled. "I've sparred with him, on the days this hip lets me. Nice young man. Good choice, Dyna. Does Owyn know?"

Dyna shook her head. "Not yet."

"If you want me to speak to him and Alanar, I will."

Dyna shook her head. "It's too soon for that," she said, her words tumbling over each other. "I mean...it's just a walk. Maybe later. If there is a later." She reached out and took Aeris' hand. "I mean... you don't mind, do you?"

"No," Aeris said. "Of course not. I like him. If you want to get to know him better, then we'll welcome him."

"And if he hurts you, we'll thump him," Tiras added.

"You will not!" Dyna gasped. She looked at Tiras and Gannet, who were both nodding. "You would?"

"Of course we would," Gannet answered. "You're ours, and we're yours, and we're all Aeri's. We take care of each other. And anyone else who comes into the Circle. No one hurts our Circle."

Aven chuckled. "Nice to know you've learned that lesson, Gannet."

"I have a hard head," Gannet answered, "not an empty one. I learn. Slowly, but I learn." He looked up at the sky. "We should pack, shouldn't we? If we're leaving the day after tomorrow?"

"We'll all need to prepare, but you won't need to do too much packing. Lexi and her staff will take care of most of it." Aven sighed. "This will be the first time we've all left the Palace at once since your Progress, Aeris, and we prepared for that for over a month. So things will be somewhat frantic today and tomorrow. I hope the coaches are still in good order."

Aeris looked back down the beach at the sea, and realized something. "I'm not getting my tattoos until we get back, am I? We were going to do that this trip, since I'm old enough."

Aven frowned slightly. "We could wait. Or...if you want, we may still be able to do it. Othi is here, after all. If you get up early tomorrow, he might be able to have it done in time for your party. We can go ask him."

Gannet coughed. "That's hours! It'll take hours?"

"Mine took days, but I had a lot of catching up to do," Aven answered. "It's ritual, Gannet. It can't be rushed. We'll need to talk to Othi. He's the expert." He stopped walking and winced. "Sand is hard."

"Because it isn't?" Dyna asked.

"Because it isn't," Aven agreed. "It shifts, and it's unstable, and it makes walking harder."

"I can work on the hip when we get inside," Dyna volunteered.

"Thank you, but I'll ask your fathers," Aven said, and started walking again. "Alanar is more familiar with it, since he was there when they rebuilt it. And Elaias has been working with him and my father to try and replicate what Pirit did to rebuild it in the first place. I wish Grandmother had left better notes on what she did."

"Grandfa hasn't found anything?"

"No, and they haven't been able to recreate it, either, for all that he was in the meld when she did it." Aven sighed and draped his arm over Aeris' shoulders. "It may have been one of those '*the Mother helped us when we needed it*' times, and it's not something that we'll be able to do again."

"Here's hoping that we won't ever need to know how to do that again," Dyna said. "Fa told me about that meld. It sounds terrifying. Everything about that sounded terrifying."

Aven stopped walking. He turned to face them, his lips pressed tightly together. He nodded slowly.

"Mother grant you never have to know how terrifying it actually was," he said softly. "Now, let's go in."

Chapter Four

Aeris yawned and tried to ignore how much her right shoulder itched. Othi had agreed there was enough time for Aeris to have her family tattoo before the party, but only if they started before dawn. So Aeris had slept alone the night before the party, and Aven had fetched her in the dark hours before dawn, taking her down to the canoes where Othi and her grandmother Aleia waited. For hours, Othi had sung the chants and worked with the ink and hammer, inscribing Aeris' lineage into her skin. Every line, curve, and symbol was a legacy that traced her bloodline back to the first canoe, to Abin and Axia. By the time the tattoo was done, it was near midday, and Othi could barely speak. After eating something, Aeris had staggered up to the Heir's suite, and had fallen into bed, and her Companions had gently teased her for almost missing her own naming day party while they admired the dark ink etched into her skin. Her father had done something to make certain it healed cleanly, but it still itched.

"Is it supposed to take that long?" Gannet asked. He was sitting across from her in the coach, in the middle of the bench. Tiras sat next to him, and was leaning against him, sound asleep and snoring gently. Dyna was sitting next to Aeris, her hands full of the fine stitchery that she enjoyed when she had the time.

"Fa says that it's normally supposed to be spaced out over several days," Aeris answered. "But we all agreed that it was better to get it done before we left, since we won't have the time on the road."

Dyna nodded. "And if it bothers you, I can take care of it. Fa and Fa Eli and Fa Aven all sat down with me to make sure I knew what to do."

Aeris smiled. "They would. And I just realized that I never asked you. Did you get to spend time with Lancir?"

Dyna blushed. "It stopped raining, so we did go out and walk on the Water Walk. It was nice. I'd have told you about it, but you were barely awake, and then there was the party—"

"And you were barely awake," Gannet murmured.

Aeris laughed and gently kicked Gannet's shin. "We're none of us awake," she replied. "Anyway, Dyna, how was it?"

Her blush deepened. "He's very sweet. He likes being in the Palace guard, and he likes serving under Captain Karse and Copper. He's working on learning to read, so that he can be something more than just a guard. So... when we stop, if he's not on duty, I'm going to read with him."

"He's with us?" Aeris grinned. "He's only been with the palace guard for a year. Captain Karse would say he's as green as new grass. How did he get assigned to this trip?"

"Dyna, if you turn any redder, you'll burst into flames," Gannet said. "Did you get him assigned to the guards coming with us?"

"I asked," Dyna admitted, "and I think I caught Captain Karse in a good mood. He's brought Lancir along to further his training."

Gannet coughed. "He was in a good mood, wasn't he?"

"Or Fa had a word with him," Aeris murmured. "Do you want to ask him?"

"No!" Dyna laughed. "No, I don't want to know. And it's not like we can really do anything — he's going to be on duty most of the time."

"Yes, but only most," Tiras murmured without opening their eyes. Gannet chuckled and looked down at them.

"How long have you been awake?"

"Who says I've been asleep?" Tiras opened their eyes and sat up.

"You drooling on my sleeve says you were asleep."

"And snoring," Aeris added. "You were snoring."

"I was not!" Tiras protested. "I don't snore!" They looked up at Gannet. "Do I?"

"Not much," Gannet admitted. "Except when there's Maiden's Lace blooming. Then you get all red and blotchy, and you snore at night."

"And Maiden's Lace is in season now. There must be some growing along the road." Dyna set down her stitching and held out her hand. "Let me see."

"I hate Maiden's Lace," Tiras grumbled. "My head gets all foggy and my visions get weird. Owyn says he's never heard of a Smoke Dancer whose visions are controlled by their nose before."

Aeris frowned. "But Smoke Dancers used to train in the vents of the Smoking Mountain, and they were breathing in the smoke. Owyn was one of the last ones trained that way. So why is smoke different from the scent of flowers?"

Gannet looked thoughtful, then shrugged. "Because Smoke Dancer sounds more impressive than Perfume Dancer?"

Tiras hooted with laughter, hard enough to give themself the hiccups, setting Gannet off. Outside the coach, Owyn rode up alongside and peered in the window.

"What's funny?" he called.

"Perfume Dancers!" Tiras broke down in another peal of giggles.

"Perfume Dancers," Owyn repeated. "I... what *are* you talking about?"

"Smoke Dancer sounds more impressive than Perfume Dancer," Gannet repeated.

Owyn looked puzzled. "I...we'll talk about this when we stop. Because that was just enough to confuse me even more. I have got to hear the rest of it."

"How is your horse behaving?" Aeris asked. "You said you weren't sure about him."

"He weren't too sure of me, either. But we've only just met each other. He seems to be settling, but it'll take us a day or two to get to know each other." Owyn smiled. "Pepper here looks almost exactly like his grandfa Freckles. I hope he's as smart."

"He's got a good bloodline. He'll get to know you," Alanar said, riding up on Owyn's other side. Past him, Aeris could see Del, who waved at her.

"How far are we going today?" Dyna asked. "And when can we come out and ride?"

"If Mama has her way, we'll be in a coach all the way there and all the way back," Aeris muttered.

"I heard that," Owyn said. "Aeris, be kind. You can't really blame her."

"No, but this is suffocating," Aeris answered. "I can't just be kept in a box and only taken out for special occasions. I need to learn. We all do."

"True," Alanar said. "But if you're going to ride, then you're riding with guards."

"I'm fine with that," Aeris said, hearing Tiras echo her words.

Alanar cocked his head to the side and smiled. "Dyna? Your heartrate just spiked. So... which guard?"

"Fa!" Dyna gasped. Then she laughed. "I should know better. You always know. Lancir."

"I'll tell you about him," Owyn said to Alanar. "Our girl has good taste."

They rode on, and Aeris glanced at Dyna. "Did you know he could do that?" she asked. "That he could pick your heart rate out of the group? That... that's beyond level five, isn't it? Is there a beyond level 5?"

"I think it's just that Fa is more sensitive, because he can't see," Dyna answered. "Now, I want to hear more about Perfume Dancers! Gannet, what do they use to dance?"

"Fans," Gannet answered without hesitation. "Big ones."

By the time the coach rolled to a stop, they had created the entire arcana for the lost Perfume Dancers of the Fire tribe, including mythology and lore, and none of them could keep a straight face. To Aeris' surprise, the wealth of the information came from Gannet, who proved to be a very talented storyteller, and who appeared oddly satisfied by the whole venture.

"It's just storytelling," he said. "I was good at telling stories to the little ones around the fire back with the flock. I haven't done it in ages, though." He smiled. "This, though... think I could start another cult in the mountains with this one?"

"Don't you dare!" Aeris laughed. Someone knocked on the coach door, and she looked out to see Lancir smiling up at her.

"Time for a rest break," he announced. "The Firstborn and her Companions are at the head of the line. What was so funny? I could hear you laughing from the rearguard."

"We have to tell Owyn, too, so we'll tell everyone when we camp tonight." Aeris got out of the coach and spread her wings wide to stretch. The sides of the road were a riot of color — purple Lady's Passion, vivid yellow Maiden's Lace, pink and red Lover's Blush, and tiny blue Sea Stars. Tiras took one look at the blanket of flowers and sneezed violently.

"Are you all right?" Lancir asked.

"Outside makes me sneeze," Tiras answered, tugging a handkerchief from their pouch and wiping their nose. Dyna put her hand on their back, only for Tiras to shake their head.

"It won't help for long," they said. "I'll be sneezing again in an hour."

"How have we not seen it this bad before?" Gannet asked. "I don't remember you looking this poorly last year."

"Because I haven't been out around this many flowers since I came to the Palace," Tiras answered. "We haven't all been out on the road like this ever, and I take my season in the fall, when the flowers are done." They rubbed their nose again. "There are a lot of flowers this year, too."

"It's a good year for them," Owyn said as he came toward them. He stopped and looked at Tiras. "Oh, Tiras. You don't look good."

Tiras nodded and sneezed again. "I don't feel good either."

"Oh, no. Is Tiras flower sick, or do they just have rotten timing?" Alanar asked.

"Flower sick," Tiras answered, and sniffled. "It's not usually this bad."

Alanar nodded. "I've heard this refrain already this year, from multiple sources. Come on. Elaias has honey drops. He swears it helps."

"Honey drops?" Dyna repeated. "Fa, why would honey drops help?"

"I'll let Elaias explain," Alanar said. "It's apparently a remedy used by non-healers in the mountains, and he says it works. Elaias? Explain how the honey drops work?"

"What?" Elaias asked, turning toward them. His brows rose. "Oh. Come here, Tiras." He looked around. "Tris? Where's my carryall?"

"Still in the coach, I think," Trista answered. "Let me see." She went to the coach and looked inside, coming back with a canvas bag. Elaias took it from her, giving her a kiss in return. He rummaged through it, coming up with a small packet.

"Here," he said as he handed the packet to Tiras. "Take two of these a day, every day. And talk to the Senior Healer. He'll make sure you have more."

Tiras opened the packet, then looked up. "They're boiled sweets," they said, their brow furrowed. "I don't understand."

Elaias grinned. "Tell me what you know about honey," he said.

Tiras' frown deepened. "Ah... not a lot," they admitted. "Bees make it."

"From?"

Tiras looked around, then blinked. "Oh. Flowers. They make it from flowers."

"Specifically, they make it from the same part of the flower that makes you sneeze. And that makes me sneeze, although I'm more sensitive to the flowers we find in the mountains than I am to the ones down here." Elaias leaned against the coach. "And there is enough of that left in the honey after the bees make it that it helps your body build up a tolerance. You just have to take a spoonful a day, every day. But it has to be honey made from the flowers that make you sneeze."

"That part is easy," Tiras replied. "Everything that blooms makes me sneeze."

"So take two of those a day," Elaias said. "Two of them is equal to one spoonful. When you're in the Palace, get honey from the hives at the home farm. It'll take a few weeks to really start showing any signs of working, but it will help. And next year, start taking them when the snows melt, and you'll be ready for when the flowers bloom."

Tiras nodded, took two of the honey drops from the packet and popped them in their mouth. They grinned. "Mama never let me have too many sweets," they said. "She said it made me wild."

"Now you tell us!" Gannet said with a laugh. "Right. We need to ride. We need to be outside the coach, or Tiras will be bouncing off the walls."

"What's this?"

Aeris turned to see that her parents and Treesi had joined them. "Tiras, you don't look well," Aria said, gently bouncing Yana in her arms. "Is it from being in the coach?"

"They're flower sick," Elaias said. "And there are a lot of flowers this year. It's not serious, but they'll feel like they've been beaten with a bag of rocks for a bit. Until we get into the hills where the flowers are different, I think."

"It won't help," Tiras sniffled. "I've never been anywhere where the flowers don't make me sneeze."

"I understand that," Elaias said, "but these are different flowers, so your body will take a few days to figure out that it doesn't like them either." He took a deep breath. "I'm usually sensitive to the ones that bloom first, in the early spring. Summer flowers aren't as bad, but this year it seems that there are more of them. More of everything growing. We'll have a good harvest this year."

"From your mouth to the Mother's ears," Treesi said. "When I took my season, Othi and the girls and I just sort of meandered. Everything was in bloom. Every farmer we saw said the same thing — that this is looking to be the best year since Aria took her Progress. They're wondering why. There were a lot of questions about if Aria was pregnant again when we were near the foothills."

"That would be no," Aria answered. "Not after I frightened you all the last time." She smiled down at her youngest daughter. "As much as I love my children, I don't want to be pregnant again. Why would they ask that?"

Treesi blushed slightly. "Because apparently Father Adavar is still paying attention to you and your cycles?" she said. "And every year you have been pregnant has been a year with an excellent harvest."

Aria's eyes widened. "No one has pointed that out to me. Not a single person!"

"I don't know that we'd notice it," Owyn said. "I mean, we're not as close to the land. We have the reports on yield and everything, but... I don't think anyone correlated the two. Well, maybe Afansa did and just didn't say anything?" He paused, then asked, "Treesi, is it just Aria?"

Treesi shook her head. "Hard to say. We can ask Afansa when we get back."

"I'd be curious to see how the numbers line up, and if it's just Aria, or if it's both of you," Aven said. He grinned. "Oh, there's a thing I haven't thought of in years."

"I bet I know what you're thinking," Owyn said with a laugh. "Hilarious pots?"

Aven burst out laughing. "Yes!"

"You'll explain that," Aria said. "Once we're in the coach."

"Mama, could we ride for a while?" Aeris asked. "If Lancir rides with us?"

Aria paused, then nodded. "It's been quiet this morning. If we're lucky, it will stay quiet the entire trip."

Tiras frowned slightly. "Three days," they murmured.

"What?" Aeris looked at her Fire, at their distant expression. "Tiras?"

"Three days of quiet, then it begins," Tiras said. Then they crumpled, and Gannet caught them before they hit the ground.

"Tiras!" Gannet knelt, lowering Tiras down to the ground. Owyn knelt next to them, and Dyna dropped to her knees on Tiras' other side.

"I didn't think they were more than flower sick!" she said as she reached for Tiras' hand.

"They're fine, Dyna," Owyn said. "Don't touch them. That was a vision. Tiras? You with us?"

Tiras nodded, sitting up and rubbing their face. "I'm going to have visions all the way there, aren't I? There's going to be flowers all along the roads, and I'm not going to see a single thing that's really in front of me."

"Three days," Aria murmured. "Three days and it begins. What begins?"

Aven shook his head. "We find out in three days?" He sighed. "We've had twenty years of quiet. Twenty years of balance. What's starting now?"

"I...it really already started, didn't it?" Aeris asked. "It started when I didn't find my Water. We're not balanced. Because I'm not. We're not." She looked at Dyna, at Gannet and Tiras. "We're missing part of us."

"She's got a point," Owyn said. He stood up and dusted off his knees. "And apparently it's been growing. Whatever it's coming, Frayim is seeing again, and it's starting in three days."

"*Will it be as bad?*" Del signed. "*It can't be, if things are growing and blooming.*"

Owyn sighed. "I don't know. I don't think so. I mean... I don't feel anything coming. But we'll find out. And we'll handle it." He helped Tiras back to their feet. "Come on. I'll ride with you and you can explain this whole Perfume Dancer thing to me."

Aria blinked. "Perfume Dancer?"

"I have no idea, but from the laughing we could hear from inside their coach? It was fucking hilarious."

Aven chuckled. "As hilarious as pots? Maybe I should ride with you."

"More."

CAMPING THAT NIGHT was quiet. Prompted by Owyn, Gannet told the others about Perfume Dancers, and Aeris got to see her mother laugh until she cried. And, while everyone was sitting at the fire, Aeris watched Dyna walk into the shadows with Lancir.

The next day was more of the same, with some traffic going west who reported nothing of import on the road. They shared a meal, then rode on.

The third day left Aeris feeling uneasy, too fidgety to sit in the coach, too nervous to ride. Her horse danced underneath her, and she sighed and tried to get her emotions under control.

"You feel it, too?" Owyn said, riding up next to her.

"Like summer lightning," Aeris said. "Whatever Tiras saw, it's close enough that I can feel it."

Owyn nodded. "Aria feels it, too. She sent riders ahead to scout for a campsite. There should be someone coming back..." His voice trailed off as he squinted into the distance. Aeris looked, and saw dust on the road.

"Someone coming, at speed," Owyn said, and reached into his belt pouch for his whip-chain. "Go to the coach."

"Owyn—"

"Do what I said!" He urged Pepper into a gallop and rode off. Aeris turned Lace back toward the coach, riding past it, then turning to ride alongside. He hadn't said to get in the coach, after all.

"What's wrong?" Dyna asked.

"I'm not sure," Aeris answered. "A rider, coming toward us at speed. And Owyn and I are both feeling as if something is about to happen—"

"Now," Tiras' voice came from inside the coach. "It's now." They looked out. "It begins."

Aeris looked at them, then tapped Lace's sides with her heels, riding forward. Whatever it was, she needed to know. She joined the group at the head of the line as the rider came into view.

"I thought I told you to go to the coach," Owyn grumbled.

"I didn't listen," Aeris answered. "That... that's Lancir!"

The young guard drew in his horse as he reached them, threw himself down from the saddle, and ran toward them.

"Firstborn..." he panted. He bowed and took a deep breath. 'I... we found something. A burned-out camp. And a body. We found a body."

Chapter Five

The campsite was set well back from the road, far enough that Aeris didn't think that you'd find it if you didn't know it was there. She wasn't sure how the guard had found the site, and she wasn't entirely certain that she was happy they did. She and her Companions hung back with Aria, Del and Treesi, watching as her father, Owyn, Karse, and Othi went through the site and Howl circled the area, sniffing the ground.

"Is there anything that might identify them?" Aria asked. "Anything at all?"

Aven shook his head. "It looks as if everything was burned — there's not a blasted thing in this camp that wasn't put to the torch." He looked around. "Whoever did this, they were thorough."

"It was deliberate?" Astur asked. He and Elaias had helped Aven examine the remains of the body that had been found in what probably was a tent, confirming that there was nothing left to it that would allow for identification. The state of the body was so bad that Elaias thought that it might have been a man, but it wasn't anything he would swear to it. "It wasn't... the campfire burning out of control? Or... or lightning?"

"It's too complete," Karse answered. He crouched next to a charred pile, poking at it with a stick. "A campfire burning out of control wouldn't burn everything this completely. Whoever did this even killed the horse and burned it." He gestured with his stick to another charred pile, then snapped the stick in two, sighed and stood up, brushing off his hands. "I hope the poor fuck was Fire."

"We'll bury what's left," Owyn said. "Just... just in case." He sighed. "I don't get it. This is more than a robbery. This... there's no way to tell who they killed. Or why. They did this so no one would know who it was they killed."

Howl whined softly, and started to dig near the remains of the tent. Karse glanced at Aven, then went over. "What have you found, old man?" he murmured, going to one knee. Howl whined again, and Karse took his dagger out, using it to dig down into the ash and uncovering something that glittered. "What's this?" he murmured, picking it up. It was a pendant on a chain, and he let it dangle from his fingers. "Definitely not a robbery," he said, showing the others. "This is gold. They'd have had this."

"May I see that?" Astur asked. He took the pendant from Karse and rubbed his fingers over it. "I... I've seen this before. Or one like it. But... I can't think where." He frowned. "I know I've seen it."

"It'll come to you," Elaias said. "Hold on to it. We'll keep it safe, and see if we can find where it came from. It's distinctive."

"That's why I recognize it," Astur said. He shook his head. "I know I've seen this before!" He closed his eyes. "I... it's been a while. A long while."

"Maybe when you were still living out in the hills?" Owyn suggested.

"That's probably it," Astur sighed and tucked the pendant away. "Right. Are we burying the body?"

"I think that would be for the best," Aven said. "That way, if they were Earth, there's at least a chance of the Mother finding them." He looked over at Karse. "Do we have shovels? Something to dig with?"

Karse nodded. "We've got tools. Let's go back to the coaches. We can come back and get to work while they get the camp set."

"Do you want help?" Gannet asked, sounding hesitant for the first time Aeris could remember. Karse looked at him and shook his head.

"We'll take care of it, lad. It's been a time since we last had to deal with raider leavings, but I think the lot of us still have the knack of it. You'll be more help if you go help Trista with the kids, or help with the kitchens."

Gannet looked startled. "I... I'm not a child. I can help."

Del tapped Gannet's arm. "*There are different kinds of helping,*" he signed. "*This sort of helping? Isn't going to be helping, because you've never done anything like this before.*"

Gannet blinked. "You went too fast."

"He said that this isn't something for us to help with, because it's not something we have experience with," Aeris said. She took Gannet's arm. "And I agree. Fa and Owyn and Del and Uncle Captain have all been through harder times than we have, because they had no choice. They don't want us to experience that if we don't have to."

Aria nodded. "That's exactly it," she said. "And I wouldn't have had you this close, but it was pointed out to me that protecting you from everything leaves you ignorant of the real risks we face." She gestured toward the camp. "This... will we see more of this? And from where?" She sighed. "I'd hoped you would never have to see this sort of thing, and now we must make certain you know how to face them when they come. But for now, we'll do as Karse suggests. You can help with the camp, and we will talk around the fire after we eat."

Aeris looked back at the charred ground, then followed her mother back toward the coaches. Her mind was racing, and she didn't let go of Gannet's arm as they walked; by the time they reached the road, she could tell that her Companions were worried.

"Aeri?" Gannet murmured. "What is it?"

"I... I'm still getting my mind around it," she answered. "I..." She frowned and looked back. "That was because of me."

"What?" Dyna gasped. "Aeri, no!"

"It was," Aeris said. She let Gannet's arm go, clasping her hands in front of her. "I... I'm not sure how, but it was. And there will be more. Because of me. Because of who they think I am."

"As much as I wish I could say you're wrong," Aven said from behind them, "I don't think you're wrong. I think this is still that same... conflict that's been simmering for years, and it's finally coming to a boil."

"So how do we stop it?" Aeris turned to look at her father, and pointed past him, toward the burned-out camp. "How do we keep that from happening again? How do I make them see that I'm not this mythical Child that they think I am? I'm me, and I'm here, and I don't want people fighting over me!"

"You can't," Tiras said. "You can't make them. They believe that legend."

"Tiras is right," Aven said, nodding. "We all learned how important lore can be — it's part of our people, our place in the world. And we learned the hard way that while some people will use that lore to build, like the Penitents, other people will use that lore to tear things down. Possibly whoever did this is of that sort. We don't know."

"That makes this my fault," Aeris said in a soft voice.

"No," Gannet said gently, sliding his hand over her lower back, underneath her wings. "It's not your fault. They'll say they're doing it because of the Child, but really, that's just an excuse." He looked up. "Right?"

"He's right, my dove," Aria said as she joined them. "People who will do something like this do it because they think they have the right, that the lore gives them permission. We saw it with Risha, with the raiders who terrorized people in the hills, and with the

Wanderers who thought that Air and Water were animals, and not people. They will say that they do the things that they do because that's what the lore says, and that's the way they were taught, and others will say that it's because that's the way things should be, but at the heart of it, I think that it's just to give themselves an excuse to hurt others. Because what they're doing isn't in the lore — there's nothing in any of the stories or songs that tells them to kill." She paused. "Some of them will change when those beliefs are challenged."

"Like the Penitents at the Temple," Dyna said. "They learned better."

"Or Frayim," Owyn added. "Once he knew that what he'd learned was wrong, he tried to teach his people they were wrong and they hunted him because of it. Because for everyone who is willing to think for themself and change, there's a whole handful of people who'll fight back because someone dared to question their ways." He sighed. "Look, the people who are doing this are grown adults. They know what they're doing. They're still chasing the lies that Risha and her lot told them. They don't even know your name, Aeri. They're not doing anything because of you. They're doing it because it's easier to follow than it is to think and go against the crowd." He shook his head. "We don't know, though. Maybe whoever it was had enemies, and we're all following the wrong tunnel. I mean... it's possible."

"Here's me hoping we're all jumping at shadows," Karse said. "Come on."

They returned to the road, and Karse called Copper over. "We're camping, but on the other side of the road," he said. "Find a good spot, and get the camp set. Then... I'll need half a dozen guards, and as many shovels as we've got."

Copper nodded. "Yes, sir. How bad is it?"

Karse looked back over his shoulder. "You know, let's have fresh eyes on this. Come with me. Aven, we'll be back." He led Copper away. Owyn took over giving the orders, while Aven turned to Aeris. "You all know what to do with the kitchen tent, don't you?"

Aeris nodded. "Yes, Fa."

"Would you mind?" He looked around. "I want to get this done, and I'll need Owyn with me. Once the kitchen tent is set up, get supper started, and we'll be back as soon as we can." He paused to share breath with Aeris, kissed her cheek, then went to Aria. They stood for a moment, foreheads together, before Owyn joined them. They both kissed Aria, and headed back the way they'd come.

"Right. Let's pick a good spot for the kitchen tent..." Tiras looked around, then pointed. "There. That's a good spot."

"Let's go get started, then," Aeris said. "Dyna, go see if your fa needs help first."

"Mama Treesi is with him," Dyna said. "I'll go check on them once I help with the kitchen, since you don't need me to cook."

"Woman, you can't cook," Gannet grumbled.

"Which means you won't need me once you start cooking." Dyna smiled sweetly. "But I can help set up the firepit and fill pots with water. Then I'll go see if Fa needs help."

They got to work — once the tent and the trestle table were set up, and the equipment unpacked, Gannet dug the firepit while Tiras and Dyna collected firewood. Then Tiras set up the tripod for the big kettle and got the fire started while Dyna and Gannet carried water. While they worked, Aeris got to work at the trestle table, cutting vegetables and measuring millet into the kettle, adding spices and one of the seasoning balls that Lexi made to add to soup. Owyn had taught her to cook from the time she was tall enough to see over the edge of the counter in the little kitchen off the Salon, and it was honestly something she enjoyed. Doing it helped her get her thoughts in order, helped her work out knotty problems she might be facing. Hopefully, it might help her understand what she was feeling.

"Did any of the guards go hunting?" she called without looking away from her work.

"Half a dozen rabbits." She glanced over her shoulder to see Lancir. "Some of the others are getting them ready, and they're saving the offal for Howl." He came up next to her at the table, watched her for a moment, then blurted, "What are you doing in the kitchen? You're the Heir."

"I'm doing my share of the work," Aeris answered. "If I wasn't cooking, I'd be helping clean up afterward. Being Heir doesn't mean I don't do my part in camp."

"But... why do you even know how to cook? Why are you doing servant work?" Lancir walked around the table to face her. "You're the Heir..."

"And the Heir is not too good to peel potatoes," Aeris finished. "Or wash pots. Or do what needs doing. I'm not afraid to get my hands dirty. Owyn taught me to cook. Del taught me what to do on the trail. My father taught me to hunt and to navigate. All of my fathers and uncles taught me to fight and to heal. Mama Lexie taught me to keep accounts and manage a household staff, and Aunt Afansa taught me to keep the Palace running and all the dozens of things that it takes to do it. Because my mother taught me that I have to know what my people are doing so that I can help them do it." She poured wine into the kettle, then looked up. "I'm no better than anyone else, just because I'm my mother's daughter."

Lancir blinked, then nodded. "I never thought of it that way. So... is there anything you can't do?"

Aeris grinned. "I'm a lousy gardener." She pushed the kettle across the table. "And... only half a dozen rabbits? Anything else?"

Lancir shook his head. "I think we scared off the game. Or that fire did. We can go back out, but I don't think we'll bring anything down in time to eat it tonight."

Aeris nodded. "Right. Stew, then. And I'll mix up some flatbread. If you'll get them, I'll add them to the pot once I butcher them." She looked up to see Lancir staring at her. "Yes, I know how to do that, too."

He laughed, shaking his head. "You're amazing. Did you know that?"

Aeris looked up to see him smiling at her. "Lancir, are you flirting with me?"

He grinned. "You noticed!"

"I also noticed you spending time with Dyna." Aeris rested her hands on the tabletop. "And I noticed that she greatly enjoys that time."

His grin faded. "You think so?"

"I know so." Aeris looked around. "You're not still on duty, are you?"

"Guarding you is my duty."

Aeris shook her head. "Flirting is not guarding. And Uncle Captain will take it out of your hide if he catches you at flirting when you're supposed to be guarding." Lancir looked over his shoulder, and Aeris laughed. "He's not there. Now, go fetch those rabbits if you want to eat tonight. And if you're interested in Dyna, focus your flirts on her. And save them for when you're off duty."

Lancir backed up and swept into an elaborate bow. "My Heir," he pronounced. Then he headed off, leaving Aeris shaking her head. She saw movement from the corner of her eye, and turned to see Dyna coming toward her.

"I saw Lancir?" she said as she joined Aeris at the table. "Is he off duty?"

"No. He's supposed to be guarding," Aeris said. "Does he flirt with all the girls, or are we special?"

"Was he?" Dyna looked past her. "Flirting with you?"

"He started to, and I told him to save it for you." Aeris smiled and leaned her shoulder into Dyna's. "I'm not going to get in the way of what you might be building. I want you to be happy."

Dyna blushed slightly. "I don't know if we're building anything. Or if we can. I just... I like him."

"Then why don't you go help him?" Aeris nudged Dyna again. "He went off to fetch the meat for supper." She nodded. "That way."

Dyna smiled and walked in the direction Lancir had gone, and Aeris started measuring out flour and salt for the flatbread. Making the dough would wait until she'd butchered the rabbits. As if the thought conjured them, Lancir and Dyna appeared, each of them carrying a string of skinned and gutted rabbits.

"Where do you want these?" Lancir called.

Aeris turned and picked up a bowl, setting it on the table. "Here," she said.

"What other help do you need?" Dyna asked as she put her string into the bowl.

"Nothing I can think of," Aeris said. She looked around. "I think you can go help your fa now."

Dyna nodded. She stopped at the wash basin and scrubbed her hands before walking away; Aeris noticed how Lancir's gaze followed Dyna as she left.

"I'm not sure if there's a guard on the healers," she murmured softly. "And Gannet and Tiras are right here. I'm fine." She looked up to see Lancir looking at her.

"And the healers aren't that far," Lancir said, glancing in the direction Dyna had gone.

"Just a shout, really." Aeris nodded. "Go on."

Lancir grinned. "You really are amazing," he said, then followed Dyna. Aeris laughed softly and went back to making supper. She was kneading the flatbread dough when her father and Owyn came toward the fire.

"It's done," Aven said. "Where's your mother?"

"I think she's with Trista and the children," Aeris answered. "I haven't seen her since we came back."

Aven nodded. "Let me go tell her we're done."

"You do that," Owyn said. "And I'll help Aeri with cooking." He grinned at her, and she smiled in response as he took his place next to her at the table. "What are we making?"

"Flatbread," she answered. "There wasn't a lot of meat from the hunting, so I made stew." She nodded toward the fire, where Gannet was minding the pot. "I wanted to save the preserved meat for if hunting failed completely."

"How poor was the hunting?" Owyn asked.

"Six rabbits."

He whistled. "Yeah, that's not a lot. Right. What can I do to help?"

They worked in comfortable silence, for which Aeris was grateful. Owyn always seemed to know when she needed to be quiet to think. And now, she did. There was something wrong underneath the surface, something that made her uneasy. When it started, she thought it was something to do with Tiras' vision and today being the third day. Now? It hadn't stopped, and she wasn't entirely sure it had anything to do with the burned-out camp.

"Fa?" she said softly. "Are you... feeling anything?"

Owyn looked at her. "You don't call me that," he said. "Just Fa, and not Fa Owyn. You don't do that. Not unless something is bothering you. What is it?"

"I'm not sure," Aeris admitted. "I still feel... something is off. I can't tell what. And it's not stopping. Remember I said it felt like summer lightning? Right before they found the campsite? I'm still feeling it. Something is..." She frowned, then shook her head. "I don't know."

Owyn nodded. "I'm not feeling anything. Did you ask Tiras?"

"Not yet." Aeris nodded toward the fire. "They sat down with Gannet and almost immediately fell asleep. Being flower sick is keeping them awake at night."

Owyn sighed. "I'll talk to Allie and see if he has any ideas about that. There's got to be something. And I can go looking tonight, after the children are asleep. See if I can see anything. Now, give me some of that dough."

Chapter Six

"So..." Karse said as he laid aside his empty bowl. "The children are all out of earshot. What do we know?"

"Not much," Owyn answered. "There weren't much to find out there. Someone did a good job of completely wiping away anything that could tell us who that was."

"We know a little," Elaias corrected. "That site... it's not that recent. There was some growth through the ash near the center, and more on the edges. Not new growth, either." He frowned. "It's been a few weeks at most? No longer than that, I don't think."

Karse snorted. "I grew up in Forge. I don't know a blasted thing about growing things. So I'll take your word for it. A few weeks old. Long enough for someone traveling to be missed. We can start asking, showing that pendant as we go. See what we can find."

"We can be pretty sure that they were Fire or Earth," Astur added. "So... they're taken care of one way or the other."

Elaias turned and looked at his brother. "What did you see that I didn't?"

Astur grinned. "Oh, now that's a compliment. You didn't notice? Their bones. They weren't hollow, and they weren't heavy. So they weren't Air—"

"And they weren't Water," Aven finished. "Not that Water would be this far inland without good reason. And if they were, we'd have known. When the tribe comes on-land, they tend to come via the Palace harbor." He nodded. "Good catch, Astur."

"It was." Elaias stretched and stood up. "I'm going to go find my wife and let her have a break. It's not fair to her that she has to chase the little ones all day."

Del got up too. "*I'll come with you. Yana will want one of us to put her to bed.*" He kissed Aria's cheek, then followed Elaias away from the fire.

"Aria, are you feeling anything?" Owyn asked. "Tiras? Any hint of anything wrong?"

Aria frowned and shook her head. "No. Why?"

Tiras sneezed. "I can't tell what I'm feeling right now," they said. "Everything is all mixed up. I don't think..." They paused. "Maybe? Something... like a shadow."

"That's it," Aeris said. "It's a shadow, in the middle of a sunny field. There's something there that shouldn't be, and I can't tell what. It's just... there." She sighed and pulled her wings in tight to her back, leaning into Gannet's comforting bulk. On her other side, Dyna took her hand. "It's darkness," she said. "It's lurking at the edges."

"I am not feeling anything like that," Aria said.

"Neither am I." Owyn turned to look at Aeris. "But Aeri is, and Tiras is." He frowned. "I wish Fisher had come with us. Maybe it's something we're not feeling because we're older?"

"Or because it is something that doesn't center on us," Aria said. "Whatever it is, it is focused on Aeris and on her Companions."

Aeris sighed. "Which... we knew that. The fighting in the mountains, it's because of the stories about the Child. This conflict, it's all centered on who they think I am." She shook her head. "It's coming, and we can't stop it. People are going to get hurt, and there's nothing we can do."

"There is," Aven said. "But it won't be easy. It's never easy, when you're at the heart of prophecy." He looked at Aria, who was sitting at his right. "We know that all too well. I could wish that you wouldn't have to learn it the way we did."

"Oh," Owyn breathed. "Oh, yeah. That... fuck." He leaned forward, resting his elbows on his knees as his twists fell over his shoulders. "Yeah, let's not have any more massive storms or exploding mountains, right?"

"We're not that far out of balance," Treesi said. "The land says we are not. Things are green and growing. When we first started, back at the beginning, the land was dead."

"It's a little out of balance, but it can be pulled back in," Othi agreed. "We're a little off course. But a little off course for a long enough time? Then you're lost."

"We're not lost," Aven said, his voice firm.

"The last time, it was twenty-five years," Aeris said. "This time, it's two or so. We're not lost. Not yet." She looked around to see the entire group staring at her. "We know why we're out of balance. The lore says I have to have my Water first."

"You know, I thought we were done hearing about lore," Karse said. "I mean, everything to do with getting Aria on the throne was driven by the lore, and by things being done wrong. And it went all the way back to Milon taking the wrong road on his Progress, because of the floods that year. Right?" He looked around. "Aven, am I remembering that right?"

"You are," Aven agreed. "And I thought we'd fulfilled the requirements for the lore, too. But now—"

"You haven't," Gannet blurted. "Because you're missing part of the lore entirely."

"What?" Aven frowned, looking across the fire. "Gannet, what do you mean? What lore are we missing? We've done everything—"

Gannet shook his head, his wings flaring slightly. "You haven't!" they insisted. "Because you're not looking at all of the lore." He looked around. "Ever since I came down from the mountains and started really learning, I've been wondering about it. But it didn't seem my place to say anything. I thought... you all lived the lore already. But I haven't heard anyone talking about anything to do with the lore that I learned when I was small."

"Which lore?" Aria asked.

"Firstborn, no one talks about Axia as a child. I haven't heard anyone talking about the High Meadows lore, which means that no one is looking at all of the lore. No one is talking about the Heir becoming the Heir. And the stories they tell in the mountains, about the Child, those are based in the High Meadows stories. Aren't they? Does that make them lore, too? The people in the mountains, that's their lore. That's why they're doing what they're doing. We were just talking about that."

"I... it's..." Owyn started. He frowned and looked around. "Aria, you told us those were lore. Years ago."

"That was what I was taught, the same as Gannet," Aria said. "That they were the early lore, from before Axia came down from the mountains."

"They are lore because they are stories about Axia," Gannet said.

"I... I don't think that's how it works—" Owyn started.

"Why not?" Gannet asked. "Tell me why stories about Axia as a child are not being taught as a source of lore, when every other story about her *is*? The Progress is the path she took to find her first Companions. The order that the Heir is supposed to find the Companions is the same order that she found hers. And not following that lore is what started the whole downhill slide the last time." He looked around. "All of our lore started as stories about Axia. These are stories about Axia, but they're not taught as lore anywhere but in the mountains. Why not?"

"That... those are some very good questions," Aven murmured. "I wonder what Steward will have to say to those?"

"I want to know what Del will say," Owyn added. "He'll know more about this than any of us. He's been studying these stories since we first learned about them, because he'd never heard all of them either. I don't think we were ignoring them. Not intentionally, anyway. Somehow, we lost that part of the lore." He frowned. "Fire doesn't tell those stories. Or they didn't, until Del got them written down and we spread them out again."

"I never heard them outside the mountains," Astur said. "I knew them from when I was small. Mam told us those stories. But when we got Del's books and read the stories to the children in Terraces, no one knew them at all."

"And Water doesn't tell them," Aven said. "I'd never heard them until the Progress. Aria, you knew them."

"They're common stories among the Air flocks," Aria said. "Or they were."

"They still are," Gannet agreed. "I've told them. I'm not sure how they're lore, though. The ones we call lore... those are instructions. Ways to do things. How is beating King Frog at riddles an instruction?"

Tiras laughed. "Because there's the story, and there's the meaning. What's the meaning?" They poked Gannet with one finger. "The heart of the story is the lore."

"My question about those stories about the Child is how old are they?" Aeris asked. "Are they new, like the silliness about the Perfume Dancers that we came up with the other day? Or are they the same lore, from a different angle? How do we tell the difference? Gannet, you were making jokes about how you could start a Perfume Dancer cult based on what we came up with in the coach. Remember?"

"That's a frightening idea," Owyn said. "And we had the same questions when we first learned about the Child and Del told us about the High Meadows stories. He's been working on that answer for years." He sat up. "And here he comes."

Del joined them, sitting down next to Owyn. He looked around and arched a brow. "*I missed something?*"

"Something you might be the only one who can answer," Owyn replied. "We were talking about the High Meadows stories, and how they're lost lore. Which means that when we're following the lore, we're not following all of it, and that might be a problem."

Del's brow furrowed. *"If it's a problem, it's been a problem for a very long time. No one in Milon's circle knew the stories. Fa didn't know them before I learned them."*

Owyn translated, and Alanar leaned forward. "Del, where did you first learn them?"

Del cocked his head to the side, frowning. He slowly shook his head. *"I don't remember,"* he signed. Then he coughed. "Nestor," he said aloud.

"Nestor, the old steward? The one Risha killed?" Owyn said. "He told you those stories? How did he... oh. I remember now. He was wingless Air."

"And Air didn't lose that lore," Gannet said. "Huh..." His voice trailed off, and he frowned and hunched over in his seat.

"Gan?" Aeris put her hand on Gannet's arm. "What is it?"

"Wondering," he murmured. "I've been telling those stories since I learned them from my grandmother. Who taught her? And...did we learn them from the people in the mountains? Or did they learn them from us?" He gestured toward the eastern sky. "Is that what the fighting in the mountains is about? It's all over which lore is right? But it's the same lore, isn't it?"

Owyn looked at Del. "You want me to say it?" When Del nodded, he grinned. "Right. Too many words, and it's getting dark. Del says that it probably is all the same lore, and that it probably came down from the mountains from the winged flocks to the wingless ones and spread from there. Given how isolated the Air flocks are, and how the Wanderers in the mountains tend to be isolated, too, Del says that would lead to... wait, what?" He paused. "Really? All right. It leads to less drift."

"Drift?" Aven repeated. "Like tides?"

"Oh," Othi breathed. "I understand. It's a problem we have with tattoos. Every time an artist works, they make small changes. They can't help it. Nobody can make the same mark the same way every time, no matter how hard they try. And every time there's a small change, it's replicated. So small changes become big changes..." He paused. "And we were just talking about that. That's where we are. Small changes became big changes became stories that aren't even told anymore because no one recognizes them as being lore."

"But the stories are spreading again—" Astur said.

"As stories," Treesi interrupted. "The books that Del compiled and had printed are storybooks. It's like *The Stars Dance*. They're entertainment for children. They're not being read as lore. Which... how do we teach people the lore if we don't know what it's supposed to mean? What is it telling us?" She gestured toward Tiras. "They're right. We need the meaning at the heart of the story. And it's changed so much, how do we know?"

"We find out," Owyn said. "Del says we have to find out. Which means we have to talk to the Air tribe and find out which is the oldest version."

Gannet snorted. "Good luck with that," he said. "Every flock will say that their version is the oldest."

"Do we have time to do that?" Aeris asked. "This is happening now. The mountain folk are fighting over this now. We need to know how to stop this."

"We've got time before we get to the Temple," Gannet said. "I'll tell you the stories. All of the ones I know. And we can compare them to the ones the Firstborn knows, and the ones Del knows, and see what's the same. And maybe find something that way."

"That sounds frighteningly like a plan," Karse said. "And it'll give you a way to pass the time in the coach."

"Write them down," Owyn said. "Del says to write them down. Who writes with the best hand?"

"Tiras." The answer came from three directions, and Tiras scowled at them.

"I can't embellish, can I?" they asked. "I just have to write it down the way you tell me. That's boring."

"It's important." Gannet hugged Tiras to his side. "I'll try to be entertaining."

"We should get some sleep," Aven said. "We need to be on the road early to make up time."

Aeris nodded and let go of Dyna's hand, standing up. Gannet rested his hand on the small of her back, and she leaned into his side. Tiras offered Dyna their arm, and the four of them left the fire and headed toward their tent. As they reached it, someone whistled from out of the shadows. Aeris turned and saw Lancir. He smiled and came toward them.

"I just went off duty," he said. "And... well, I was hoping to steal Dyna away for a little while? For company, while I eat?"

Aeris looked back at Dyna, who blushed. "I'd like that," she murmured. "Aeris, if you don't mind?"

Aeris smiled and shook her head. "I don't. Go on. And if you stay up too late, you can sleep in the coach tomorrow." She laughed as Dyna hugged her and kissed her cheek, then watched as Lancir took her hand and walked off toward the kitchen tent with her.

"Do you think they'll just be having dinner?" Tiras whispered.

"I think she'll tell us in the morning," Gannet whispered back. "And that we shouldn't wait up for her. She's likely to come in late, and she'll crawl in with us when she does."

They entered the tent, finding that the bed boxes had been set up for them — there were two beds set up side by side. Gannet went to stand by one of them, then looked back.

"Who's sleeping where tonight?" he asked. "All together, and we can put Tiras in the middle?"

"Threaten me, why don't you?" Tiras said with a laugh. "In between two of my favorite people? How is that a bad thing?"

Gannet chuckled. "Come on, then. I'll tell you both a story."

They prepared for bed, and all climbed in. Gannet laid down on his right side, and Aeris was on her left, facing him. Tiras rested between them, on their back, their hands tucked behind their head.

"Story?" they prompted.

Gannet laughed. "Right. I'll start from the beginning of the cycle. And I'll tell it again tomorrow so you can write it down, Tir." He paused, closing his eyes, then began, "World begin. Worlds end. Worlds begin again. So it is with worlds. In the young days of the world, in the days when the Mother and Axia dwelt in the hidden meadows of the high places, Axia went out from her mother's house in search of her own purpose. Her entire world, and all that she knew was her mother's house and the meadow, but she had seen more in her dreams. So she followed those dreams, leaving the meadow and her mother behind her as she climbed higher into the mountains, seeking answers to the questions that she held in her heart, and seeking the places that she saw in her mind.

"High in the mountains, far from the meadow she had known, Axia lay down to rest by the shores of a lake. While she slept, she was discovered by the frogs who lived there. They had never seen anyone like Axia before, and fled to their king, terrified of the monster sleeping in their back garden. The king summoned his army, and they marched out to defeat the threat to their people. They discovered Axia awake; the king challenged her, and she assured him that she meant his people no harm. She spoke to them kindly, telling them about her life with her mother, and about her search for answers. And she asked them questions about their lives and their world, and the Frog King grew to desire this gentle stranger, and demanded that she remain with them and become his queen—"

A snore interrupted the story, and Aeris muffled a laugh as Tiras rolled toward Gannet in their sleep.

"I think that's the end of story time," Gannet said in a low voice. "Did you get anything out of what you did hear?"

"Nothing that I didn't already know," Aeris admitted. "Axia trying to find her place in the world, and trying to make sense of who she was. Which... doesn't everyone have that?"

Gannet nodded. "Truth. I think that's part of growing up. We have it easy."

"We do?" Aeris shifted closer, draping her arm over both Tiras and Gannet.

"I think so," Gannet answered. "You're the Heir. Your place in the world is pretty solid. And as for the Companions? We find out who we are and our place in the world when you give us these." He touched the cloudy white gem at his throat.

Aeris smiled. "Have I mentioned recently that I love you?"

Gannet looked thoughtful, then shook his head. "Not today. But that's fine. I know it. Go to sleep."

Chapter Seven

A eris woke up hearing movement outside the tent. People were calling and there were the sounds of the camp being broken down. Gannet was still sound asleep, but Tiras had somehow gotten out from between them without waking either of them. She shifted closer to Gannet, and he sleepily pulled her into his arms and sighed. Then he jerked slightly and opened his eyes.

"We're missing one," he mumbled.

"They got up without waking us," Aeris said. "I only just noticed."

Gannet chuckled and pulled her closer. "Well, since we're alone..." His voice trailed off, and he raised his head. "Aeri, we are alone. The other bed wasn't slept in."

Aeris rolled onto her front to look — the blankets on the other bed were still tucked in. "Dyna didn't come in?" She looked back at Gannet. "We're getting up?"

"We're getting up."

They scrambled into clothes and left the tent together. There was a group sitting around the fire, but Aeris could see that Dyna wasn't there. Owyn, however, was, and he smiled and waved at them. Then his smile faded, and he touched Alanar's arm.

"Oh, fuck," Aeris whispered.

"Do you see her?" Gannet asked.

"No." Aeris didn't move, waiting for Owyn and Alanar to come to them.

"Is Dyna still asleep?" Owyn looked at the tent flap. "That's not like her. She's never the last one up, and Tiras came out a bit ago."

"She's... not in there," Aeris said. "She went for a walk with Lancir last night, and she didn't come in. We only just woke up and found out."

"She..." Owyn stared at them for a moment, then turned around and bellowed, "Dyna!"

Immediately, the group at the fire moved — Karse and Elaias both came running, with Aven and Othi following behind.

"What's is it?" Elaias asked.

"Dyna never came in last night," Aeris repeated. "She went for a walk with... Lancir!" Aeris gasped as the young guard appeared from behind the kitchen tent, hand in hand with Dyna. Both of them were wearing the same clothes as they had been the day before, and both carried baskets.

"Where have you been?" Owyn demanded.

"We were up early, and we went foraging," Dyna answered. She looked mystified. "We told the guard on duty where we were going."

"I wanted to help with the supplies, since the hunting was poor yesterday," Lancir added. He grinned sheepishly. "Turns out, I don't know a thing about mushrooms."

"Or anything else you could gather while foraging," Dyna jibed gently. She turned to face them. "I'm sorry we frightened you. We didn't mean to."

"And where were you last night?" Owyn asked in a low voice.

"And that's our signal to leave," Karse said. "Lancir, with me."

"Captain, if I may?" Lancir said. "I... I asked Dyna to come and keep me company while I ate. We went for a walk, just past the guards. They could see us the entire time. Then we went back to the fire to talk and... well, we fell asleep sitting there." He looked around. "There's Lestri. He's the one who woke us up. You can ask him." He drew himself up. "Fireborn, nothing untoward happened."

"Keep it that way," Owyn said, his voice firm. Dyna narrowed her eyes, and Owyn coughed. "Really?" he sputtered. "That's your argument?"

"What?" Alanar asked.

"Right... maybe I'm being a bit overprotective. Maybe." Owyn grumbled. "Dyna, if you're going to throw that in my face, even privately, then you're old enough to know the whole story. Go put those in the kitchen tent to be packed."

Dyna blushed. "Yes, Fa. I... I'm sorry. That was... I shouldn't have..."

"No, you shouldn't have. And it's past time that we talk, Dyna." Owyn led Alanar away, and Aeris could hear them talking in low voices. Dyna bit her lip, but shook her head when Aeris stepped toward her. She turned and walked toward the kitchen tent. Lancir and Karse followed, and Aeris could tell that Karse was furious.

"What was that about?" Gannet whispered.

"I'll explain later," Aeris answered. "Let's go eat."

They headed toward the fire, and Aven fell in next to her. He didn't say anything, which was fine with Aeris. She wasn't sure how she'd have answered any questions. Then he took a deep breath and broke the silence. "Aeris?"

She stopped walking and sighed. "Yes, Fa?"

"How long has this been going on?"

Aeris shook her head. "I'm not sure what 'this' you mean, Fa. You know when Dyna and Lancir started. It was right before we left. We talked about it on the beach, after you took us out on the canoe. Remember?"

Aven nodded. "I remember now."

"I'm not sure of the problem," Aeris added. "We all like him. You like him. Fa Owyn likes him, too. At least, I thought he did."

"I can't speak for Owyn, but I think the problem may very well be that Dyna isn't an adult yet."

Aeris frowned. "Fa, she's been my Companion for two years. We weren't any of us adults when we first came together. Fa Owyn didn't have any trouble with that."

"But that's the difference," Aven said. "She's your Companion. You four are made for each other. He knows that none of you will ever hurt Dyna, and he trusts all of you. He doesn't have that same level of trust with Lancir, for all that he's one of Karse's men." Aven grimaced. "We've had... trouble with one of Karse's men before. Karse has been more careful since then, but still... Owyn is wary."

"Trouble?" Gannet repeated. "With the Captain's men?"

"It was years ago, during Aria's Progress," Aven said. "And that's all you need to know. The rest isn't important. At least, not to this conversation." He took a deep breath. "Go and eat something, Aeri. We'll be on the road soon enough."

"Can we ride this morning?" Aeris asked. "If we stay with the guard or Fa Owyn and Fa Del?"

Aven smiled. "I'll tell the guard to have your horses saddled. Now go eat."

Aeris nodded, taking Gannet's hand. They walked to the fire and sat down with Tiras, who watched them coming without moving.

"Why didn't you come see?" Gannet asked softly.

"Because Othi told me to stay." Tiras looked over their shoulder. "When someone that big tells me to stay, I'm staying. What happened? I noticed Dyna wasn't in the other bed when I got up."

"She and Lancir fell asleep out here," Aeris answered, keeping her voice low. "And Fa Owyn isn't happy."

"You said you were going to explain," Gannet said. "Is now good?"

Aeris looked around. There was no one in earshot. "Tir, would you get us some porridge?" she asked. "We need to eat so we can get ready to go."

Tiras nodded and got up, going to the fire and filling two bowls. They carried them back, sitting down on the ground at Aeris' feet once she and Gannet had taken the bowls. "Tell."

Aeris looked around again. "You don't tell," she murmured. "Understand?"

"Understood," Gannet answered.

"Fa Owyn grew up on the streets of Forge, and before he was adopted by Grandfa Mem, he was a street whore," Aeris said. "And he started way too young."

Tiras whistled softly. "That... I didn't know that."

"You didn't need to know," Aeris answered. "Fa Owyn doesn't talk about it much, because people are funny about it when they find out. But that's the brand on his shoulder — the crossed lines? He was caught one too many times, and sold as a slave because of it."

"Owyn was a slave?" Gannet gasped. "I... I didn't think there were slaves anymore!"

"There were, when they were our age," Aeris said. She looked around again. "Mama changed the laws. Well, Grandfa Milon did because she asked him to do it. He made it so that whores aren't punished anymore, and she outlawed slavery in all of Adavar. Owyn may be the last person to have those marks."

"Why didn't anyone tell us that?" Tiras asked. Then they frowned. "No, nevermind. Why would they? It's not important."

"Except that may be why Owyn is reacting the way that he is," Gannet said. "Aeri, did you know that he could hear Dyna in his head?"

"No, but it makes sense. She's his daughter." Aeris stirred her porridge and took a bite. "We'll see what happens next."

"Do you think Lancir is going to be sent back?" Gannet asked. "Or sent away?"

"I hope not," Aeris answered.

Gannet nodded, eating his own porridge. He finished his bowl before saying, "Tir, what do you think of him? Really?"

Tiras shrugged. "What time I've spent with him has been with you all. I haven't had any alone time with him, so I don't have any impression that isn't..." They paused. "Ah... colored? I suppose that's the word. Colored by what others think of him."

"Especially Dyna?" Aeris asked, scraping the bottom of her bowl.

"What about me?" Aeris looked over her shoulder to see that Dyna had come up behind her. Her face was pale, her eyes red. Aeris put down her bowl and held her hand out, but Dyna ignored it, coming around to sit facing them. "What about me?" she repeated.

"Wondering if we need to thump Lancir," Tiras answered.

"You do not need to thump Lancir," Dyna snapped. "You're all overreacting. Honestly, you said that if we got closer, you'd welcome him!"

"We did," Aeris agreed. "And in the very next breath, there was the promise that if he hurt you, we'd thump him. So... which is it? And are you all right?"

Dyna grimaced. "I was... I was wrong. I said something I shouldn't have to my father, and now he's upset with me." She clasped her hands in her lap. "And if Lancir gets put out, it'll be my fault."

"You both did it. Why would it be your fault?" Tiras asked. "Isn't it part his fault? Why do you get all the blame?"

Dyna blushed slightly. "I suggested going foraging. He reminded me about how bad the hunting was, so I suggested we go foraging, and we didn't find any of my parents to tell them we were going before we left."

Aeris nodded, then looked past Dyna to see Karse and Lancir coming toward them. Lancir had a look that Aeris knew — Karse had taken him to task, then forgiven him and given him a second chance. All the younger guards in the Palace wore that look at least once. There was a different look for guards who were taken to task a second time, one that was usually paired with them being dismissed.

"Captain?" Aeris called. "Were you looking for us?"

"Just your Earth," Karse answered. "If I could borrow her?"

"Captain, I don't mind saying this in front of them all," Lancir interjected. "The Heir and her Companions are... well, they're a whole. And if I'm speaking to one of them, I should speak to them all. Shouldn't I?"

Karse nodded. "If that's how you want to do it. Make it handsome."

Lancir nodded, tucking his hands behind his back. "Earthborn," he said. Then he grimaced. "It feels strange to say that. Dyna, I'm sorry. I know better. We shouldn't have left the camp. I was under orders to keep you and the rest of the Heir's circle safe, and going off alone with you... if something had happened, it would have been a disaster. I violated the trust placed in me by the Firstborn and my captain, and I apologize."

Karse folded his arms over his chest. "New rules, Dyna," he said. "If you continue to go walking out with my guard, you stay inside the camp at all times. No going out foraging without my express permission, and without a half-dozen guards. We don't know who did for that poor wretch in the other camp, and until we find out, I'm not taking chances with any of you." He looked at the others. "And that goes for all of you. Understood?"

"Yes, Captain," Aeris said, hearing Gannet and Tiras echo her words. "Thank you."

Karse smiled. Then he turned and pointed at Lancir. "You've got latrine duty from now until we reach the Temple. Understood?"

"Yes, Captain," Lancir answered.

"Good. Go on, then. We'll be ready to ride soon."

THE REST OF THE JOURNEY was uneventful, and even pleasant in spots. They met with farmers and traders along the road, stopping to share news. No one recognized the pendant from the campsite, and while there were reports of bandits, they were all second-hand reports witnessed by someone who knew someone who'd seen them. In the coach, Aeris and her circle studied the different variations of the High Meadows stories that they'd collected from Aria, Elaias, Astur and Treesi, and compared them with the ones Gannet knew, looking for differences and arguing about what they might mean. The evenings were quiet, and Lancir and Dyna sat together every night after supper, reading by torchlight.

The group grew smaller at the crossroads, when Elaias and the other healers left them. Astur gave the pendant to Owyn for safekeeping, and made them promise to stop and tell him if they found out who it belonged to. From there, it was only a day before the road started sloping up toward the Solstice village and their next stop.

They reached the Solstice village a week after they left the crossroads, and spent two days camped there, hearing the news from the Headwoman, Aeris' great-aunt Sarita. On the third morning, they set out for the Temple. The last time Aeris had been on this road, it was during her own Progress, when they'd brought Dyna, Tiras and Gannet to meet the High Priest and see if he had any answers about what not finding Aeris' Water might mean.

"Looking forward to seeing them?" Owyn asked, guiding Pepper up next to Aeris' horse. They could see the Temple ahead of them, close enough that they could see people waving.

"Yes. I've missed them," Aeris answered. "You, too?"

Owyn nodded. "When Aunt Rhexa told me she was coming up here, I thought she was insane. But... she's happy. All her letters say she's happy. I just... I miss her being only a couple of hours away on the cutter." He straightened. "And there she is!" He urged his horse into a trot, heading toward the Temple and the woman standing in front of the door.

"Owyn!" Aeris heard the shock in her voice. "What are you doing here?"

"That's a funny thing to say," Gannet said, coming up on Aeris' other side. "They sent for us."

"Something isn't right," Aeris said, and goaded Lace into a canter. Gannet and Tiras followed, and they reached the Temple just as Steward came outside. He was alone, and Aeris felt cold.

"Rhexa, what is it?" he said. Then he stopped. "Owyn? What..." He stopped, looking around, squinting hard.

"They're here," Rhexa said. "They're all here. Steward, the children are here!"

"No," Steward breathed. "No! Aria! What are you doing here? And you brought Aeris? Why?"

"You sent for us," Aria answered as she reached them. "Did you think we wouldn't come?"

Steward looked blank. "I... I didn't send for you! I sent for guards! We needed help. I told Iantir to tell you not to come, and to guard Aeris and her Companions like your lives depended on it!" He squinted again. "Where is he? Where's Iantir?"

"Oh...oh, no." Owyn reached into his pouch. When he took his hand out, Aeris could see the chain dangling from his fingers. "That's why Astur knew this," he murmured. He went to Steward and opened his hand. "We found this on the way here," he said softly. "In... we couldn't identify the body. I'm sorry."

"Body?" Steward took the pendant and brought it close. His breath caught. "No," he whispered. "He... no." He closed his hand around the pendant and took a deep, shuddering breath as Rhexa took his arm. "Mother hold him," he whispered. "He was ready to take his vows as a priest. He was going to follow me... where are the guards?" he asked, his voice shaking. "You... you didn't bring guards, did you?"

"Karse, and a squad of his men," Aria answered. "Steward—"

"Frayim is missing," Steward's voice caught, and it took a moment before he could continue. "Fray... he took some of the novices and went out to visit some of the local villages. He does it... every sixth day, or thereabouts. This time, he never came back, and when we went looking for him, we found the villages burned to the ground. I sent Iantir to the Palace. We need guards to help us search, and he was supposed to warn you."

"The messenger that came to us was a stranger, and he said that Frayim had a vision and wanted to see Aeris," Aven said.

Steward shook his head. "A lie. A trick." He sighed. "Half truths. Frayim did have a vision, but it was a warning. That's what Iantir was supposed to tell you." He looked around, and stopped when he saw Aeris. "I still say your father indulges you far too much."

Aeris laughed and went to hug him. "I'm fine, Uncle."

He nodded, his cheek brushing against her hair. "And I worry. But you're here now. And we'll do the best we can."

"We can send Aeris and her Companions back to the Palace—" Aria said, stopping when Steward shook his head.

"Don't make rash decisions, Aria," he said. "Stop and think. Right now, we can keep her safe. The Temple is defensible."

"And if we need to, I can take her to my flock," Gannet added.

Steward nodded, keeping his arm around Aeris' shoulders as he turned. "On the road, Aeris would be a target. A lightly guarded one, if that. Here in the Temple, or up with the flock? She's safe." He smiled down at Aeris, hugging her to his side. "I'm sorry to see you here," he added. "But it's good to see you. I've missed all of you. Come into the Temple, and we'll talk."

Chapter Eight

Setting the camp up took priority over talking, and by the time the tents were set and guards posted, it was too late to talk — Steward was asleep.

"Is he not well?" Aria asked Rhexa when she came to tell them. "We have enough healers to see to everyone in the Temple, and more setting up a healing center at the crossroads..."

"He's fine," Rhexa said. "He's perfectly healthy. He's just... well, he's not getting any younger. And he's worried. About Frayim. About Aeris. About what is happening out in the mountains. It takes a toll on him, and there are days when he's asleep practically as soon as the sun sets. Then he doesn't sleep well, because he's worried and..." She sighed. "And I should go back. If he wakes up and I'm not there, he'll rouse the entire Temple looking for me."

"I'll walk back with you," Owyn said, getting up and dusting off his trousers. "We can talk. I want to know more about what Frayim saw."

"I don't know the details, I'm afraid." Rhexa took Owyn's arm. "And I'm not sure that Steward does either. At least, he didn't tell me."

"We'll find out in the morning," Owyn said. "Come on. I missed you." They headed off to the Temple, and Aria sat down. Aeris knew what her mother was going to say before she said it.

"Aeris and her Companions must go back. It's not safe here."

"And the road won't be any safer," Aven said. "We can't protect her if we're not there. She's safer with us."

"And she doesn't appreciate you discussing her as if she wasn't sitting right in front of you," Aeris added. Both of her parents looked shocked. "Did you forget I was here?"

"The High Priest said that we needed to talk to him, and we can't do that tonight," Gannet added. "Nothing is getting decided tonight."

"They both have valid points," Treesi said gently. "Aria, you can't make a decision in the heat of the moment. You... you don't make the best decisions when you do that."

Aria scowled at her Earth, then sighed. "You're right. You're right, and I thought I'd grown out of that." She took a deep breath. "Aeris, I apologize. I just..." She wrapped her arms around herself and drew her wings in. "I already almost lost you once. I don't want to face that ever again."

Aeris got up and went to kneel in front of her mother. "Mama, you and Fa and all my other parents have taught me the best you know how to take care of myself."

"That doesn't change anything, my dove," Aria said, taking Aeris' hands. "But you all are right. I can't make this decision in haste, and I can't make it alone. We will talk with Steward in the morning, and we'll decide on the best course of action. And in the meantime, we should eat."

THE FOLLOWING MORNING, everyone assembled in the High Priest's apartments in the Temple.

"There aren't enough seats, I'm afraid," Steward said.

"We'll be fine," Aven replied. Aeris and her Companions all sat on the floor in the middle of the room, and the adults ranged around them, finding seats on chairs and tables.

"What do you know about Frayim's vision?" Owyn asked.

"He didn't go into specifics," Steward answered. "I think he was more startled than any of us that he'd had a vision after all this time. He told me it was a warning, that there was a darkness in the mountains, and that it was coming for Aeris."

"A darkness?" Aeris blurted. "Like... like a shadow?" She turned and looked at her mother. "Like what we were feeling, all the way here."

"You had the same vision? And you came anyway?" Rhexa asked.

"Not the same, and not until we were three days on the road," Aeris answered. "It wasn't a real vision. It was... a sense of something." She shrugged. "I get that, sometimes. I'm not a Smoke Dancer. Not like Mama, or Tiras."

"I didn't have more than a sense, either," Tiras added. "But I was addled most of the trip."

"Flower sick," Aven answered Steward's questioning gaze.

"Which makes Tiras have all kinds of waking visions," Owyn added. He frowned. "I could dance. See what I can see. But that might not be the best idea. It might change things, make them worse."

"Wait," Karse said. "How would looking for visions make things worse? We'd have a better idea of what to do. You might see what Frayim saw."

"It doesn't really matter what Frayim saw," Tiras said. "We're in it. If we try to change what we're doing..." They shrugged. "Bad things."

"Is that hyperbole, or a vision?" Steward asked. "Bad things?"

Tiras shrugged again. "Hard to say. But changing what we're doing may put us closer to the shadow, and sooner than we should be." They frowned. "The only way is through the shadows."

Steward's brows rose. "I see what you mean about waking visions. All right. We can move Aeris and her Companions into the Temple for the duration. It's the most defensible." He smiled at them. "And we'll be glad of the company."

"Thank you, Uncle Steward," Aeris said. "While we're here, we need to talk stories with you."

"Stories?" Steward looked over to where Del was sitting with Yana on his lap. "You should be talking to Del about stories. He's the expert."

"We have been, and he's not sure," Gannet said. "There are stories that we tell in the flocks as lore, but that in the lowlands are just... stories. The High Meadows cycle."

Steward frowned, nodding slowly. "I remember when we first heard of those. I know that the Wanderers think of them as lore. But so much of what they believe is different from what we follow. Are their stories part of our lore?"

"The Air tribe thinks they are. Which means that the Wingless think so, which may be where the Wanderers got it." Gannet spread his hands wide. "But no one in the lowlands teaches them as lore. Which may be a mistake. I mean... Air held on to the lore because we're slow to change. We're like our mountains like that. Other tribes are more... flexible. So if we can understand why the Wanderers held on to that lore when no one else did, and what they're trying to do, then maybe we can stop it? Or... or convince them they're doing it the wrong way? Or something?" He dropped his hands in his lap.

Steward looked thoughtful. "We'll talk to the Penitents and see what they can tell us. I'm sure that there will be some who'll be willing to tell you their stories from before they turned to follow Aria." He sighed. "Now, tell me what happened to Iantir."

Aeris looked back to see her father looking at Owyn. Owyn shook his head, and Aven sighed. "Are you sure you want to know?" he asked.

Steward went pale. "I think I have the right to know," he answered. Rhexa rested her hands on his shoulders.

"Aven, how bad was it?" she asked.

Aven grimaced. "Bad. It was... it was bad," he said. "Owyn told you we couldn't identify the body. They... whoever did this killed him, and his horse, and they put the entire campsite to the torch. The body was burned beyond recognition. We buried him properly."

"Mother hold him," Rhexa murmured. She leaned down and hugged Steward. "Don't you start," she warned. "It was not your fault."

"I sent him," Steward said, his voice shaking. "I let him go alone. I knew there was a threat out there..."

"You didn't let him go alone. He insisted," Rhexa interrupted. "You argued over it, and he insisted because he'd be able to travel faster."

"Given what we saw?" Karse offered. "It wouldn't have made a difference if he'd been with others. Whoever did this knew what they were about, and had the numbers to do it fast and hard. They took Frayim and did for those villages, knowing you'd send word to the Palace. Then they did for Iantir, and sent their own man in to lure us out." He took a deep breath and shook his head. "They know what they're doing. That tells me there's more going on out here than we've been told."

"What have you been told?" Rhexa asked.

"The reports we've had from the Solstice village and the Air flocks have told us that there's fighting, but not who or why," Aven answered. "Now... this has to be connected. The fake priest, the attack on the road, it's all too convenient to be isolated incidents. There's something else going on here. So what do you know?"

Steward took a deep breath. "Not much. I have some contacts among the Penitent communities in the mountains, but they told me that they didn't want to involve the Temple or the Palace in their troubles." He smiled slightly. "They said it was nothing to bother the Blessèd Mother with. I accepted that. It may have been a mistake."

He shrugged. "What I was told was that the Wanderers appeared to be coming together, and the Penitents have forces working against them."

"Wait." Aria held up one hand. "Wait a moment. Did you... are you saying that there's a *war* going on in the mountains? And you knew about it?"

Steward looked startled. "I... a war?" He looked up at Rhexa. "I hadn't... I didn't think of it in those terms. Over the years, I've learned that there are all sorts of little scuffles and feuds out here. I didn't think this was anything more than that."

"And they didn't want you involved," Karse said. "They tried to protect you."

Aven nodded. "Right. We need to meet with your allies, see what they know. Get search parties out. I wish Ama was here. This is her strength." He stood up and started pacing, his limp more noticeable than usual. "We can send riders down to the healing center at the crossroads, have them send messengers back to the Palace for more men. They have the men to spare, and we don't. They'll also be able to bring in more supplies. We were only planning for a month." He stopped and looked at Aeris, then shook her head. "And you are safer here. And perhaps you'll be able to find something in the stories that can help us."

Owyn shifted in his seat and looked at Del. "Del wants to know if you've found anything yet?"

Aeris shook her head. "Nothing that doesn't line up with other stories we already know from the High Meadows cycle. Everyone so far is telling variations on the same stories."

"So what's fueling this, then?" Karse asked. "What's made whoever is out there stand up and get people to follow them?"

"I'll send word to the Penitent communities," Steward said. "We'll see what we can find."

Aven nodded. "And we'll see what we can find here in the meantime."

THAT AFTERNOON, AVEN and Othi led a group of guards and Penitent priests out to search, while Copper took two guards back to the Solstice village, carrying urgent messages that would be sent on to the new healing center and on to the Palace. Aeris and her Companions moved into the Temple, trying to arrange themselves in a room that would be small for a single person but now had to hold four.

"Normally, we'd have visitors stay in the guest house," Rhexa said as she helped them settle in. "But this is more secure."

"We'll be fine, Aunt Rhexa," Dyna said. "It's just to sleep."

Rhexa smiled. "Now, Steward went and talked to some of the newer novices. They'll be waiting to tell you their stories whenever you're ready. I'll leave you to get settled." She left, closing the door behind her. Aeris looked around and sat down on the narrow bed.

Dyna sat down next to her and took her hand. "This—"

"If you're going to say it won't be so bad, don't," Gannet said, keeping his voice down. "How are we all going to sleep in here? There's barely room in here for four people without wings."

"We'll manage," Aeris said. "We don't have a choice." She sighed. "I don't want to go up to the flocks. It would mean leaving two of you behind, and in possible danger."

"So we'll have all four of us in possible danger," Tiras said, dropping to sit on the floor at Aeris' feet. They rested their head on her knee, taking a deep breath. "The shadows are getting darker. Have you noticed?"

Aeris stroked Tiras' hair. "I haven't. I've been too busy to see."

Tiras nodded. "They're darker. Closer. It's coming. And the only way out is through."

"Like sailing into a storm," Aeris said. "We'll do what we have to. Together."

Tiras shook their head. "No, this is yours to do, Aeri. The path to becoming is yours."

"Becoming? Becoming what?" Gannet asked.

Tiras sat up. "I... I don't know," they said. "It blew away." They frowned. "I want to go find Owyn. I'm having more waking visions, and I don't know what's real anymore."

"We'll all go," Dyna said. "We should stay together."

"And then we'll go listen to variations of the same stories, and see if we hear anything different." Gannet pushed off of the wall and opened the door. "Let's go."

Owyn wasn't available, so they sat down with the priests and Penitents first. To Aeris' surprise, when they met with the Penitents, one of the older novices offered a fragment of a new story — one involving Axia and a cloud.

"I don't mind it much anymore," the novice said, his thick mountain brogue making him hard to understand. "Tain't one that's told much, and I never heard no one tell it among this lot. I hain't heard it since I was a wean."

"A what?" Tiras asked, their pen hovering over the paper.

"A wean," Dyna answered. "It's hill dialect. It's a combination word — wee and one. Wean. Fa Elaias uses it, sometimes."

"Elaias?" the novice said. "Now that's a name I hain't heard in an age. Healer lad, no?"

"Yes," Dyna answered, looking surprised. "He's my mother's husband."

The novice smiled. "He was a good sort. I mind him well. I'll see if I can call the rest of the tale to mind." He got up and wandered away, and Tiras looked down at the page.

"That's interesting," they said. "A cloud. That's new."

"And clouds cast shadows, don't they?" Gannet murmured. Tiras looked up, their eyes wide.

"And sometimes clouds are shadows!" they blurted, scrambling to their feet. "Yes! This is the story we need! Let's go find Del!"

They found Del and Owyn in the Temple library, going through records. Owyn smiled as they came in, setting aside the book he was holding.

"You all look like you've found something," he said. "What is it?"

"We think we might have found the story," Tiras answered. "One of the priests mentioned a story about Axia and a cloud. He didn't remember much of it, though. But... a cloud."

"Like what you and Aeris were feeling on the way here," Owyn said slowly. "Del, have we found anything about clouds?"

"No," Del said. He looked down at the book he was reading, then at the shelves and shook his head. "No' yet."

"He said that he hadn't heard it anywhere around here," Gannet added. "No one here tells it. And he hasn't heard it since he was... what was that word?"

"Since he was a wean," Dyna said. "And if he's saying it that way, he's from far up in the mountains, where Granna Gisa is from. Because she's the one Fa Elaias gets that accent from."

Owyn nodded. "Meaning... he's from Wanderer folk. Dyna, you never heard that story from Elaias or your grandmother, did you?"

"No," Dyna answered. "And Fa didn't volunteer it when we were collecting stories, but he knew the rest of the High Meadows stories, so I don't think he knows it."

"Right. Well, now we know it's out there. We'll keep asking. Del and I are going back to the Solstice village tomorrow to send word up to the flocks for more guards." He grimaced. "Plain forgot to send that message with Copper, and Karse is kicking himself. So I said we'd go. Gannet, you want to come? You can send a message to your flock, maybe see if there's anything you weren't taught?"

Gannet glanced at Aeris, and she smiled. "You can go, Gan. It might be helpful. You can share that fragment, and see if they can ask in the flocks."

"I don't want to leave you," Gannet protested. "Not when we're not sure what's happening or what's out there. It isn't safe. I should stay."

"And you sound like you're trying to convince yourself when you really want to go," Aeris pointed out. "Gan, I'll have Tiras and Dyna with me, and all the guards. If necessary, I'll stay in the Temple. I'll be fine."

"Owyn, I need to talk to you," Tiras said. "The waking visions, they're getting more frequent. I keep... I never know when I'm going to fall into one."

Owyn frowned. "And when did you have the last one?"

"An hour or two ago, I think," Tiras answered. "In the middle of a sentence. All of a sudden, I was talking about shadows getting darker, and the only way out is through. And it was before we heard the bit of story about Axia and the cloud." They frowned and looked at Aeris. "Did I say anything else? It's all foggy now."

"That it was mine to do. Tiras said that becoming was mine to do."

Owyn nodded. "Sounds like a vision. Clear as mud." He sighed. "I understand how Mem and Granna Meris felt now. You and me, we're not like other Smoke Dancers, and what I was taught doesn't always apply to you. This...wait... are you hearing anyone yet? And how's your appetite?"

"I'm not having heart visions yet," Tiras answered. "And I already eat like I'm never going to see food again."

"Well, let me know the minute it happens, even if you have to wake me up." Owyn glanced at Del. "Maybe we should take you with us too? We'll be gone most of the day, and I really want to keep an eye on you."

"If Tiras is going, then I really should stay," Gannet said. "I'm not comfortable with both of us leaving Aeris and Dyna alone."

Owyn nodded. "Right. Especially since Aven and Othi aren't here. We'll talk to Steward and Aria tonight, see if they think it's a good idea." He turned to Del. "Anything?"

"No," Del answered. He closed the book and stood up, gesturing toward the door.

"Oh, we're done?" Owyn laughed. "Fine, let's go find them now."

They found Aria, Steward and Alanar in the meadow, surrounded by a large group of people. Aeris could see familiar wagons and carts.

"Dyna, isn't that your mother?" she asked. "Those... those are all the healers. What are they doing here?"

"What?" Owyn stopped, then started jogging toward the group. "Trista?"

At the sound of her name, Trista turned. She waved, then hugged Owyn as he reached them. Aeris and the others caught up with him just in time to catch the end of what Elaias was saying.

"—the village asked us to leave." He ran one hand through his hair. "And to be fair, I don't blame them. Having us there puts them at risk. So I figured we'd follow you and decide where to go from here."

"Honestly, I wouldn't mind if you stayed," Steward said. "There's more than enough room to support a healing center here."

"They sent you away?" Dyna asked. Elaias turned and smiled.

"I didn't see you there, lammie," he said. "And... yes. The village headman had a visit from some of the hill folk, who weren't happy that any of Elan's kin were back in the hills." He grimaced. "So... rather than put the people in the village at risk, we left."

"Won't they be unhappy that you're here?" Gannet asked.

"If the Temple sanctions the healing center, they'll let it be," Steward said. "And we already send novices down to the crossroads on a regular basis. Having a healer ride with them won't be an issue."

"We'll discuss how to make it work." Elaias nodded. "Where should we set up?"

Steward turned and looked around. "Rhex?"

"I'm here," Rhexa called. "And I heard the question. The far end of the meadow should be good. It's close to the stream, and it's fairly level."

Elaias turned and raised his voice. "You heard them. Let's get settled!"

People started moving, and Astur made his way through the group to them. Owyn grimaced.

"Astur, walk with me," he said. "I... we have answers for you."

"Answers?" Astur frowned slightly. "Oh. You know who it was." He stopped and bit his lip. "I... it was Iantir, wasn't it?" Owyn nodded and took the pendant out of his pouch. He handed it to Astur, who looked down at it, rubbing his thumb over the surface. "It's been a long time since I saw this last, but... I remembered. I... I was hoping I'd see him again, once we got out here." He sniffed once. "He asked me to go with him."

"He did?" Elaias asked.

"Yeah. The last night before we went west and the Penitents went north. He asked me to go north with him. He wanted to show me that he'd changed. That he wasn't... that he wasn't the same person who'd followed Mitok. I mean, he was the best of that lot, but he wanted to show me that he could be more." He shrugged. "I thought about it. But I needed to be with Jin and the girls, and with Mam and Minna and Versi. He... he understood that."

Steward made his way through the group to Astur's side. "He was more," he said gently. "And he talked about you. About how you gave him a chance, that you let him see that he could be more."

Astur smiled slightly. "I just... I slept with him. I spent time with him. I... I talked to him. Listened when he talked to me."

"And you fell in love with him, didn't you?"

Astur jumped at the sound of Treesi's voice. Aeris hadn't noticed her approach. Apparently, neither had her brother. "I... you know us, Trees. We're healers. We always fall in love with the ones who need us the most. I just..." He shrugged. "I wasn't sure if I still was. I wanted to find out." He looked down at his hand. "Steward—"

"It's yours," Steward said softly. "Come spend some time with me, and I'll tell you about the man you helped make."

Astur nodded. "I'd like that. Thank you."

Chapter Nine

"**M**y Heir?"

Aeris jerked in surprise, her wings flaring as she looked up from the book she was reading. She felt unusually jumpy, which she attributed to being alone for the first time in ages. Her Fire and Air had gone with Owyn and Del to the Solstice village, and her Earth was helping plan the new healing center with Alanar and Trista. So for the first time since her Progress, Aeris didn't have one of them within earshot. It was strange, and she wasn't sure she liked it. Gannet had reminded her of her promise to stay in the Temple four times before he and Tiras had left for the Solstice village that morning, so she couldn't even go help in the healing center. Rhexa was keeping her company in the library, which helped a little.

"Lancir?"

"Good afternoon," Lancir said from the doorway. "I'm sorry. I didn't mean to startle you. I wouldn't bother you, but there's another group for you to talk to about stories. They came from the hills. Said that the High Priest sent for them. Captain says that I'm to go with you."

"Thank you, Lancir," Aeris said. She stood up and smoothed her long skirt. "I'm presentable, at least. Let me get the Diadem, and I'll come meet them. Are they in the Temple?"

Lancir shook his head. "Out near the edge of the meadow. They didn't want to come too close to the Temple, they said." He shrugged. "I don't know. It doesn't make sense to me."

"Some of the hill folk told Steward that they don't want the Temple involved in whatever they're doing out there," Rhexa said, looking up from the notes that she was taking from another text. "That might be it. Give me a minute to clean up, and I'll come with you."

They walked out of the Temple and around the building, toward where Aeris could see a small group waiting just on the edge of the meadow. "Is it just me, or do they not look like the other Penitents?" she said softly. "They seem... rougher."

"We can't expect them all to look alike," Rhexa said. "That would be like expecting all Air flocks to look alike, or every family in every house in neighboring villages." She paused. "We should have more guards, though."

"They're waiting, though," Lancir said. "Leaving them standing there would be rude. Wouldn't it?"

Aeris grimaced. "It would be. And they won't come closer?"

"No, they—"

"Aeris!"

Aeris turned at the sound of her name and saw Elaias and Astur following them. Elaias carried a heavy walking stick, and Astur had a whip coiled at his hip.

"You're armed?" she asked. "Why?"

The brothers looked at each other and grinned. "Owyn," Astur said. "And he threatened us with Othi. That's reason enough."

"And you were supposed to stay inside," Elaias said as he came closer. "Dyna was pretty insistent. Where are you going?"

"We have visitors," Lancir said. "Penitents who are here to share their stories. The Heir is supposed to collect them."

"Right. Treesi mentioned that." Elaias glanced at Astur, who nodded. "All right. Let's go and talk with them. We'll see if they need anything from the healers while they're here, and they can carry word back to the others that there'll be a healing center near the Temple when they leave."

They started walking again, and Aeris realized that having her honorary uncles behind her was comforting. She relaxed slightly, dropping back to keep pace with them.

"I'm sorry that the healing center at the crossroads didn't work," she said.

Elaias shook his head. "We can't go where we're not wanted. And honestly, given how our father was? I don't blame the hill people for being afraid that we might be cut from the same cloth. This is better for them. Better for all of us. They'll see that the Temple lets us stay, and they'll get to know us for ourselves. It'll take time, but you have to go gently when someone's been hurt before."

Aeris nodded. "Granna Dyna taught me that."

"Dyna is an excellent mind healer," Elaias said. "You had a good teacher."

"It will be good to have you here," Rhexa said. "I've been missing having little ones around. It's peaceful here, but sometimes... I just miss happy noise." She smiled. "Welcome to the Mother's Womb," she called. "You're here to share stories?"

One of the ragged men stood up and faced them, bowing slightly as they approached. When he spoke, his accent was thick enough that Aeris had trouble understanding him.

"Name's Pelin. We've come to seek the Child."

Aeris fought the urge to grimace. "I'm the Heir," she said. "The High Priest asked you to come to share your stories with me. I appreciate you answering his call."

"You're the one," the man said. He looked past her. "And you... you're both healer boys, no? With that hair? You're Gisa's whelps."

Astur stepped forward, but Elaias stopped him. "Our mother's name is Gisa, yes," he said slowly. "Did you know her?"

"Knew of her." The man spat onto the ground, then nodded toward Rhexa. "And you're who?"

Rhexa blinked. "I... I'm the High Priest's partner. One of them."

The man nodded slowly. "Ah. You can go, then. We've no quarrel with you."

"Quarrel? What are you—?"

"Rhexa?" Elaias said, his voice low and serious. "Take Aeris back to the Temple. Now. Lancir, escort them back." He stepped between Aeris and the man, holding his staff in both hands. "Go."

Aeris stepped back, walking into Lancir. He grabbed her upper arms, pinning her wings to her back. For a moment, she thought she might have knocked into him, but he was steady, and his grip on her arms tight.

"Lancir, let go!" Aeris tugged against his hold, wincing as his fingers dug into her skin. "That hurts!" All at once, warmth started spreading up and down her arms. She recognized the feeling as her limbs went leaden. "You're a *healer*?" she gasped, trying to keep her eyes open. She heard the sharp crack of a whip, and Lancir let her go, howling in pain. She crumpled, unable to get up.

"Aeris," Rhexa sounded frightened as she tried to get Aeris to her feet. "I can't lift you. You have to get up."

Aeris shook her head, hearing the sound of fighting around her. It sounded like it was happening somewhere far away, distant whip cracks and shouting. She tried to tell Rhexa to go, to get help, but the words were lost in the darkness.

"ONCE OWYN COMES BACK, it'll be a day or two before any Air warriors start showing up," Karse said. "Then we'll have the extra manpower to send Aeris and her Companions back to the Palace." He paused. "She's going to hate this. You know that, don't you?"

Aria nodded, resting her hands on the desk in Steward's office. She and Karse sat on one side, with Steward facing them. "I know. And if she can give me a good reason to stay, then we'll have extra men to go and search for Frayim."

Steward nodded. "Thank you. Have you discussed this with her?"

Aria shook her head. "Not yet. That's where I am going from here. However, we need the men, regardless of whether she goes back to the Palace or not."

"True. But perhaps you should have talked to her first?" Steward said gently. "So as not to alienate her? She's an adult —"

"And I am her mother," Aria interrupted. "I'd rather have her angry and someplace safe than in a dangerous situation because she thinks that being a week past her naming day gives her the wisdom of age."

"Now wait a moment," Karse said, scowling. "You can't be talking about the same Aeris we are. You can't be. She's possibly the most level-headed person in the entire Palace. I honestly don't think that she could even imagine some of the fuckheaded things her parents got into, let alone do them."

Steward chuckled. "Karse is right, I think. You're not being fair to her. She doesn't seem at all... foolhardy. Now that Air and Fire of hers?"

"Just remember that she chose them," Aria said.

"The Mother chose them. And she chose Aven and Owyn for you," Steward replied. "That says... what, exactly?"

Aria stared at him for a moment, then sighed and rubbed her forehead with her fingertips. "Fine. You're right. Both of you. I'm reacting instead of thinking. Aven would —"

"Be reacting right alongside you," Karse finished. "He's not even a little bit rational where his first baby is concerned. And I don't blame either of you. You both carry some pretty deep scars." He stood up and held his hand out to Aria. "Do we know when he'll be back?"

She took his hand and let him help her up. "I'm hoping today or tomorrow. And I hope that they'll have Frayim with them."

"From your mouth to the Mother's ears," Steward said solemnly as he stood up. "Now, Aeris and Rhexa are in the library. Shall we go find them?"

The library was empty, and a chill ran down Aria's back. "She said she was staying inside," she said. "She promised Gannet. I heard her."

"Maybe she went out to the healers?" Karse suggested. "If she's with Elaias and Astur, they'll take care of her."

"And Rhexa is probably with her as well. She told me that she was going to stay close to Aeris today." Steward gestured toward the door on the far wall. "Let's go and see."

To Aria's surprise, there was crowd outside the Temple, walking toward the building. At the front of the group, limping heavily, was Aven. He looked tired.

"Aven!" she called. He smiled when he saw her, and waited for her to come to him. She shared breath with him, then kissed him and stepped into his embrace.

"Anything?" Steward asked.

Aven sighed. "No," he admitted, shifting to stand at Aria's side, his arm around her shoulders. "We found signs of passage, but nothing we could follow. We came back because we were running out of supplies. When we go back out, I want to take Del. He's the best tracker we have, and we should have had him with us from the start." He looked up at Othi joined them, then frowned. "What's that over there? Where did the tents come from?"

"We have things to tell you," Aria said. "We were going there anyway, so we'll explain on the way."

Othi nodded, then turned as they all heard a distant crack and a scream. "What was that? Sounded like a whip."

"Beyond the Temple," Aven said, pointing. "It came from that way." He glanced over his shoulder. "Othi, take your men around the left. I'll go right. Karse, get your men. Aria? Up high."

Aria nodded, taking to the air and watching as Aven and Othi led their men around the Temple. She circled, then flew over the Temple. On the edge of the meadow, near the tree-line, she could see what looked like a fight, and as she watched, a figure with bright red hair fell to the ground, a whip falling from his hand.

Then she noticed the small, winged figure on the ground, and the older woman trying to protect her.

"Aeris!" Aria screamed her daughter's name as she dove toward them. She armed her wrist crossbow as she flew, fitting a dart to the string. As she stooped to strike, she fired, and a man yelped and fell back. Behind him, another man raised a bow, tracking her flight... then changed and fired at the enraged Water warrior running unevenly toward them. The arrow missed, and Aven and his men hit the attackers, cutting them down. Othi reached them at the same moment, roaring in fury. In the tumult, Aria lost track of Astur, but saw Elaias with two halves of his walking stick in his hands, trying to fight his way out of a circle of ragged men. She saw a man shove Rhexa to the side and grab Aeris, scooping her up and running for the woods.

"No!" Aria heard Aven echoing her, saw him trying to follow. Saw the archer raise his bow again.

Saw Aven fall.

More men came around the Temple, all wearing Palace livery. At the sight, the ragged attackers abandoned their dead and fled, taking Aeris and the healers with them.

ALANAR CAME OUT OF the tiny Temple room and folded his hands in front of him. "He'll live," he said. "He'll be weak for a time, but he'll live. Dyna is monitoring him." He sighed. "It was a near thing," he added. "The arrow was entirely too close to his heart."

Aria swallowed. "Thank you, Alanar," she said. "Please, keep me informed. I need to speak to Karse now." Her relief at the news was fleeting. Now that she knew her Water would live, she could focus on the attack.

"Aria, what happened out there?" Alanar asked. "They took Elaias and Astur. Why?"

"I don't know," Aria answered. "My question is what was Aeris doing out there?"

"I have an answer." Aria turned to see Steward coming toward them. "How's Aven?"

"He'll be fine," Alanar said. Steward sighed, his shoulders visibly lowering.

"Thank the Mother," he murmured. "Now, Rhexa said that one of the Palace guards came in. He said that Karse sent him to escort Aeris to discuss stories with a new group of Penitents. But Karse was with us all morning."

Aria closed her eyes, trying to pull her frayed nerves together into something that would be able to control her temper. "We were betrayed. Again. By one of Karse's men. Again."

"What?" Karse appeared in the corridor. "I heard that. First, tell me how Aven is. Then... tell me how I fucked up this time."

"Aven will be fine," Aria answered. "Rhexa says that one of your men came and collected her and Aeris to speak to Penitents about stories. And that guard claimed you sent them."

"Which you didn't, because you were with us," Steward added. "Rhexa said he was young—"

Karse went white. "Lancir. Fuck me, it had to have been Lancir."

"Aren't we jumping to conclusions?" Alanar asked. "He might have been taken, the way Elaias and Astur were."

"He lied to get Aeris out there," Aria answered. "If Elaias and Astur hadn't gone with her, we probably wouldn't have missed her for hours—"

"There's one more thing," Steward added. "Rhexa said that he put Aeris to sleep so she couldn't fly off. He's a healer."

Alanar blinked. Then he knocked on the door. "Dyna, come to the door," he called.

The door opened. "I could hear you," Dyna said. "I knew he had healing potential. He asked me not to say anything because he was afraid that you'd make him stay behind with the healers for training. He told me he'd talk to you or to the Senior Healer when we got home. I didn't know he had any training." She stepped closer to Alanar, who put his arm around her. "He used me, didn't he?" she asked. "He courted me so that we'd trust him, so he could get close to Aeris. So she'd believe him when he told her to go with him. Now... now they have Aeris, and Fa Elaias, and Uncle Astur, and... it's my fault, isn't it? I... I should have seen through him."

"It's not your fault," Alanar said. "You had no reason to think he was anything more than what he said he was."

"If it's anyone's fault, it's mine," Karse said. He turned to Aria, then knelt with a wooden lack of grace, going to one knee in front of her. "I'll get her back," he said. "I swear that on everything I am. I'll bring her safely home. And once I do, you can have my resignation, if that's your will." He paused. "Or my head. If that's your will."

"Karse, get up and stop being dramatic. We don't have time for it," Aria snapped. "Your head? Really?"

Karse got up. "I've failed you. Twice. Twice in exactly the same way."

"I don't think it's the same as Wren," Alanar said. "You didn't just take him at face value. You took precautions this time. Or am I remembering wrong? I thought you looked into Lancir's history?"

"I did. I did and this still got past me. We went as far back as we could," Karse answered, tucking his hands behind his back. "His service in Terraces was exemplary, and he came to the Palace with recommendations from Captain Leesam. He told Lee that he was on his own for a few years, and where he was before that. When he came to the Palace, I sent people to check that out. Found the place, but the people were long gone. And the village he said he came from was one of the ones Mitok's folk burned out back when we were on Progress. We passed it."

"Then it sounds like you did everything you could," Steward said. "I think we'd be better off not trying to find fault, not when it appears that someone went to a lot of effort to set this plan in motion. Now, you sent men out after them?"

Karse nodded. "Othi went out. Copper's back, too. They took every man we could spare, and a round dozen Penitents who know the area. I could wish Del was here, but I might as well wish for all the trees to fall down so we could get a clear view." He clasped his hands behind him. "I'm getting old, Aria. I'm slipping. I should have caught this. Not... Meri liked him. Copper liked him."

"We all liked him," Alanar said. "He was a very attractive trap." He sighed and hugged Dyna to his side. "Go back to Aven, love. He's fighting the trance."

"Yes, Fa," Dyna murmured. She disappeared back into the room and closed the door. Aria closed her eyes and tried to think.

"How old is Lancir?"

Aria opened her eyes. "Rhexa? Are you all right?"

Rhexa waved one hand. "I'm fine. Just... not as young as I used to be, and I don't bounce anymore. Now, how old is Lancir?" she repeated. "I... I have a theory. But I'm not sure if it's possible, and... well, one of them, one of the ones who took Aeris and the healers... they called Aeris the Child. And... well, how old is he?"

"Lancir is twenty-five," Karse answered. "Near enough, anyway. Why?"

Rhexa looked thoughtful as she counted on her fingers. "Math was never my strongest talent," she murmured. "Sixty-eight minus twenty-five is... forty-three?"

"Yes," Alanar answered. "Wait... Rhexa, are you thinking what I think you're thinking?"

"And I think I'm wrong," Rhexa sighed. "There's no way he can be Risha's son. That was right about the time that the main healing center fell, and we all moved to Terraces."

"You would have noticed a pregnancy," Steward said. "Or I would have. We both saw her often enough."

"But you think he's connected to the Wanderers?" Aria nodded. "It makes sense. And now... I don't remember. Do any of the Penitents have any idea what they want the Child for?"

Steward frowned. "They say that the Child is going to change the world. How is... open to interpretation. I'll... who's shouting?"

Aria turned, hearing her name. "That's Owyn!"

A moment later, Owyn appeared in the door from the Temple. "What the fuck is happening?" he demanded. "Tiras about lost their mind in the Solstice village, and we had to drug them to get them back here! Gannet's about to molt, he's that worried!"

"Keeping it short?" Karse answered. "I fucked up again, Lancir betrayed us, the Wanderers have Aeris, Elaias and Astur, and Aven damn near died."

Owyn stared at him for a moment, his jaw hanging open. "Well... fuck me." he breathed. "Aven's going to be all right?"

"He'll be fine if we can keep him in bed for a day or two," Alanar answered. "Ah... go look in on Trista. Treesi is with her, but I think she'll need you."

Owyn swallowed. He nodded, then went to stand in front of Aria. He looked into her eyes and opened his arms. "She don't need me as much as you do right now. Come here."

Aria stepped into his embrace, letting his strength sooth her, feeling the walls starting to crumble.

"We'll find her, Aria," he murmured as she cried into his shoulder. "No matter what it takes. We'll find her."

Chapter Ten

Aven paced the length of the Temple, silently cursing. The search party had come back after two days with no word, and had gone back out this morning with more men, more supplies, and Owyn's solemn promise that they'd find her. Alanar had refused to let Aven ride out with them, and had threatened to knock him out and tie him to a bed if he so much as thought about going.

"You're going to make yourself sick."

Aven stopped. "So?" he asked as he turned. "Uncle, I should be out there!"

Steward nodded, coming over to join him. "Come in and sit," he said. "I know it's hard. Trust me. I know."

Aven nodded. "We're going through the same thing for different reasons."

"We're going through the same thing for the same reasons," Steward corrected. "Don't think I'm not worried about Aeris, and I know you're worried about Frayim. But you and I... we're not up to being out there. For you, at least, it's temporary." He sighed and shook his head. "Come and sit with me. We'll try to plan. I've been making lists... well, I've been dictating lists. Penitent contacts, people who we can send messengers out to who might be able to help."

Aven followed him into the High Priest's apartment, where Rhexa was sitting at a table. To Aven's surprise, Tiras was sitting with her.

"How are you feeling?" Tiras asked. "I...I wanted to help. And I'm not really good at doing much in the healing center, and I couldn't ride out with Gannet and the others—"

"I'm feeling better. And I understand how it feels to want to ride out and not be able to," Aven said, sitting down. Rhexa filled a cup of tea and put it in front of him, then pushed a bowl closer.

"Salt in that one," she said. "There's honey in that crock."

Aven nodded his thanks and poured some salt into his tea. As he sipped, he studied Tiras.

"You're not sleeping, are you?"

Tiras shook their head. "Not really. I... I keep thinking that I should have seen something. I should have known. I should have known that we needed to be here, and not in the Solstice Village. All these visions from being flower sick, and not a single one warned us not to go! I'm starting to think I haven't seen anything useful at all."

"Owyn would be the first person to tell you that with some visions, you sometimes don't know what's useful until after it's over," Rhexa said. "Sometimes, visions don't make sense until you know what they really mean."

"Have you heard anything else about the shadow story?" Steward asked.

"Nothing yet," Tiras answered. "No one else knows it."

Rhexa sipped her tea and sighed. "So, who else should be on that list, Steward?"

Steward sat down with his own cup of tea and closed his eyes. "Let me think. We've got Vilar. Jenis. Oh... did I say Araglar?"

"No," Rhexa said, writing down the name. "It's been quite a while since we last saw him. Before the first snow?"

"That's about right," Steward said. "He's overdue. I think this visit he's going to send his son to Terraces to train to be a healer. He said he might."

Rhexa smiled. "He's a good boy," She looked at Aven. "You'd like him. Very quiet. He has the most beautiful eyes. I've never seen eyes like his."

Aven sat up and looked across the table at Tiras. "Two different colors?" he asked slowly.

"Yes! How did you know?" Rhexa asked.

"Tiras, go get Owyn's book," Aven said. "I think you and Owyn had the answer all along."

AERIS WASN'T SURE HOW long it had been, or even where she was. In a wagon of some kind, possibly one like Fa Owyn's house on wheels. She couldn't tell more — her captors seemed to think that her wings meant that she would react like a falcon, and had blindfolded her before she'd regained consciousness. She could hear muffled voices outside when they came close — Lancir giving orders, other people shouting and fussing. The voices all seemed to be men, all with the same thick hill accent that made it difficult to understand them. There were at least eight of them, she thought, although it was hard to tell. No matter, there were still too many. Help was coming. She was sure of it. Fa Del was the best tracker in the world, and her parents wouldn't stop until they found her. They'd done it before. She just had to stay alive until they came for her. So she stayed quiet, refusing to speak when anyone spoke to her and refusing to eat what they offered. And she listened. There wasn't much else she could do — they'd wrapped her wings and chained them to immobilize them, then bound her wrists behind her back. The ropes weren't tight enough to cut off circulation, but there wasn't enough slack for her to try and slip them.

They'd stopped, apparently for the night. She could smell fire, and something cooking. Hear men coming and going. And now... footsteps, coming closer, and the squeak that heralded the door opening. Aeris stayed still, turning her face away. She heard the clink of chain.

"Aeri?"

Aeris jumped at the familiar voice. "Astur?"

She heard him chuckle. "Surprise," he said. "They took Eli and me, too. And... well, you're worrying them. So, I got sent to make sure you're not pining like a caged songbird."

Aeris snorted, making Astur laugh again. "I'm not pining. I'm just not cooperating."

"That's the other thing," Astur said slowly. "They want you to cooperate." He paused. "They're going to make you cooperate." He paused again. "I'm not saying it. You want her to know, you tell her."

"You're more trouble than you're worth."

Aeris sat up straighter. She recognized the accented voice. "I don't care what you have to say, Pelin."

"You should, Child," he replied. "You see, you're the only one I have to bring back. These two? They're extra. And if I leave them in pieces along the way? No one will care. It's up to you. Either you start behaving and doing as you're told, or I start removing fingers. Do you understand?"

"I won't—" Aeris' protest was cut short by Astur's yelp of pain. She breathed in, and could smell blood.

"I said, do you understand?" Pelin repeated.

"I... yes." Aeris swallowed. "Astur?"

Astur didn't answer immediately, and when he did finally say something, she could tell he was lying. "I'm fine," he gasped. "I... I'm fine."

"Don't lie to me," Aeris whispered.

"I'm fine," Astur insisted. "It's... it's not bad."

"It'll be worse," Pelin crooned. "And I'll enjoy it. So behave, Child. Someone will bring you food soon."

The wagon bounced and jostled, then shook as the door was slammed closed. Aeris closed her eyes behind the blindfold, drawing her knees up to her chest. Her heart was hammering in her ears, and she wanted to cry until she was sick. Her parents were coming. She knew that. But they needed to hurry.

Outside, she heard a shout. More shouting. The unmistakable sound of metal clashing on metal. She raised her head, frightened and hopeful all at once. "Fa?"

More shouting. More sounds of fighting, coming closer. She heard Lancir, shouting to move the prisoners. Pelin shouting orders that countered Lancir's. The sound of something thumping against the side of the wagon. The creak of the door.

"Here!" She didn't know the voice, but the wagon shook as someone clambered in. "Got you," a man said as he tugged at the blindfold. The cloth fell away, and Aeris found herself looking up at the scarred face of a man she'd seen only in drawings and dreams. A man for whom she'd been looking for two years. Her parents had been right — the man Tiras and Owyn had seen in their visions was her Water. Mismatched eyes met hers, and he smiled. "Come."

"Kas, come on!" someone shouted. The man nodded and drew a knife, turning Aeris and cutting the rope binding her wrists. He backed away, out of the wagon, and held his hand out to her. Outside, it was nearly dark, and she could see a fire burning across the campsite, with dark figures darting around the gloaming like bats.

"Come!" Aeris followed him, taking his hand and jumping to the ground. He nodded and pointed toward the woods. "There. Now."

"My uncles," she protested, tugging against his hand. "They have my uncles."

"Who am I looking for, my Heir? And how many?" someone asked from behind her. She recognized his voice as the one who'd shouted. His face was obscured by shadow, but his hair was bright gold.

"Two," Aeris answered. "Both of them with red hair—"

"I've seen them," he interrupted. "Go with Kaspin, he'll keep you safe and get you to a safe place. I'll bring them." He looked past her. "Kas, get her out now."

Kaspin tugged on her hand again. "Come!"

This time, Aeris followed him, hiking up her skirts and running toward the trees. She heard Lancir shouting, ordering people to follow them, to stop them. Someone charged toward them; Kaspin snapped his free arm to the side, and Aeris saw the shimmer of firelight on a blade before the attacker fell. They kept running into the trees, and the sound of fighting behind them gradually faded away. Aeris followed Kaspin without hesitation — he knew where he was going, and if she fussed or tried to slow down, they'd be caught. This way was safety. And maybe answers.

It was nearly dark when Kaspin stopped. He let Aeris' hand go and bent, resting his hands on his knees as he panted, clearly trying to catch his breath. Aeris dropped to her knees, feeling the sweat running down her back.

"Rest," he said softly. "Then go." He took something from his belt — a bottle. He unstopped it, held it up so that she could see, then took a sip before handing it to her. She smiled and took it, and was surprised when she tasted salt water.

"Good?" he asked, then tugged the scarf around his throat down. It was too dark to see them, but Aeris knew he was showing her his throat. His gills. "Water?"

"You're Water," she whispered. "I am, too. Partly."

"All tribes," he said, and there was something odd about the way he spoke. The way he hesitated before each word, and the over-enunciation. It reminded her of the way Del spoke, when he spoke. "You. All tribes."

She nodded. "Yes. Do... do you not talk?"

He grimaced. "Not good," he admitted. Then he held one hand up, clearly listening. He shook his head. "Not safe. Not here. Come."

Aeris got to her feet, and rolled her shoulders. "Can you free my wings?" she asked.

"Rags can." Kaspin held his hand out again. "Heir?"

"Aeris." She took his hand. "I'm Aeris."

He squeezed her hand. "Aeris. Come." They started out again, walking through the darkness. Kaspin seemed to know the woods well enough to walk them blindfolded, and had a clear destination in mind, leading them silently along until the trees started to thin, and Aeris could once more see the sky and the stars. Then Kaspin stopped. He gestured to Aeris to stop, then howled, sounding almost exactly like Howl or the other wolves around the Palace. He did it twice more, then looked back at Aeris. He was frowning.

"No answer," he murmured. "Bad."

"Oh, no," Aeris whispered. "What do we do now?"

Kaspin stepped back behind the tree and leaned against it, wrapping his arms around himself. "Home." He looked back over his shoulder, and there was hope in his voice when he added, "Rags knows."

"Who is Rags?"

Kaspin looked back at her and shrugged. "Fa, not Fa."

Aeris nodded. "Rags is your adoptive father?"

He cocked his head to the side. "Again?"

"Adoptive?"

"Doptive," he repeated, then shook his head. "No. Not right. Adoptive. Means Fa, not Fa?"

"Yes." Aeris smiled. "Where are we going?"

He held his hand out. "Home. Long way. Tired?"

"I'm fine." She took his hand again, and let him lead her back into the trees.

As Kaspin had warned, it was a long walk, and the moon was high before they left the trees behind for a rocky plain that led them into a canyon. Aeris was tired and hungry, and her back ached from not being able to move her wings. But Kaspin's hand was warm in hers, and his presence was soothing. She kept catching him glancing at her, and she wondered if his heart was racing as much as hers. Her Water. The last part of her heart. She wondered what her other Companions would think of him. What he'd think of them.

He stopped so abruptly that she nearly bumped into him. He looked down at her, then tapped his nose. "Smell?" he asked, his voice low and quiet. She understood why — their voices would echo off the walls, and if anyone was hunting for them, it would give them away.

She sniffed, then sniffed again. "Something is burning?" she whispered.

He nodded. "Careful." He started forward, keeping to the shadows. She followed, trying to stay as quiet as Kaspin. He turned into a narrow gap in the stone wall that Aeris would have missed if she'd been alone. The passage was only a dozen paces, and opened out into a moonlit nightmare.

They were on a ledge overlooking what Aeris thought had once been a small village. There was nothing left of it but ruins and ash—houses burned to the ground, and bodies strewn between them like broken dolls. There was something in the center of the village, something Aeris was almost certain didn't belong. In the moonlight, it looked like a thin obelisk, but she suspected it was no such thing. She heard Kaspin whimper softly, and took his hand. He looked at her, his eyes wide.

"Go," she whispered. "Go see if you can find him."

He hesitated, then tugged her hand. "Come?"

"I'll come with you."

He nodded, then led her down a twisting track that followed the curve of the rock wall. It came out behind one of the burned-out houses, and there were three bodies at the bottom, two men and a woman, all of them armed. Kaspin stopped.

"Taal," he said, pointing. "Amal. Nisa." He swallowed, squared his shoulders, and led Aeris on. More bodies, and Kaspin named each of them as they passed, getting closer and closer to the center of the village. Aeris could see now that it was the remains of a bonfire, and that what she'd taken for an obelisk was in fact a stake, and there was a body hanging from it. Kaspin let her hand fall and walked all the way around the stake before rejoining her. He met her eyes and shook his head.

"We go," he said softly. "Ah...things. Need things." He turned, and headed to the still smoldering ruins of a small house. Aeris followed him, and hadn't quite caught him before he darted inside. He came back out with a bundle under his arm, which he handed to her. "Clothes," he said. "Rags say... Heir needs clothes." He looked around. "Need blankets. Food. I find. You... you clothes."

"Hurry," Aeris said. "They might come back." She looked up, suddenly afraid. "They might have left people to watch. We have to hurry."

Kaspin nodded. He touched her arm, hesitated for a moment, then darted off. Aeris looked around, and stepped into the shadow of a wall that was still standing. The bundle held a pair of trousers, a belt, and a jacket made for someone with wings. She stripped off her skirts and underthings, grimacing at the dirty garments. At the first chance she had, she was going to wash, but for now, there was no time — she put the trousers on, and folded the jacket to take with her. The way her wings were bound, she wasn't going to be able to get her shirt off. Then she remembered that Rags was supposed to have been the one who could free her. She was stuck like this until they found someone who could undo the chains. She picked up her skirt and carried it over to a smoldering pile, dropping it into the embers and poking it with a stick until it caught fire. When she looked up, Kaspin was coming toward her, carrying a pair of bundles. He handed her one, then gave her a sheathed knife.

"You use?" he asked.

"I can use a knife. Thank you."

"What?" he asked, nodding toward the blaze.

"If there's no one watching, then I don't want them to know we were here if they come back," she answered. "And... this was your home. They have to expect you to come back."

He nodded. Then he looked back at the stake and the remains of the fire. Aeris stood up and touched his arm. "I'm sorry, Kaspin."

He nodded. Then he drew himself up and turned to her, offering his hand. "We go."

Chapter Eleven

They crept up the track and along the passage, back the way they'd come. Every kicked pebble was a sentry, every night bird someone revealing their presence. By the time they were back under the trees, Aeris was nearly in tears. Kaspin's hand kept her anchored, kept her safe, and she clung to him like a child. As the moon dipped toward the western horizon, Kaspin stopped. He looked to his left, then his right, then nodded and led Aeris to a fallen tree. He let her hand go, dropped to his knees, then swung his legs underneath the tree and disappeared from view.

"Kaspin?" Aeris whispered. She knelt next to the tree, looking down into darkness. A moment later, a light flared, and Kaspin stepped into view.

"Come," he whispered, holding his hands up to catch her.

"Will I fit?" she whispered back. He nodded, so she shifted to dangle her legs over the edge, then pushed off. There was just enough room for her wings; Kaspin caught her legs and gently lowered her to the ground, his arms warm around her as she settled onto her feet. Her hands rested on his chest, and she could feel his heartbeat hammering against her palms. She looked up into his eyes, and the fear faded away.

Then he let her go, backing up a step. "Safe here," he said, his voice strained. "Rest. Eat." He moved away from the opening, carrying a small lantern that he must have had in his pack. The roof of the cave was low enough that he couldn't stand upright, and the tops of Aeris' wings brushed against the stone as she followed. In the very back of the cave, there was a tiny rivulet filling a small pool. Kaspin sat down near it, opening his pack. He pulled out a wrapped something and handed it to Aeris. "Sit. Eat."

Aeris took the wrapped bundle and sat down, unwrapping the cloth to reveal travel bread and jerky. Kaspin was already gnawing on the jerky, and had taken the bottle from his belt. He glanced at the water, then at Aeris. "Drink?" he mumbled around a mouthful.

"I can drink fresh water," Aeris answered. "Can you?"

He nodded. "Salt better."

"I agree." She tore off a piece of travel bread and ate it, taking the bottle from Kaspin when he offered it. They passed it back and forth until they were done, then Kaspin refilled it and set it aside.

"Sleep," he murmured. "I watch."

"You need to rest, too," Aeris protested.

"Sleep," Kaspin insisted. "I..." He paused. "I will rest. Later." He smiled. "Right?"

"That was right," Aeris assured him. She lay down and rested her head on her bundle, draping the coat over herself. "Kaspin? I am sorry about your father."

Kaspin made a face. Then he spat. "Rags say...take care of Heir. Important. Dark wants Child. Can't have." He looked at her. "Dark bad. Bad things. Bad people. Protect the Child. Duty." He frowned. "Re...respon..." He shook his head and made a face. "Hard word."

"Responsibility?"

He nodded. "Again?"

"Responsibility."

"Re..spons...bility." Kaspin grimaced. "Not right."

"It was close," Aeris offered. He snorted, leaning back against the wall.

"Get safe," he said softly. "Go by night. Safe."

"Are we going to the Temple?" Aeris asked. "My parents are there."

Kaspin looked thoughtful, then shook his head. "They know. Wait. Kill me, take you."

"Because it makes sense that we'd go there," Aeris sighed. "Then... the Solstice village? Or... or into the mountains? I have family in the flocks."

Kaspin closed his eyes, gently tipping his head from side to side. "Mountains not safe," he said at length. "Cold. Not right things. Not food. Village better. Still not safe. But better."

"But it's better than going into the mountains with no supplies," Aeris said. "That makes sense. And we'll travel by night. So we'll stay here tomorrow?"

Kaspin nodded. "Rest." He looked at the opening. "Drazi, maybe?"

"Drazi?"

"Uncles."

"Oh, his name is Drazi?" Aeris closed her eyes. "Thank you." Silently, she added *my Water*. Saying it aloud would wait. She fell asleep wondering what the others would think of him... and woke with a start, seeing pale sunlight filtering into the cave. The light wasn't what woke her. What...

Then she heard it again, a muffled sob. She sat up, and saw Kaspin curled up against the wall near the spring, his face buried in his hands. She crawled over to him and wrapped her arms around him. "I've got you," she whispered into his hair. "I'm here."

He clung to her as desperately as she had to him in the darkness the night before, eventually falling asleep in her arms. She shifted gently, trying not to wake him, until finally he was asleep with his head pillowed on her legs. She leaned her shoulder against the stone wall and closed her eyes.

They were alone, with no supplies, barely any weapons, and they were being hunted. Dark, Kaspin had said. Dark wanted her.

Dark, like a shadow?

SOMETHING IS WRONG.

No.

Everything is wrong.

Rags can fix it. Rags can fix anything.

No.

Rags!

Kaspin woke all at once, explosively on guard, ready to defend himself. It was something that Rags had been trying to ease him out of doing — mostly because he'd frightened people who thought he was attacking them. He heard a startled squeak and rolled away from it, coming up facing Aeris. Had... had he been sleeping *on* her?

He sat back, rubbing one hand over his face, trying to force himself awake now that the initial rush of energy had passed. Rags had always thought how he went from completely alert to groggy once he knew he was safe was funny...

Rags...

He closed his eyes and shuddered, and immediately, she was there, putting her arms around him. For a moment, he let himself rest in her arms, reveling in her warmth. He'd never allowed anyone other than Rags to be this close. He'd learned early that close enough to touch meant close enough to hurt. But her touch was soothing, her very presence calming, and he didn't understand why he had no urge to lash out at her the way he would have for anyone else who came too close. She was different. She was safe.

She was his.

Aeris. The Heir. The Child.

His.

"Kaspin?"

He raised his head and looked into her eyes. He wanted to see them in the sunlight — he couldn't tell what color they were. She looked worried. Of course — he was her only protection and her only way home.

He sat up and rubbed his face again, trying to think of what he wanted to say. "I... fine," he managed.

"You're not," she answered, keeping her voice low. "Can I help? Do... do you want to tell me about him?"

He stared at her. She'd heard him talk. Telling her anything would take them hours! He shook his head and slowly got to his feet, ducking his head to keep from hitting the top of the cave. He moved closer to the opening and peered out. Still early. They had a long day ahead of them.

"Rest," he said. "Eat. Go at dark."

She nodded. "How long will it take to get to the Solstice village, do you think? I don't know how long they had me. Do you know?"

He came back to sit down next to her, reaching for his pack. Distance. He knew how long it would take him to get to the village. Could she keep up with him? He thought so — she had already.

"Five. Six sleeps." He shrugged slightly. "To go. How long? No."

"You don't know how long they had me," she said. "Which... why would you? Five or six days. My parents must be frantic. They must be out here, looking for me." She smiled. "Maybe we'll find them?"

He shrugged again. If they did find her parents, what then? Dark was still out there.

Unless... would the Firstborn stop Dark? Rags had said that Dark was their problem to solve. But Rags was gone now. Maybe...

He unwrapped his pack and took out another bundle. "Hunt?" he asked, taking out a piece of jerky.

"I hunt," Aeris answered. She gnawed on her own jerky and looked at the entrance. "I can set snares, if we have cord."

Kaspin shook his head. "You stay."

"Then you stay, too," she said, and took his arm. "Don't leave me." She leaned against him, resting her cheek on his shoulder. He fought the urge to turn his head and bury his face in her hair, and tried to think of something to say. Before he could, she looked up at him. "What weapons do you have?"

"Sickles," Kaspin answered. He shifted, taking one off his belt and showing it to her.

"I saw this when you saved me," she said, taking it from him. "Where's the blade?"

He took it back and jerked his hand to the side — the folded weapon snapped open, revealing the curved blade. She gasped. Then, to his surprise, she laughed, muffling the sound with her hand.

"That's wonderful! May I see?" Kaspin smiled and handed her the sickle, watching as she turned it over in her hands and tested the blade edge. She opened and closed it, studying the folding mechanism. "This is beautifully made," she murmured. "Someone is an artist—"

Kaspin lost the rest of what she said, hearing something carried on the winds outside their hiding place. He touched her arm to silence her, then crept toward the entrance.

Voices. He glanced back at Aeris; she nodded to show that she heard, and moved to the rear of the cave. He followed her, taking the sickle from her and taking out its mate, shaking them both open. Aeris drew her knife, and rested her other hand on his back.

"Drazi?" she whispered.

He shook his head. "No signal," he whispered back. "Hunters."

As they waited, listening, Kaspin wondered what kind of trail they'd left the night before. How careless had he been? He swallowed and shifted in place, trying to remember if he'd done the right things to hide their trail. He couldn't think of anything, couldn't clearly remember anything after he'd looked down into the ruins of the only home he'd ever known. Everything was a fog.

He'd led the hunters straight to them. He'd failed.

The voices above got closer, close enough that Kaspin could hear them clearly, even if meaning escaped him completely. He glanced back at Aeris, she had her eyes closed and her head cocked to the side. She could tell him what they'd said later.

He hoped.

The voices slowly faded away. Kaspin heard a soft sigh of relief from behind him, and slowly crept back toward the entrance. No voices, but he didn't move until the birds started to sing once more. Only then did he relax and turn back to Aeris, folding his sickles and putting them away.

"Left a trail," he whispered.

She nodded. "We probably left a trail my baby sister could follow," she said. "We'll need to be careful when we leave."

Kaspin grimaced. "Careless. Stupid. Useless."

"Stop that," Aeris snapped. "You are not. You saved me. You're going to bring me home. And then you're going to stay with me."

Kaspin blinked. He knew the words, but he didn't think he'd understood them properly. "Again?"

She looked at the entrance, then nodded toward the rear of the cave. He followed her back, sitting down across from her so he could watch her face.

She glanced toward the entrance. "Is it safe for us to talk, do you think?" she asked in a quiet voice. "Or should this wait?"

"Birds," Kaspin answered. "Not close. Tell."

"You know about the Firstborn? And the Companions?" she asked.

Kaspin nodded. "Rags tell. Firstborn. Air. Earth. Fire. Wat—" He stopped, reaching up to touch his throat through his scarf. "No. Me?"

"Yes." Aeris smiled. "I've been looking for you for two years. The Smoke Dancers could only tell me that you were out of place. And they were right. I never would have looked for my Water in the mountains."

Two years. That was two snows. Kaspin shook his head. "Wrong. Not me."

"The Mother isn't wrong, Kaspin," she said. She reached across the space between them and took his hand. "You're mine. And I'm yours. And I think you know that."

Instantly, he felt his face growing warmer. "I...my Aeris," he whispered. "Yes."

She smiled. "My Kaspin," she murmured. "We'll get out of this." She glanced toward the entrance, then shifted to sit next to him. "You said Dark wants me. Who is Dark?"

Kaspin grimaced. "I...Dark bad. Bad people. No Air. No Water. No...broken."

Aeris looked thoughtful. "Dark wants to destroy Air and Water, and anyone who is different?" she asked. Kaspin nodded, and she sighed. "So he's a Wanderer?"

Kaspin thought about what he knew. What Rags had told him. "Wanderers follow Her. She go, Dark come." He tapped his chest. "Rags never follow. We stop. Rags say... serve Mother. Serve Blesséd Mother Firstborn."

"Rags was a Penitent?" Aeris asked.

The word was new, and Kaspin frowned as he puzzled over it. "Pen...again?"

"Penitent." She pronounced it slowly and clearly, and he repeated it. "That's it."

"Means?"

"Someone who is sorry," she answered. "Someone who was a Wanderer, and realized they were wrong and stopped hating. My mother said they followed the Seer's visions and his teachings."

Kaspin smiled. "Seer is Frayim. Frayim nice."

She stared at him. "You know Frayim? Do you know where he is?"

"Temple."

She shook her head. "When we got to the Temple, Steward said he'd vanished. He went out to visit local villages and never came back. The villages were destroyed."

"Seer gone?" Had Rags known? Unlikely, or he'd have gone hunting for his friend. "How long?"

"I'm not sure," she answered. "A month, maybe? Steward is very worried." She paused. "You've been to the Temple?"

Kaspin nodded. "Two times. Priest nice. Frayim nice. Rhex very nice."

Aeris smiled. "I agree with you." She shifted, resting her hands on her knees. "Did Rags tell Steward about Dark?"

"Don't know." Kaspin shook his head, then shrugged and rested his hand on hers. "Why?"

She took a deep breath. "Wanderers followed Her, you said? Do you mean Risha?"

At the sound of the forbidden name, Kaspin turned away and spat, then turned back to see Aeris staring at him. "You spit when you hear her name?" she gasped.

"Evil," he answered. "Forgotten. No name. Only Her."

She nodded. "I'm sorry. I didn't know." She frowned. "Should I spit?"

He nodded, then fought the urge to laugh as she shifted so that she could spit on the ground. She did it like she'd never spit before, and wasn't sure what would happen. Once she settled next to him again, he poked her shoulder. "Tell."

"She kidnapped me when I was a baby," Aeris said. "Me, my mother and my grandfather. My fathers saved me."

Kaspin nodded. "Stole the Child. Rags tell. She die. Dark come."

"Someone took her place," Aeris murmured. "And... do you call him Dark because he's evil and has no name?"

Kaspin nodded. "Rags say Mother turn face from Dark."

Aeris blinked. "I think that's the longest full sentence I've heard you say," she said.

He grimaced, looking away. "Still learning speaking," he said in a low voice. "Understand most, but not talk. Sound...idiot."

"You do not," Aeris protested, her voice spiraling up. He hissed at her, and she covered her mouth, her cheeks turning red. "You don't," she repeated in a lower voice. "You remind me of one of my fathers. His name is Del."

Kaspin knew that name, but it took him a moment to remember from where. "Del? Priest son?"

She nodded. "Yes. He was injured, and he doesn't talk well. When he does, he talks like you do. Most of the time, he uses Water signs."

Kaspin nodded. "Priest tell. Offer to teach." Kaspin raised his hands, then shrugged. "Not remember."

She chuckled. "I understand. It takes time, and you've only met him twice. There's not a lot you can learn in that short a time. I'll teach you." She took a deep breath. "We need to get to my parents. We need to tell them that someone took Her place. When do we leave?"

Kaspin looked at the light shining down into their den. "Sunset."

She nodded. "Can you see if you can free my wings? The chain shifted; it's digging in, and it hurts."

Kaspin nodded and gestured toward the light. "Come."

They moved to where the light was better, and Aeris turned around so that she was kneeling with her back was to him. Kaspin got onto his knees and leaned in close to better see what they'd done. Her wings were wrapped in canvas, and the canvas was held on by chains that wound around and between them, and around Aeris' body. He ran his fingers between her body and the chain, resettling it as he looked for where it joined, and finding the lock underneath her wings, against her back. He studied it for a moment, then growled softly.

"Lock," he grumbled. He continued resettling the chain, finding where it had pulled tight into the top of Aeris' left wing. He shifted it, then closed his eyes and concentrated on soothing the hurt.

"Kaspin?" she whispered. "Are you... you're a *healer*?"

"Wait," he answered, checking to make sure there was nothing left, nothing he'd missed. He moved his hands, and she turned to face him.

"You're a healer," she repeated. "Who taught you?"

"Rags," Kaspin answered. "Some. Rhex say go Terraces. Learn. Rags say perhaps."

She looked horrified. "Perhaps? You mean... you wouldn't go? You wouldn't learn how to use your gifts?"

"I learn," Kaspin protested. "I heal." He shrugged. "I go..." he paused, then sighed. "They laugh. Stupid Kas."

"You're not stupid," Aeris said. "You're wonderful. And if you don't want to go to Terraces, you can learn from my father. He's Water and Earth, too."

Kaspin wasn't sure that she understood. And he wasn't going to argue with her. He ran his hand over her covered wing. "Better?"

She smiled. "Much better. Thank you."

Chapter Twelve

"What's going on?" Owyn demanded as he walked into the Temple library, with Del and Othi right on his heels. Aria was sitting at the head of the table, with Aven at her right. Steward sat across from Aven. "Why did you call us back? What happened?" He paused, seeing his book open on the table, resting on top of an unrolled map. "And why do you have my book?"

Steward touched the page with the picture of the young man that Owyn had seen before they left the Palace. "His name is Kaspin. His father is one of my Penitent contacts. The one who told me not to bother the Firstborn with the news of the Wanderers, as a matter of fact."

Owyn stared at him for a moment, then took a seat next to Aven. "And this is important why?"

"Because of who Kaspin's father is." Steward paused. "Araglar is a Penitent, but he wasn't originally a Wanderer."

"*Araglar is an Air name,*" Del signed as he sat down next to Owyn.

"It is, and I thought at first that he was wingless Air. I was wrong," Steward answered. "I've known him for... quite a few years now. He came here perhaps two years after the Mother called me to be High Priest, and he knew who I was. Who I had been. Frayim stopped him from cutting me down where I stood, and they became friends. Now he comes every few months or so, to tell me the goings on in the hills and hear about what's happening in the rest of the world. The last two times he came, he's brought Kaspin." He paused. "I feel as though I'm betraying him to tell you all this. He told me his history in confidence. But if it will save Aeris, I think he'll forgive me."

"If he wants to be angry at someone, let him be angry at me," Aria said. "I am ordering you to tell me."

Steward smiled. "Yes, my Firstborn. He goes by Rags now. When I met him, he was very... very angry. It took years before he was willing to sit with me without Frayim's intercession, and it took Rhexa recognizing him for him to trust me enough to tell me his reasons." He looked around the table. "He was one of Risha's victims. He's Air and Earth, and he was a student at the main healing center. Based on his age, he may have been her first victim after she got the idea from having to take Alanar's wings." He looked at Owyn. "I asked Alanar. He thinks he remembers Araglar from when he was a boy. And Rhexa remembered him when he came here after she joined us. That's when he told me who he was."

"He was one of the ones who vanished," Rhexa added. "We never knew what happened to him. Pirit was... well, she never really got upset, but she missed him terribly. He was one of her personal students. Incredibly talented."

"Yeah, we know what Risha did with anyone who was incredibly talented," Owyn muttered. "So how'd he end up out here? And why didn't he go to Pirit and tell her?"

"I asked him that question, and he never answered it," Steward said. "And he's out here because he tried to go back to his flock, and they cast him out."

"Because he was broken," Aria said.

Steward nodded. "Because he was broken. He stayed out here because he thought he had no place left to go, and he built a community, a safe place for other broken people." He touched a spot on the map. "Sanctuary. It's about six days by foot, two to three days on horseback."

"How many other victims did he take in?" Owyn asked. "Risha's victims, or Wanderer victims?"

"I think pretty much the entire community are one or the other, and that's why you need to go there." Steward tapped the map again. "Because of Kaspin."

Othi leaned over Owyn's shoulder to look at the picture, then at Steward. "He's Water, isn't he? Like we suspected? He's Earth and Water, if he's a healer. That means we were right. They were breeding for the Child, and he's the son of one of the lost Water."

"And what's more, he's Aeris' Water," Owyn added. "This is why she couldn't find her Water, and why she said he was important when she saw that." He gestured to the open book. "Fisher and I both said it — he was in the wrong place. Who's going to look for a Waterborn in the mountains? And she said that if we'd told her about it before, that there might be Water up here who were victims of Risha's hate, then she'd have had us looking here. We... we failed a lot of people by keeping things from the Heir." He glanced up, saw that Othi had stepped back, and pushed his chair back. "I need that map."

"You're right. We did fail. And we're not going to again. So we're all going," Aria said. "Trista and Rhexa are going to take care of Yana while we're gone. Preparations are already underway."

"CLEAR."

Aeris heard the quiet call, and lifted herself out of the buried den. Kaspin seemed to have a knack for finding underground hiding places that were nearly invisible in the pale light of dawn. This was the third one since they'd started, and the first one where they'd felt secure enough to hunt before they'd gone to ground, and to have a fire. They'd shared a meal of something other than trail bread or jerky, they'd both eaten their fill, and Aeris had fallen asleep in Kaspin's arms. Now the sun was setting, and it was time to move. She was getting used to sleeping through the day and walking all night. She smiled when she saw him crouching next to a stream, refilling his bottle. She joined him, kneeling downstream from him and splashing water on her face.

"Oh, I want a bath," she said as she sat down, reaching up and combing her fingers through her hair. He glanced at her and nodded.

"Soon," he answered. "Safe soon. Halfway now." He pointed upstream. "Follow, go right to village."

"Really?" Aeris started braiding her hair. "Are there going to be good places to hide during the day? It looks like we'll be leaving the trees." She tore a strip from the hem of her shirt and tied off her long braid, then got back to her knees. In the distance, she heard... barking? "Kaspin?"

Kaspin nodded, then looked over his shoulder, going very still. "Dogs," he whispered.

Aeris got to her feet. "Upstream or downstream?"

He looked up at her, then got to his feet and held out his hand. "Down."

Keeping to the shallows, they splashed down the stream as the sound of dogs grew closer and closer. Aeris looked over her shoulder at the clear view of the spot where they'd been.

"If they come out of the trees, they'll see us," she gasped.

Kaspin looked back and nodded, then pointed to the far bank, and a tiny rivulet running down the rocks. "That way!"

Aeris followed him up the slope, slipping and splashing on the slick rocks. Ahead of her Kaspin fell, and she heard a sharp crack. He yelped, struggling to get back to his feet. Aeris caught up with him and grabbed his arm.

"Lean on me," she hissed. "Where are we going?"

"Up," Kaspin answered through gritted teeth. He draped his arm over Aeris' shoulder, waving his other arm. "Waterfall."

"Waterfall?" Aeris repeated, then jumped, looking back. Men were shouting behind her, and the dogs sounded much closer.

"Go!"

Aeris grabbed onto Kaspin's belt and they started up the slope once more, staying in the water. She tried to dampen the pain she could feel radiating from Kaspin's knee, but she couldn't focus long enough to do any good. Hopefully, once they found a place to hide, she'd be able to do more.

"Where are we going?" she panted, catching him as he slipped once more.

"Waterfall," Kaspin answered. "Swim?"

"I can swim."

Kaspin nodded. "Under waterfall. Follow me."

"There they are!" Aeris fought the urge to look back when she heard Lancir's voice. "Put him down and get the girl!"

She heard a distant snap, and Kaspin grunted; she felt the wave of pain wash over him, and nearly fell.

"Not bad. Keep going!" he growled. She shuddered and kept moving, half supporting, half dragging him around a spill of rocks that blocked them from view... she hoped.

On the far side of the rocks, she could hear the waterfall, and as they crested a rise, she could see it, spilling over the edge of the cliff where they stood.

"Under the waterfall?" she said. "How do we get down there?"

"Jump," Kaspin answered. "Safe." He glanced at her and grinned. "Fun."

"*What?*"

He limped forward, dragging her by the hand. "Flyer, no? Afraid?"

"Yes! I'm a flyer, not a faller." Aeris followed him to the edge, then looked back. She could hear the dogs baying, getting closer. The water was a very long way down. "Is it deep enough? What do I do?"

"Trust." Kaspin met her eyes. "Trust me."

Aeris answered immediately. "Always."

He smiled. "Three, then run. Feet first, arms close. Ready?"

"No." Aeris took a deep breath. "One..."

On three, they ran and leapt. Every instinct screamed for Aeris to spread her wings, to fly, to escape the water that was rising toward her, but she crossed her arms over her chest and tried not to scream. Then she hit the water, the shock of it enough to make her dizzy. She opened her eyes underneath to see Kaspin swimming toward her.

She could taste blood in the water.

He gestured, turning and swimming down, and she followed, down toward the bottom of the lake. Swimming deep usually gave her trouble — her Air bones made her too buoyant. But the chains acted as weights, helping her as she followed Kaspin underneath a rock overhang and into a dark cave. Unable to see, she trilled the way she would have in the deep, listening as the sound bounced off the walls. There was nothing in front of her, so she kept going, starting to feel her lungs burning. It couldn't be far. She trilled again, hearing an echo just as she noticed there was light coming from above. A tunnel! She swam up, seeing Kaspin above her, and surfaced next to him. Panting, trying to catch her breath, she looked around — a cave, with light coming through a sheet of roaring water.

"We're behind the waterfall?" she asked. Kaspin nodded and swam toward the edge of the pool. He lifted himself out, and Aeris saw the blood staining the side of his shirt.

"You said it wasn't bad!" she gasped, climbing out of the water. "Take your shirt off. Let me see."

Kaspin tried to stand, then grimaced and sat down hard. Aeris stopped him from trying again. "I'll look at your knee in a moment. Take your shirt off," she repeated. "Let me see how badly you're hurt."

He frowned slightly, pulling his left knee to his chest. "Healer?"

"Level two," she answered. "Enough of a healer to take care of this."

Kaspin looked puzzled. "Level?"

"It's how strong a healer you are," Aeris answered. "And I'm not telling you more until that shirt comes off."

He scowled at her, then tugged his shirt up over his head, letting it fall in a sopping wet pile on the ground. Aeris bit her lip — Kaspin's upper body was covered with old scars.

"Oh, we're going to have a time of it when you get your tattoos," she murmured, peering closer at his side. The wound was a deep graze, and she laid her hand over it, focusing her healing into convincing the blood vessels to close, the muscle and skin to reform, cleaning out anything that shouldn't be there. The wound was an angry red line when she moved her hand, but that would fade.

"Tattoos?" Kaspin asked as she shifted to look at his leg. "You?"

"I have my family tattoo, yes," she answered. "Among Water, when you're counted as an adult, you get your family tattoo to show your family canoe. And there are other tattoos, depending on how you set your sail."

"Show!" Kaspin demanded.

"Once I'm done," Aeris assured him. "Now sit still!" She rested one hand on his knee. "Can you straighten your leg?"

"No. Broken?" he asked, and she heard the wobble in his voice. She shook her head.

"I don't think so," she answered. Gently, she examined the leg. "No, nothing broken. You dislocated the kneecap. Lay down." Carefully, she numbed his leg, then rubbed her hands together, trying to remember what she'd been taught. Kaspin lay back, but propped himself up on his elbows.

"Lie down," she said. "You need to be flat. I'll explain what I'm doing."

Kaspin scowled, then lay all the way down. "Want see," he grumbled.

She chuckled. "What I'm going to do is move the bone back into place," she said. She moved to his feet, taking hold of his ankle with one hand and putting her other hand over the displaced bone. She slowly straightened the leg, applying pressure to the kneecap; there was a resounding 'pop' as the bone snapped back into place. At the sound, Kaspin winced.

"It's all right," Aeris assured him. "It's over. It'll be fine tomorrow." She concentrated on setting healing power into the abused knee, then sat down. "We're not going anywhere until the day after," she added. "You need to rest this."

Kaspin propped himself up again. "What do? And... sit?"

"You can sit up," Aeris said. She touched his uninjured leg. "There's a cap of bone here," she said. "Can you feel it?" Kaspin prodded his knee and nodded. "You knocked it all the way over here," Aeris said, tracing the outside of his knee. He shivered, and she looked up at him. "Kaspin?"

"Fine," he answered quickly, and his face went red. Aeris could feel his heartrate increasing. She smiled, and he went even more red. He looked around, then pointed. "Things there."

"Things?" Aeris looked around the dark cave. "You mean supplies?" She got up and followed Kaspin's direction, and in a niche found chests, a collection of jars on a ledge, lanterns, and a firepit. More hunting on the ledge turned up a flint and steel, and she lit one of the lanterns. Then she went back to Kaspin. "What is this place?"

"Den," Kaspin answered. "Safe place." He pointed into the darkness opposite the waterfall. "Tunnel there."

"There's another way in?" Aeris looked at the niche. "Oh, of course there's another way in. Those supplies got here somehow."

Kaspin laughed. "Halfway to Temple. Stay here. Safe." He gestured. "Tunnel near stream."

"Oh!" Aeris laughed. "Was this where we were coming the whole time?"

Kaspin nodded. "Supplies. Pocket soup in jar. Pot in chest. Blankets in chest."

"Pocket soup?" Aeris looked at the jars. "Which jar?"

Kaspin growled. "Come help."

"Help?" Aeris came out of the niche and found Kaspin trying to get up. "What are you doing?"

He froze, and for a moment, Aeris was reminded of her brother Fisher when he was caught doing something he wasn't supposed to. He looked up at her and smiled hesitantly. "Helping?"

"Hurting yourself is not helping, and your leg is still numb. You won't even be able to tell if you hurt yourself more," Aeris pointed out. "But you should be near the fire." She went to his left side. "Keep that foot off the ground," she said. Getting him up while he was balancing on his right foot was more difficult than she thought it would be, and getting him into the niche was a slow process made even slower by Kaspin starting to laugh halfway there. By the time he dropped gracelessly onto the ground next to the firepit, they were both whooping with laughter.

Aeris sat down next to him and shook her head, then rested her hand on his thigh. She closed her eyes and slowly examined his leg, then looked at him.

"You didn't do any more damage," she said. "But you're not moving until morning. Now, what's pocket soup?"

He pointed. "Small jar." When Aeris brought it to him, he opened it and took out a small square. "Pocket soup. Hot water. Soup."

She took the square from him and sniffed what proved to be a stiff gel. "I put this in hot water?"

Kaspin nodded. "Soup."

Aeris handed him the square and got back up, going through the chests. She shook out blankets and handed one to Kaspin. "Take off your wet clothes," she said. "I'll hang them to dry while the water boils." She carried the pot out of the niche, picking up Kaspin's wet shirt and draping it over rocks. When she came back with the pot of water, Kaspin had wrapped the blanket around himself, and his wet clothes were in a pile next to him.

"Wood there," he said. Then he paused and frowned. "I...I will...start fire." He paused. "Yes?"

"Yes, you said it correctly." Aeris set the pot down. "No, you're not starting the fire. You've been taking care of me. It's my turn. I'm taking care of you."

AFTER ALL THE DAYS they'd been running, it shouldn't have been a surprise that Aeris could take care of a camp. Finding out she was a healer was a surprise. Finding out that she knew how to lay a fire, and how to cook? That shouldn't have been.

Kaspin watched as she rummaged through chests and jars, finding things to fill out the soup that was simmering on the fire.

"Wet," he called. "Clothes. Off."

She smiled. "Once I'm done." She picked up a jar sealed with wax. "What is this?"

"Meal. Add to soup?"

"No, we'll save that for the morning." She filled two smaller bowls with soup and carried one over to him, sitting down next to him.

He nodded, then remembered. "Tattoo?"

She tapped her shoulder. "It's under here. I'll have to cut the sleeve." She looked down at her arm. "It's already torn. You can see part of it." She tugged open the tear in the cloth, and he could see blue-black ink in her skin.

"Canoe?"

She nodded. "Among Water, families are called canoes. Your canoe is your bloodline, going back to Abin." She tore her sleeve, showing more of the tattoo. "This is still new. I just got it before we left the Palace. But it says I am daughter of Aven, who is the son of Aleia, of Neera's canoe, and a direct descendant of Abin." She smiled, "I'll show you the whole thing when I can take my shirt off."

He nodded. "What canoe?" he asked. "Me?"

Aeris shook her head. "I don't know. We'll try and find out, but I don't know what canoe you're from." She paused. "Your parents. Your birth parents, I mean. Not Rags. Do you know them?"

Kaspin grimaced. "No. Never knew. Never..." He tapped his forehead. "Memory?"

"Remember."

He nodded. "Never remember. I..." He paused. "Animal."

"What?"

Kaspin drank his soup, then set his bowl aside and looked down at his hands. "Was... animal. Not person. No mother. No father. No home. Cage. Straw. Scraps." He gestured to his cheek, then his chest. "Whip."

"Mother of us all," Aeris breathed.

"Like dog," he continued. He leaned against the wall and tipped his head back. "Broke cage. Ran. Five, six snows. Sick. Rags find. Rags tame. Rags teach. Teach talk. Teach heal. Teach... person." He looked at her and shrugged. "Still learning talking. Still... some animal."

"You're not an animal," Aeris said. She put down her own bowl and took his hand. "You're my wonderful Kaspin. My Water."

He ran his thumb over her fingers and wondered... what would she say?

"Wet clothes," he offered. "Off?"

She met his eyes and smiled. "Will you keep me warm?"

"Always."

Chapter Thirteen

The passage in the rocks was narrow — too narrow for Othi, so he stood guard at the head while Karse led Aven, Owyn and Del along the path marked on the map. Aven leaned on his walking stick and tried to ignore the pain shooting through his right hip — he hadn't ridden horseback in years. Not since he'd broken his already-damaged hip when he'd fallen off a horse. He accepted that this wasn't going to be anything but painful, and had argued for nearly an hour with Alanar over coming with the search party — Alanar had finally relented, but only because Treesi and Dyna were both going. Aven already knew that Treesi was going to sigh and give him *the look* when he got back to their camp. *The look* was usually reserved for one of the children, and was to be expected when they'd done something they ought to have known better about. Aven and the other men in Treesi's life were not immune from *the look*, and he'd already gotten it at the end of each the past two days when he'd hobbled to her for help relieving the pain from riding.

But if Aeris rode back to the Temple with them tonight? *The look* would be worth it.

"Oh, fuck," Aven heard Karse from the head of the line.

"What is it?" Aven called.

"There's no one left alive down there is what," Owyn answered. "Come up and see."

Aven joined them at the end of the passage and looked down into carnage that was at least several days old. "Mother of us all."

"What do you want to bet the poor fuck on the stake was Rags?" Karse asked, pointing to the center of the ruins. "Or that they made the others watch him burn?"

"No bet," Owyn answered. "I don't get it. Why?"

"Wrong question. The question is who?" Aven said. "Who did this? How did we not know they were out here?" He looked at the others. "We thought we solved all the problems. We thought it was over. But it was festering, right under our noses."

"And people were keeping it from you," Karse said. "Aven, this isn't your fault. You can't do something about a problem you don't know about."

"Try convincing Aria of that," Owyn said. "I want to watch." He looked back out over the town. "No, we should have known about this. Treesi and Othi have been out here on her season every year for years — we don't have any excuses. This is on us."

Del snapped his fingers, then pointed up. "Gan."

Aven looked up to see Gannet circling. He waved. Gannet waved back, made a broad gesture, then banked and flew back the way they'd come.

"He wants us to follow him," Owyn said. "No alarm, though. No warning horns or anything."

"There's nothing we can do here, except bury the dead," Karse said. "And we don't even know if that's right. Rags, he was Air, you all said? What about the rest of them?"

"We'll send people in," Aven said. "We'll talk to the Penitents, and see if they can see to the dead. Let's go back."

They made their way back through the passage and out into the open. Gannet had landed, and was standing with Othi.

"The Firstborn asks that you come back," Gannet said. "We found something. Someone." He paused. "Someone found us."

⟿ ◌◌ ⟾

BACK IN CAMP, GANNET brought them to the tent that had been set aside for the healers. Treesi met them outside.

"Copper found him. He said that it looked like the boy was trying to get to us and collapsed. Dyna is with him," she said in a low voice. "He's in bad shape, and Aria wanted you to hear what he had to say."

"Did he tell her?" Aven asked.

Treesi shook her head. "He said he had to tell the Blesséd Mother and her Companions. That's why she called you in." She licked her lips, and her voice wobbled when she added, "He knows who I am. He called me Gisa's daughter. I don't know how. He said that he saw Eli and Astur. He tried to get them out."

"Oh, Treesi." Othi went to her and put his arms around her. "We'll find them."

She nodded. "Go in. Tiras is in there, too."

Aven paused long enough to kiss Treesi's cheek before going into the tent. There was a young man on the narrow cot. He'd been badly beaten, and his pale hair was still matted with dried blood. Dyna sat on a stool next to him, one hand resting on his chest, while Aria and Tiras stood near the foot of the bed.

"Healer Dyna?" Aven asked. "Report."

Dyna looked up. "Someone is rather stubborn," she said. "He refused to let me put him into a trance until he made his report to the Firstborn and her Companions. And fought it so hard that Healer Treesi decided it would be easier to just hold him stable until he did so." She tapped his chest. "They're here, Drazi."

"I hear," Drazi mumbled. "Thank you." He opened one eye. "Blesséd Mother, we tried. Our father sent us to stop them, and when we couldn't, he told us to rescue the Child."

"Where is she?" Aria asked.

Drazi shook his head. "Kaspin took her. We tried to free Gisa's sons, because she asked it of us, but we failed. Barely got away, then

Dark's men set a trap at Sanctuary. The rest of my brothers... they all fell so that I could get away."

"Dark?" Owyn asked. "Who's Dark?"

Drazi swallowed, and Aven felt a surge of pain. Dyna winced and flattened her hand on his chest. "Talk faster," she ordered. "You need to be in trance."

"Yes, Healer." Drazi turned his head to face them. "Dark carries on what She started. But worse. He doesn't want the Child to control her. He wants to sacrifice her. He says that she and the animal tribes are tainted, and only fire will cleanse the world of them."

"Fire..." Aven murmured. "Drazi, your father is Rags, isn't he?"

Drazi nodded. "You're going to tell me he's dead, aren't you? I know. We went home first, to get more people to try again. Dark's men were waiting for us. I don't know how Kas and the Child got past them. Maybe because Kas is quick, so they'd be in and out."

Aria joined Aven, taking his hand. "Do you know where they were going?"

"He left a trail a child could read, which isn't like him," Drazi answered. "Seeing what happened... that must have rattled him bad. They're going north and west, but Dark's men are close, and they have dogs. I hid what I could of their trail."

"North and west?" Owyn repeated. "What's north and... the Solstice village!"

Drazi took a deep breath. "If they went to ground, there's a den near the steam that runs right to the Solstice village. Rags would stop there when he went to the Temple, so Kas knows about it. Stream is west. You'd have crossed it coming here. You have to know the den is there to find it, though." He closed his eyes. "Show you when I can. Maybe they're still there. I hope they're still there."

"May I ask a question before you put him to sleep, Dyna?" Tiras asked.

"Make it quick," Dyna warned.

Tiras stepped forward, rubbing their hands together. "You called the person behind this Dark. Why? And you knew Treesi. How?" They paused. "Two questions. Sorry."

Drazi smiled. "In order? Rags called him that. We don't speak his name, so he'll be forgotten by the Mother for his crimes. Dark is from a story—"

"Axia and the Cloud?" Tiras blurted out.

"The Shadow," Drazi corrected. "*Axia and The Shadow.* Rags had a dog he called Shadow, though. So he called that one Dark." He looked up at Dyna and smiled slightly. "I'll tell you the story when I wake up. And everyone in the hills knows Gisa's get. It's the hair."

"Is red hair that uncommon in the hills?" Treesi asked. "I didn't think so, but I'm related to all the people I've ever known with red hair."

Drazi closed his eyes and took a deep breath. "Marks you as hers. Which marks you as his. Hill folk worry they can't trust her get, because her children are his children, and blood tells."

Aven looked at Treesi, saw the horror in her face. Owyn had gone ashen.

It was Aria who asked the question. "Drazi, is the man you call Dark named Elan?"

Drazi turned his head and spit. "We don't speak his name," he murmured.

"Enough," Dyna said. "He needs to be in trance. Is that all, Drazi?"

He nodded, then sighed softly. Dyna closed her eyes, then nodded.

"He's out," she said. "Healer Aven, will you help me with seeing to him? We want him hale as soon as possible."

Aven nodded. "Right. Everyone out."

THE SUN HAD SET WHEN Aven came out of the tent. He could see everyone sitting around the fire, and went to join them.

"How is he?" Owyn asked as he approached.

"He's responding well," Aven answered. He took a bowl that Del offered him and sat down next to Aria. "When he wakes up in the morning, he should be healthy enough to ride out, but we'll reassess before we do anything." He looked around. "Where's Treesi?"

"She and Othi are in the tent," Owyn answered. "She's really torn up about this. I mean... that's her father out there hurting people, and she didn't know he was even alive."

"No one knew," Aria murmured. "We discussed it while you saw to Drazi. She thinks this is why no one came to her and told her what was happening while she was taking her season all these years. Because they never trusted her to do what was right for her people."

"*Othi told us he always thought it was his fault. He thought that people didn't want to talk to Treesi because they were frightened of him,*" Del added. He poked Aven. "Eat."

Aven nodded and started on his bowl of stew. "In the morning," he said between bites. "We'll head out to this den. If they're there, then we can take them both back to the Temple. If they're not, we can follow them to the Solstice Village."

"And what about Dark?" Karse asked. "We don't know where he is."

"No, but we will," Aria said. "Copper, in the morning, I want you to go back to the Temple. Tell Tiercel what we've learned, and tell him that we need this entire area mapped from the air and he is to make it happen. Dark is out here, counting on the fact that Air has never patrolled this far from our ranges. That's how he's stayed hidden. That changes now."

"Firstborn?"

Aria and Aven both turned to look at Gannet, who had gotten to his feet. "Yes, Gannet?" Aria replied.

"Let me go back," Gannet said. He paused, his wings flaring slightly as he fidgeted from foot to foot. "I'd be faster, so we'd have eyes in the air sooner than if you sent Copper back. Here, you need boots on the ground, and that's not my strength. But I can be back at the Temple and have Tiercel and his men in the air by the morning after tomorrow. Copper wouldn't even be halfway there by then." He paused. "And... it would be safer."

"Safer how?" Karse asked. "How do you figure?"

Gannet waved his arm toward the woods. "Anyone could be out there, and we'd never see them until we were on top of them. I heard you saying something like that earlier. That means Copper and his people could be waylaid before they ever got to the Temple, and we'd never know." He looked at Copper. "No offense."

"None taken," Copper said. "You're right. These woods are thick enough that we could trip over an army. It's a huge risk."

"But it's a risk we don't have to take," Gannet said. "If I go up and stay at cloud level, or just above, they won't see me and they definitely won't be able to hit me." He paused again. "I think. Crossbows don't shoot that high, do they?"

Karse chuckled. "Not as fast as you lot fly. They might try, but it would be a difficult shot, and they'd only have one shot at it. You'd be out of range before they could reload. But all it would take would be one lucky shot, so stay above the clouds, out of sight. Aria?"

Aria nodded. "If you go at dawn, and go high and fast, you'll be there long before a rider would." She paused, then nodded. "You might even get there by sunset, if you rode the thermals all the way."

"Wait, really?" Owyn blurted. "I've been yours for how many years, and I never once asked how fast you all fly."

"It was never a question that needed an answer," Aria answered.

"That first time we saw the Palace, it was still four or five days by horse. I said it was a good day's sail," Aven said. "Do you remember?"

Aria nodded. "I do. And that would have been a few hours flight." She smiled and turned back to Gannet. "You are correct in your assessment, Gannet. You may go."

"Gan?" Tiras took Gannet's hand. "Be careful."

"I'll be fine," Gannet assured him. ""You keep your head down. You're still seeing things that aren't there."

Tiras shook their head. "Not today. Today, I haven't seen a single thing that wasn't there in front of me."

"Could you?"

Aven looked up to see that Othi had come up behind him. He was alone, and he wasn't smiling. "Treesi is asleep," he said. "I'm going back in a moment. I just...can you see anything? Anything at all about Eli and Astur?"

"I can get my blades," Owyn offered. "See if I can see anything. Let me finish this."

"Thank you. I just... anything will help. Anything at all will give her a little peace," He looked out into the darkness. "We could have stopped this. If one person had just trusted us — trusted her — we'd have known. We could have stopped all of this."

Owyn put his bowl down. "Let me get my blades. Tiras, would you find a good place for me?"

Tiras nodded and got up, and they walked off into the dark together. Aven turned to look at Aria.

"Of course we're going to watch," she said.

Owyn was already barefoot and holding his smoke blades when they found him in a small clearing near their tent. He nodded, gesturing for them to stand next to Tiras. "Stay over there. There's not a lot of room, but this is the best we've got."

Aven nodded and rested his hand on Tiras' shoulder. Owyn smiled, then lowered his head, and took a deep breath. Aven felt Tiras take a mirroring breath, mimicking Owyn's three deep breaths, and wondered if Tiras knew they were doing it. He'd ask them once

Owyn was done. Then Owyn started to move, and almost immediately fell to his knees as the vision took him.

A heartbeat later, Tiras collapsed.

OWYN OPENED HIS EYES to find himself in a place he never thought he'd see again — a green meadow, and a large rock.

"This is not making me feel better. It's that important?" he called. "Owyn?"

Owyn spun. "Tiras? What are you doing here? How?"

Tiras shook their head. "I... I don't know. I was watching... and then I was here. Which... where's here?"

Owyn licked his lips and sighed. "Well, you're about to meet someone important. Mind your manners."

"Who..." Tiras looked past him and smiled. "Wait... that's the Bright Lady! I... how do you know about her?"

Owyn glanced over his shoulder and saw the Mother, sitting on the rock. He bowed his head to her, and she smiled in response.

"Go ahead," She said. "See to your student."

"Thank you," Owyn called. He turned back to Tiras and asked, "Reverse that question, will you? How do *you* know her?"

Tiras looked startled. "You mean... she's real? Really real? I... I thought I dreamed her. When I was small. My mother said that I'd made her up as a... well, as an imaginary playmate, because I was lonely. None of the other children wanted me playing with them because I was strange."

"Your mother should have known better," Owyn said. "I mean, she's a Smoke Dancer, too. But then, I never saw her dance, so I have no idea how strong a dancer she is. She might not know better. But you do. I mean, you will." He put his arm around Tiras' shoulders and brought them toward the rock. "Tiras, this is the Mother."

Tiras jerked. "No! Owyn... I... really? I...." They stopped, pressing their hands over their mouth. "I don't know what to do!" they whimpered, their voice muffled.

The Mother smiled and opened her arms. "It's been a long time," She said. "You've done so well."

Tiras hiccupped, then threw themselves into the Mother's arms, sobbing. "I've *missed* you!"

"I was never gone, my dear." The Mother smoothed Tiras' hair gently, then let them go.

Owyn smiled, then looked around. "So... it's this important, is it?"

The Mother met his eyes and nodded. "Tomorrow, when Drazi wakes, he will tell you the entire story Tiras and the others have been seeking. But it won't tell you where you need to go, and Gannet will not have my Airborn children back in time to show you the proper way."

Owyn shivered, suddenly cold despite the sweet, warm air. "Mother, we're not still at 'everyone dies if Aeris does,' are we? I thought Father Adavar went back to sleep!" He frowned. "She... she's isn't really Axia come again, is she?"

The Mother laughed. "No, she is not. Axia's time is gone."

"She was there, though," Owyn said. "When Aria took the Crown. She told us."

The Mother smiled. "That was an exception, and it will not happen again. No, Aeris is not Axia. But the people who have turned from me, they believe that she is. And if she should fall, or join them —"

"Aeri wouldn't do that!" Tiras blurted.

"If it was the only way to save the lives of people she loves?" the Mother asked.

Tiras started to answer, then stopped. They looked at Owyn, who sighed.

"Yeah. She'd do it. She'd hate herself every minute, but she'd do it."

"Exactly," the Mother said. "The Child will change the world. But whether she changes it for good or ill? That will be determined by her choices. If she chooses to join them, her presence will give the shadows power, and their numbers will grow. And without an Heir to stand with her... Aria will fall. And this time, there would be no stopping Adavar when He woke."

"Oh," Owyn breathed. "Oh, so we are doing this again. Right. Where are we going?"

OWYN WHEEZED AND COUGHED and sat up, feeling a strong arm around him. Aven's arm — he could tell just from the touch.

"Gannet, give me the book!"

"Don't need it," Owyn wheezed. "Tiras. Where's Tiras?"

"They collapsed when you did," Aria said. "Owyn—"

"They were in the vision with me. But it weren't no vision. The Mother pulled us both in. I know where we gotta go."

Chapter Fourteen

Kaspin woke up slowly, gently, then lay there wondering why. For him, waking up was always violent, always desperate. But not this morning.

It probably had something... no, it had *everything* to do with the woman asleep on his chest. Aeris weighed barely anything, but it was enough to anchor him, and she radiated heat like a brazier. He closed his eyes and ran his hands over her hips to rest on her back, just underneath her shirt. She sighed in her sleep, and he shivered, closing his eyes. She'd been patient. Kind. She'd taught him to love her, and taught him that he could be loved in ways that no one else had ever done. He could wake easy because she wouldn't hurt him while he slept. He was safe with her and he knew it. And he was starting to believe her when she said that he was going to come home with her, that he'd be by her side for the rest of their lives.

She sighed again, then raised her head and smiled sleepily at him. "Have you been awake long?" she mumbled. He shook his head.

"No," he answered. "Watching you."

Her smile grew wider, and she shifted, stretching and sliding up his body so that she could kiss him, twining her fingers into his hair. He wrapped his arms around her and held on as she stopped time, and he whimpered as she pulled away.

"Could stay?" he offered. "They go."

She laughed. "Do you think they'll stop looking?"

He sighed. "No," he admitted. "We go."

"How's your knee?" she asked. He raised his head and looked down at himself as he bent his leg, testing the range of motion.

"Better."

"I want to see how you walk on it. We can stay another day, if it's not healed enough. We have enough supplies. And regardless of whether we stay or go today, we need to eat first." She shifted off of him. "If you'll build up the fire, I'll cook. Then we'll see if we can go." She let the blanket fall and went to pick up the pot. "I'll get some water and check the clothes. They should be dry."

She left the niche, and Kaspin rolled onto his knees and started adding kindling to the embers, nursing the fire back to life. He took the pot of water from Aeris when she returned, and set it over the fire, then sat back on his heels, watching as she measured handfuls of meal into the water.

"Is there salt?" she asked. "We should have salt. I don't know about you, but I'm starting to feel the lack."

Kaspin nodded and looked at the range of jars and bottles. "Blue," he said. "Take with?"

Aeris nodded, fetching the blue bottle. She poured two handfuls of salt into the water, then set the bottle aside. "Kaspin, does anyone else use this place? Should we take supplies, or leave them for someone else?"

Kaspin frowned, puzzling over the question. Then he shrugged. "Don't know. Maybe?"

She looked at him, then nodded. "We don't know if anyone got away from your home. They might come here."

He smiled. How could she understand his thoughts so well? Which led to the next question.

"Aeris," he said. "Why?"

"Why...what?" she asked. She dragged a blanket over and sat down on it.

"Why me?" Kaspin pointed at her, then at him. "Water. Why?"

She looked startled, then laughed. "Oh, that question! All of the others all asked it, too. I don't know. No one knows. The Mother chooses, and you're just the right person. You four are the people I need by my side."

He scowled. "No answer."

"I know it's not an answer. But it's all I have." She spread her hands wide. "When we get back to the Temple, I'll give you your gem. Since I never knew when I'd find you, I carried it with me whenever we left the Palace. But I didn't have it when they took me."

Kaspin nodded. "Tell? Others?"

"The others? You'll like them. Dyna is my Earth. She's a level five healer, and she's not quite a year younger than I am. She's the youngest of my Companions. I've known her my whole life — she's more like my sister. Gannet is my Air. He's big — maybe a little taller than you are, and his wingspan is huge. But he's very fast in the air, and he's a good fighter. He's also very sweet. And stubborn. And occasionally fuckheaded—"

"What?" Kaspin gasped. Rags had washed his mouth out with soap when he'd used profanity, and hearing the word used so casually was jarring.

"Fuckheaded? One of my fathers started saying that when he was our age. It means something that's either stupid, or completely wrong. Or both. Gannet's flock is from far back in the mountains, and very old-fashioned. So he had a lot to unlearn when he came to me."

Kaspin frowned. "No. Ugly."

"Ugly?" Aeris repeated slowly. "Oh, you don't like the word?"

Kaspin nodded and tapped his lip. "Soap."

"Oh, no!" Aeris clapped her hand over her mouth, her eyes wide. "Rags washed your mouth with soap?"

Kaspin nodded, and she made a soft, gagging noise. He stared at her, then started laughing. A moment later, she joined in, and their laughter echoed in the cavern.

"You should get up," she said once she could talk again. "Walk around. See how your knee feels."

"Tell," Kaspin replied. "Fire."

"Oh, how could I have forgotten Tiras?" She shook her head. "Tiras is... do you know what I mean when I say outwither?"

Kaspin nodded. "Ootwith? Not boy, not girl?"

"Yes. I like how you say it," Aeris said. She stirred the porridge. "Tiras is outwither. They look small and delicate, but they're a dirty fighter, and they're a Smoke Dancer. A seer, sort of like Frayim. You'll meet all of them once we get back to the Temple." She stirred the porridge again. "Go walk. See how your knee feels."

Kaspin stood up and walked around the fire, stopping next to Aeris. She looked up at him, tipped her head back.

"Please?" he asked.

She smiled. "Please."

He laughed and leaned down to kiss her, then left the niche, walking around the cave, testing his leg. His knee didn't hurt, but it didn't feel right, either. He crouched, bouncing slightly, feeling an odd stretch and pull. When he straightened, his knee clicked.

"How is it?" Aeris asked as he came back to the fire.

"Odd," he answered. He took a bowl from her and sat down, stretching his leg out in front of him. "Click." He tapped the side of his knee. "Here."

"Click?" She touched his leg and closed her eyes. "There's some tendon damage that's not quite healed. Does it hurt?"

"No." Kaspin frowned slightly. "Not hurt. Not right."

She nodded. "We should probably stay here another day and give this more time to heal." She picked up her own bowl. "Eat. Then... are there fish in that lake?"

His gorge rose. She must have seen it in his face, because she stared at him. "You... you don't like fish?"

"No," Kaspin answered. "Why?"

She bit her lip, then sighed. "Because you're Water. Because once we get back to the Palace, I'll be taking you out to the deep so we can find your canoe. And once we're out there..."

Kaspin coughed. "Fish?"

"Raw fish," Aeris agreed. "And seaweed. It'll take some getting used to." Kaspin shuddered, remembering the leathery, unappetizing thing that Rags had told him was fish. She patted his leg. "Maybe it was how whoever prepared it?" she offered. "If I can catch a fish, I'll prepare it for you, and we'll see if you actually like it." Kaspin made a face at her, and she nodded. "We'll see. And if you don't like it... well, you don't have to go out to the deep. It's traditional for your season, but a large part of the Water tribe stays around the harbor. You can start slow." She smiled. "I wonder what you'll look like when you change?"

"Change?" Kaspin looked down at himself. "Change how?"

"We change in salt water, to live in the deep," Aeris explained. "You'll have a tail and fins instead of legs. My scales are blue pearl. My father's are silver. My uncle Othi's scales are green and blue mixed." She paused. "You've never changed. You don't know anything about our lore, or about what it means to be a child of water. You've got a lot to learn." She paused, tipped her head to the side as she idly stirred her porridge. "I guess you already know you can't have milk or cheese?"

He nodded, then blinked. "You?"

Aeris nodded. "Me, too. And my father. It's because we're Water. We can't digest it." She finished her porridge and set her bowl aside. "Are we staying or going now?"

Kaspin looked at his knee. He wanted to be gone, to get further away from their pursuers, but if his knee failed on the way, they'd be caught. "Stay."

She nodded. "Then you should lie down. I'll put you into a healing trance and work on that leg. It should be fine once you wake up."

Kaspin nodded and returned to the blanket, stretching out. "Leave sunset?"

"We could," Aeris agreed. "But I'd rather have another night here with you." She knelt next to him, leaned down and kissed him, then touched his forehead. The world faded away.

AERIS SET THE HEALING spells on Kaspin's knee, then sat and watched him sleep. He was so much softer when he slept. How old was he? She cupped his cheek, running her thumb over the scar. He'd been so tentative with her, so uncertain...

She gnawed her lip as a thought occurred to her — had she been his first? Had no one ever touched him in love?

She leaned over him and kissed his lips gently, then got up. She needed to put the things in their packs to dry, and the dishes weren't going to wash themselves, and it was something to do. Not much, but something.

Once the dishes were clean, Aeris sat by the water and unwound her braid, combing out her hair and rebraiding it neatly. She considered jumping into the water and washing up, but decided against it — her shirt would be wet and cold, and she couldn't take it off. If she twisted her arm back underneath her wings, she could just touch the lock, but there was no way for her to reach to pick it, and she didn't have the right tools to do it even if she could reach. She sighed and got to her feet, picking up their clothes and carrying them back to the niche. She built up the fire and put their still-damp boots next to it, then went through the supplies, deciding what they should take. More of the pocket soup, and she filled a smaller jar with some of the meal. There was dried meat in a sealed jar, and she set that aside to replace what had gotten ruined in their escape. She could salvage the supplies they'd been carrying into a pottage for them to eat later.

Finally, there was nothing else she could do to distract herself. Nothing left to clean, to dry, or to organize. The pottage was cooking slowly in the coals, and Kaspin's clothes were neatly folded by his feet. There was nothing else that she could do but think.

Kaspin's village was gone because of her, and his father horribly murdered. Her uncles were Mother knew where, and perhaps they were dead as well. All of it was because of who people thought she was, and there was nothing she could do to stop it.

The only way is through the shadows.

It had been days since Tiras had said that. Said that the only way out was through.

Maybe... she was going the wrong way?

If the only way out was through, then maybe she needed to confront Dark? She turned the idea over in her mind, examining it. Confront him... and do what?

She took a deep breath and let it out. If she confronted him, with his greater strength and his greater numbers, she would either come through it in chains, or she'd be dead. Neither option appealed. There had to be another way, and she just couldn't see the course because she was in the heart of the storm.

But maybe she was looking the wrong way? Maybe she needed to look with other eyes. She lit one of the little lanterns, got up and walked out into the larger cave, pacing out an area big enough to dance. Even though she'd never had a waking vision, Owyn had taught her the smoke dancing forms alongside Fisher. Sometimes she could catch visions on the wing or when she danced. Maybe this would be one of those times?

She stepped into the center of the space and started her three deep breaths. She had no blades, but Fisher had told her once that they were just props to help with concentration. A Smoke Dancer didn't need the blades — Tiras certainly didn't. She banished random thoughts from her mind with the third breath, and started to move into the forms.

And... nothing. No visions. No answers.

She sat down in the middle of the cave and pulled her knees to her chest, wrapping her arms around her legs, feeling the weight of everything crashing down on her.

KASPIN COULD ALWAYS tell when he'd been in healing sleep. He wasn't certain why — Rags had told him that some healers could tell, but hadn't been able to explain further. It just was.

For Kaspin, it was jarring, like getting out of a hot spring into winter-cold air. He didn't wake explosively, the way he usually did, but he did come awake all at once. The first thing he noticed was the smell — something savory. He sat up, seeing the pot in the coals. His clothes were folded near his feet, and he picked up his shirt and pulled it on while he looked around. There was a small collection of containers and jars set on the ground next to their packs, which looked empty. His belt and his sickles lay next to his trousers, and he finished dressing quickly, wondering where Aeris had gone. All he could hear was the waterfall.

"Aeris?" He walked out into the larger cave, and saw her sitting curled up in a ball in the middle of the cave. Her back was to him, and she didn't appear to hear him approaching. He was almost close enough to touch her when he heard a muffled, shuddering breath, and realized why she was sitting the way that she was.

She was crying. She had her face tucked down far enough that her forehead was on her knees. The better to muffle the sound, Kaspin guessed. He went to his knees next to her.

"Aeris?" he said, touching her shoulder. She raised her head, met his eyes, then threw herself into his arms, sobbing into his shoulder. Kaspin froze. He had no idea what to do, or how to do it, or even if he should do anything. Then...something. Vague memories of crying, and someone holding him. He put his arms around Aeris the way someone had once held him, holding her tightly, but his mind was racing. How *small* had he been? Small enough that whoever was holding him seemed to envelope him completely. Who was he remembering? It wasn't Rags. Rags had never held him like that. But someone had.

Who?

He forced his attention back to Aeris, rubbing her back underneath her wings. What had upset her? Whatever it was, he wanted to hurt it. A lot.

"Aeris?" he said, keeping his voice low. "What?"

She sniffled and looked up at him. "It's all my fault," she whispered. "It's all because of who they think I am. That's why they're hurting people. That's why they hurt you, and Rags, and your whole village, and my uncles and..."

He touched her lips with his fingers. "Not your fault."

She shook her head. "But—"

"No," Kaspin repeated. He closed his eyes and tried to arrange his words the way Rags had taught him. "It... is not your fault. You...are not... a...ree...reason... for Dark. You are ex...excuse." He paused and bit his lip, then asked, "Said good?"

Aeris stared at him for a moment, then laughed. It was a soggy sound, less mirth and more relief. She nodded. "You said it just fine. And Gannet said the same thing. I'd forgotten. Thank you." She took a shaky breath. "Kaspin, let me see what you think. My Tiras said that the only way out is through the shadows. I thought... maybe if I confront Dark—"

"No!" Kaspin blurted, pulling Aeris closer, holding her tighter. "Not!"

She rested her hand on his chest. "I'm not sure why I'm surprised that would be your reaction. He'll kill me. I know. Or... well, I think he'll kill me. But I'm also too close to it to be thinking clearly."

"No," Kaspin repeated. "He will." He growled softly. "Kill me, then you."

Aeris looked up at him and nodded. "Then we keep going. Let me see your leg—"

"Well, this is cozy."

Aeris jerked, pulling out of Kaspin's arms and clambering to her feet. Kaspin jumped up, putting himself between her and the men coming into the cave. The man in front looked around and laughed.

"Why am I surprised to find a pair of animals in a burrow underground?" he asked.

"Lancir, you don't have to do this," Aeris said. Kaspin felt her tugging on his shirt, pulling him backwards a step. He glanced back at her, saw her slight head-tip toward the pool. He nodded once, the barest movement to let her know he understood. Then he looked back and let her guide him. Lancir stepped into the light cast by the lantern, and Kaspin saw fresh bruises on his face.

"Who hurt you?" Aeris demanded. "Lancir, what happened?"

"You really care?" Lancir asked.

Aeris sniffed. "You were my friend. You meant a lot to someone who means a lot to me. Yes, I care." She tugged Kaspin back another step. "You don't have to do this. You could come back with us."

Lancir frowned slightly, then shook his head. "No, I can't. You're coming back with me." He stepped closer, looked at Kaspin, and frowned. "I... know you. How do I know you?"

Kaspin shook his head and looked back at Aeris. She looked as puzzled as he felt, but her eyes darted toward the pool. She tapped his back three times, then looked at the water once more. He swallowed and looked at Lancir.

"Don't know you," he said. One tap. Two taps...

On three, he spun and followed Aeris to the pool, hearing Lancir shout behind him. The words were swallowed by the water, and he swam down and into the tunnel, and out into the lake, where he could see Aeris in front of him. He overtook her easily, and led her to the far bank. They scrambled out of the water, panting for breath. He heard dogs and shouting, and knew they had no time — he grabbed Aeris' hand and pulled her into a run. There was no time to try and hide their trail, and nowhere for them to hide. Unless....

He drew to a stop and looked around. Yes, this might work. He pulled a sickle from his belt and shook it open.

"Listen," he hissed. "Village that way. Temple that way." He pointed to the directions. "You go." He pointed again. "I go."

"What?" Aeris gasped. "No, we're not splitting up!"

"False trail," Kaspin said. He looked up, hearing the dogs. They were closer. "No time!" He reached behind her with one hand, grabbing her braid at the nape of her neck and cutting her hair with one swipe of the sickle. "Stream there." He pointed with the sickle, then handed it to her. "Stay water. Stay safe. Hide." She looked horrified and frightened and lost, and he hated that look on her face. He looked around. "I will find you."

She nodded. "Be careful," she whispered. "Come back to me."

He smiled, then leaned down and kissed her quickly. "Always. Now go!" He turned and ran, dragging the cut length of braid behind him.

--- ⟲ ---

OWYN STUDIED THE MAP, then closed his eyes and overlaid the map the Mother had given to him. "We're close," he said. "Dark should be here." He tapped the map. "How long, do you think?"

"*A few hours. Definitely less than a day,*" Del answered. "*Maybe a full day on foot.*"

Owyn nodded. "Right. I..." He stopped. "You hear that? Wolves? Karse, are those wolves?"

"Those aren't wolves," Karse said. "Those are dogs. Hunters, maybe? Sounds like they've got something's scent. From the size of that pack, something big."

Owyn looked at Karse. "Hunting in high summer? What big thing would they be... oh, no..."

Karse turned and whistled, sharp and shrill. "Mount up! Find those hunters!"

Chapter Fifteen

Kaspin could hear the dogs behind him. Hopefully, all the dogs were tracking him and not Aeris. He stopped, his chest burning, and let the braid of hair brush the ground. Hopefully, she'd forgive him for cutting her hair.

Hopefully, he'd survive to be forgiven.

He heard the dogs baying, and started running again. There was a chasm nearby, with a deceptive track that led down and stopped abruptly. If he could trick them into the chasm, it would give him time to get clear. Then he could find Aeris, and they could find another place to hide.

At the top of the chasm, he stopped, grabbing a rock the size of both of his fists. He wound the braid around it, tying the ends together tightly, then rolled it down the track. As soon as it was gone, he took off running, along the edge of the chasm and back into the trees. The dogs sounded very close; he ducked behind a tree to get his bearings...

He never saw the archer, never heard the snap of the crossbow. The quarrel drove through his shoulder and into the tree, pinning him in place. For a heartbeat, he didn't know what happened, could only stare in dull wonder at the projectile that had suddenly appeared in his shoulder, and the blood that was staining his shirt. Then the pain started; he swallowed a scream and grabbed the quarrel, trying to pull it free. It wouldn't move, and he looked up to see that he was surrounded by men with crossbows. Lancir was among them, and he turned and looked both ways.

"Where is she?" he demanded. "Where's Aeris?"

Kaspin shook his head, his voice lost in pain and fear.

Lancir scowled, then looked around again. "Where is she?" he shouted, grabbing Kaspin by the front of the shirt. He sounded desperate, and when he continued in a lower voice, Kaspin understood why. "Listen to me. I don't want to hurt you. But there's someone who can make you hurt in ways you never dreamed possible, and if I don't bring her back, then I'll be in for the same. Tell me where she is!"

A pack of barking dogs started milling around the men, and more men followed them. None of the men looked happy.

"Sir," one of them said. "The dogs followed her trail, but it was a trick." He held up a rock, wrapped in a tattered, tangled mass of hair. "We found this."

Lancir took the rock from the man, stared at it, then turned and threw it at Kaspin with all his strength. Kaspin tried to turn, but the rock caught him in the side of the head. He slumped, the only thing holding him upright the quarrel impaling his shoulder. Dimly, he heard Lancir giving orders.

"Cut him down and secure him. We're bringing him back with us."

"Sir, your orders—"

"I know what my orders say," Lancir snapped. "But there's something about him... I need answers. Bring him."

RUN, KASPIN HAD SAID. Hide.

Where?

Was this the same stream they'd been following? If it was, didn't that mean she was running straight toward Lancir and Dark's men?

She splashed to the far bank of the stream, climbed out of the water, and ran for the trees. She needed to hide now. She hadn't heard the dogs for a while, so she needed to hide. Kaspin would find her. He'd promised.

But not hearing the dogs worried her. She crouched in a stand of bushes, trying to catch her breath, listening. No dogs. No birds. Just wind in the trees and...

Horses?

There was no way she could outrun a horse. She needed a better place to hide. Maybe... maybe she could find her way back to the waterfall, and to the cave. They wouldn't look for her there. She took a deep breath, peered out of her sheltering bush, then bolted for the water. She was halfway there when a man stepped into her path, catching her as she barreled into him, grabbing unto her upper arms. She forgot every weapons lesson and all of the fight training she'd ever known, forgot the sickle in her hand — she screamed and struggled, kicking at his legs and trying to break his grip.

"Aeris!"

She recognized his voice, and went limp, staring up at her beloved uncle. "Uncle Captain?" she whispered. He smiled, and wrapped his arms around her as she threw herself at him, breaking into tears.

"It's all right, baby girl. You're safe now." Karse smoothed her hair. "I've got you. Aven! I've got her!"

Aeris heard people coming toward them, and turned to see her father appear out of the trees, followed by Owyn and Del. Aven looked pale, and Aeris wasn't sure if it was from worry or the pain she could feel radiating from him.

"Fa," Aeris breathed. She stumbled away from Karse and into her father's arms. He held her at arms' length for a moment, and she could feel his power warming under her skin. He touched her face, ran his hand over her chopped-off hair, then pulled her into his arms and started to cry.

"It's all right," Owyn said gently. "Fishie, it's all right. We've got her." He paused. "Aeri, where's Kaspin?"

The answer burst out of Aeris in a wail, "I don't know! He told me to come this way, and he cut my hair to lead the dogs away, and he said he'd find me but I don't know where he is!" She looked over her shoulder at the stream, hoping that he might be there. Then she realized something, and turned back to Owyn. "How... how did you know about Kaspin?"

"There's a young man named Drazi in camp who's worried about him," Aven answered, his voice shaking. "And Steward recognized him from Owyn's vision drawing. That's how we knew to come here."

"You found the village," Aeris whispered.

Aven nodded. "Karse is going to bring people back to see to them as best they can."

"But first, tell me where you last saw Kaspin," Karse said.

Aeris frowned. "Downstream, and that way." She pointed. "I... I wasn't really looking for landmarks."

"Captain!"

Copper and several guards came out of the woods on the far side of the stream, splashing across. Copper smiled when he saw Aeris.

"I'm glad to see you," he said. "Captain, we saw the hunters and their dogs. They didn't see us. Lancir was with them, and they had a prisoner—"

"No!" Aeris moaned. "They'll kill him!"

"They took him with them," Copper said. "Seems a lot of trouble if they were just going to kill him."

"Can you follow them?" Aeris asked. "Where are they taking him?"

"Their base," Owyn answered. "And I know where it is. We'll get him back, Aeri. Gan's gone back to the Temple for reinforcements, and they should be here tomorrow. We'll get him back."

"Tomorrow might be too late!"

"And having us go in after him and Elaias and Astur without enough men won't help anyone," Karse said. "They have hostages. We have to be careful going in."

"Del, do you have your tools?" Aven asked.

Del shook his head, signing, "*They're back in camp. Sorry, Aeri.*"

"I'm fine," Aeris said absently. "Kaspin kept it from rubbing my wings raw. I can wait until we get back to camp." She looked up at her father. "Mama must be in a state."

"I don't think her wings have gone down in days," Aven answered. He kissed her forehead, then touched his forehead to hers, breathing with her. When he drew back, she swallowed, feeling tears starting to flow.

"I haven't shown Kaspin that," she murmured. "I didn't tell him about sharing breath. Fa, he's my Water. We were right. It's him. And he's a healer, and... there's so much." She stepped back, scrubbing her hands over her face. "I want to go home."

"Take her back to camp," Karse said. "Copper and I will scout around some more, see what else we can find."

TIRAS WAS WAITING AT the edge of camp, pacing back and forth. They saw the riders and bellowed, "She's here!" before running toward them. As soon as Aeris was on the ground, she had her arms full of Tiras, who was laughing and crying all at once. Then Dyna was there, sobbing and apologizing. Aeris clung to them both, the tears starting again.

"Aeris."

Aeris looked up from her Companions, gently pulled away from them, and went to her mother's arms. A moment later, Aven joined them, wrapping his arms around them both.

"As much as I'd like to just let you be alone with your Companions," Aria said after a long embrace, "We need to know what you know. And..." She looked past them. "Aeris, where is Kaspin?"

"They found us," Aeris answered. "We got away from them, and he led them off on a false trail." Aeris ran her hand over her short hair. "That's what happened to my hair."

"Your hair is the least of my concerns," Aria said. "Getting your Water back is topmost. He is your Water, is he not?"

"Yes, Mama," Aeris answered. "Before we do anything, I want my wings free."

"Of course. Del, would you?" Once Del had gone to get his tools, Aria focused on Aeris again. "A change of clothes and a wash, too. Then you can eat while we talk." Aria gestured to Dyna and Tiras.

"I wish Gan was here," Tiras said as they took Aeris' hand. "He's been worried about you."

"He went back for reinforcements?" Aeris asked. "What reinforcements?"

"Tiercel and his sons and a lot of the rest of your flock came to the Temple to guard while we were gone," Dyna answered. "Gan's gone to get them, and they'll be flying over the area where Owyn says the base is located. He danced, and he spoke to the Mother, and she told him where."

"He did what?" Aeris stammered.

"He spoke to the Mother," Tiras repeated. "And I did, too. I fell into the vision, and I saw her and spoke to her. I used to see her all the time when I was small, but I haven't in ages. She gives the best hugs."

"I..." Aeris paused, then shook her head. "I can't think of anything to say."

"You don't need to say anything. You're here. That's all we need." Dyna led them toward a tent. "This is ours. And here comes Del."

Del trotted up to join them and held up his lockpicks. He arched a brow, and Aeris sighed.

"I didn't have my tools, and even if I did have them, I couldn't reach. Kaspin said the lock is underneath my wings, against my back."

Del nodded. He followed them into the tent, and Aeris turned her back on him, feeling the warmth of his hands through her shirt as he worked. She felt the chains fall loose, and Dyna helped Del unwind them from Aeris' wings and remove the canvas. Aeris stepped away from them and spread her wings wide, wincing as the muscles protested.

"Thank you, Fa Del," Aeris said. Del smiled and left the tent, and Aeris flapped her wings a few times. "I'm tempted to go out and fly, just to work out how stiff I am, but I'd be a target." She folded her wings again.

"I'll go get some water so you can wash," Dyna said. "Then we'll leave you so you can change."

"If Aeri doesn't mind, I'd like to stay," Tiras said. "I want to know about Kaspin. Drazi told us a little, but he's not one of us. He doesn't know what's important."

"I'll tell you everything. Then I need to see Drazi," Aeris said. "He was going to try and get Uncle Eli and Uncle Astur out."

"He told us," Dyna said. "Let me go get the water." She paused, then kissed Aeris' cheek. "I'm so glad to see you. And I'm so sorry."

"It's not your fault, Dyna," Aeris said. "He used you. And... I think someone is using him. But I'll tell you all that once I'm dressed."

Dyna left, and Aeris took off her filthy shirt and stripped off her belt, her trousers and her boots. Tiras brought her a sheet, and she wrapped it around herself and ran her fingers through her short hair.

"This is going to take some getting used to," she murmured. "I've never had it this short."

"I can trim it, if you want," Tiras offered. "Tidy it up a little. He used a knife?"

"A sickle," Aeris answered. "It's on my belt. I need to keep it safe; he'll want it back. He has a pair."

Tiras nodded, looking at the belt. "It folds? That's clever. I... what's he like? Drazi just told us that Kaspin was living wild when Rags took him in, and that he doesn't talk much."

"He's still learning to talk," Aeris said. "He was raised like an animal, he told me. Beaten and kept in a cage. He escaped, and Rags found him and tamed him. And adopted him. I...I know that they found the village. Were you there? Did you see?"

"No," Tiras answered. "I was here, helping Dyna and Treesi. Drazi was hurt really badly. He said they went back to the village and were caught there, and his brothers died so that he could get away and warn us."

"Went back... they must have gotten there after we were there. I was worried that Dark's men might come back." Aeris sighed and sat down on one of the beds.

"Dark... Drazi knows the story," Tiras blurted. "It wasn't a cloud. It was a shadow. *Axia and the Shadow.* And... and we know who Dark is. Who he really is."

"You know?" Aeris gasped. "Who?"

Tiras looked down at their clasped hands. "Treesi's father. Elan. We figure... that's why he wanted Elaias and Astur."

Aeris stared at him, her heart plummeting to bounce off the bed and through the floor. She felt sick. Dark followed Risha, so he was one of the ones that had been searching for the Child. One of the ones who were stealing Water girls to try and breed the Child, if Othi was right. And he was Mama Treesi's father, and a healer...

And Kaspin was a healer, too. Kaspin was a very strong healer. Did that mean...? "Oh. Oh, Mother of us all. I..."

"What?" Tiras knelt on the ground in front of her. "You've gone whiter than that sheet."

"I need to talk to my mother," Aeris answered. "Tir, would you pick out clothes for me?"

ONCE AERIS WAS WASHED and dressed, Dyna and Tiras brought her to the central firepit, where Owyn was sitting was a young man with bright, gold hair. The young man stood as they approached, bowing slightly.

"My Heir," he said, and Aeris recognized his voice.

"Drazi," she said. "Please, sit. You're still recovering. How do you feel?"

"Better," Drazi answered, sitting back down. "Healer Dyna is taking good care of me. And... I'm sorry, my Heir. I failed you."

"You're forgiven, Drazi," Aeris replied. "I know you tried. And you got here, to warn my mother. And you're going to help us stop this once and for all." She sat down, Dyna on her left, and Tiras on her right. "Now, I'm told you have a story to tell me? Or does this need to wait for the others?"

"We've all heard it," Owyn said. "Go ahead, Drazi. I'll check on supper."

Drazi nodded, looking down into the dust for a moment. Then he cleared his throat and started, "Worlds begin. Worlds end. Worlds begin again. So it is with worlds. In the days when the world was young, when the Mother still dwelled in the hidden places between the sea and the stars, her daughter Axia went walking out into the hills that surrounded their home. She did this often, unable to explain to her mother what it was that she sought. She would go in search of something, and come back and tell tales of what she had seen and done. This time, she did not return, and the Mother went in search of her...."

Aeris listened in rapt fascination as Drazi told the story of Axia's imprisonment in the dark, and the Mother's challenging the Shadow, and how She almost fell to them, only to be saved by Axia.

"The stronger the light, the sharper the shadows," Aeris murmured once Drazi was done. "That's very profound. How can we defeat something that draws its strength from hating us? When they refuse to admit that they're wrong?"

"We can't," Owyn answered. "Because they won't admit they're wrong." He filled a bowl, and handed it to Aeris. "We fight them by showing the people who follow them who we really are. That we're not the monsters that Shadow makes us out to be. That we're better than that. And we're doing that. We've been doing that, and that scares him even more."

"The stronger the light, the sharper the shadows," Tiras repeated. "We're stronger, and we're scaring him into doing... all this." They waved one arm expansively. "So... if we stop him, then what?"

"Then we watch to see who steps in to fill that role," Aven answered. "Because you can't unburn a candle. That hate is out there. Fear feeds it. And some people are very afraid."

Aria nodded, stirring the contents of her bowl with a spoon. "Tomorrow, the flock will be here. Then we'll be able to get more information, and we'll hopefully have the forces to go into the valley and free the prisoners."

Aeris nodded, taking a bite of the spicy stew that Owyn had prepared. She chewed slowly, swallowed, then said, "I'm going in with them."

"You are not!" Aria gasped.

"My Water is in there, Mama," Aeris said, her voice even and calm. "My Abin. I am going." She paused. "And don't tell me that you wouldn't do the same. Because I know you did."

"At least... two times," Tiras added. "I think it was two." They looked at Aeris. "Two?"

"Saving Owyn in the garden." Aeris started ticking off on her fingers. "Saving Owyn and Fa from Risha's men before you got to Terraces." She frowned. "There's more. I know there's more."

"You forgot on the Progress."

Aeris turned at the sound of the familiar voice. "Gan?" She put her bowl down and scrambled up to run into his arms. He hugged her tightly, burying his face in her neck.

"I was scared, Aeri," he murmured, his voice barely audible. "They didn't hurt you?"

"No, I'm fine," Aeris answered. "Gan, I found him. He found me. He saved me, and now we have to save him."

"Gannet, what are you doing here?' Aria asked, coming up behind Aeris. In answer, Gannet gestured behind him. Aeris looked past him, and saw people coming out of the woods — Air men and women, all of them armed.

"Gannet," Aeris said slowly. "I've flown with you. You don't fly that fast."

Gannet chuckled. "Tiercel and his flight met me halfway. I don't know why they knew to come this way. We didn't talk. We just flew. Is there something to eat?"

"There is. Maybe not enough, but there is," Owyn said. "Go sit, Gan. Good job."

Aeris took his arm and led him to the fire, where Tiras was waiting with a full bowl and a kiss. Then she went back to join her mother.

"Tierce, how did you know?" Aven asked. Tiercel laughed and came forward to hug Aven, then kissed Aria's cheek.

"This morning, Steward apparently woke up with a message from the Mother," Tiercel answered. "She told him to send us east, toward the twin spires, and to watch for a guide." He glanced back over his shoulder. "We'll set up camp over that way. We've got supplies, and we can coordinate in the morning—"

"We're not going to have time to coordinate in the morning," Aria interrupted. "We'll coordinate now. You'll need to be in the air at first light. There are lives at stake."

Tiercel bowed. "Yes, my Firstborn."

Aria nodded. Then she turned to Aeris. "My Heir, will you join us?"

Aeris blinked. "I... you want my help, Mama?"

"You know more of what we're facing than I do." Aria looked past her. "Drazi, will you attend as well, please? I want our forces to know everything they possibly can before they take wing."

Chapter Sixteen

"Your orders were to kill anyone with her."

Kaspin heard the voice and his bones turned to ice water. He already couldn't see straight, could barely walk, and his left side was on fire with pain, made worse by having his arms bound behind him. And now... they were bringing him back to Dark! He pulled back, whining deep in his throat. The men who had half-marched, half-dragged him the entire way shoved him forward. He stumbled and fell onto his knees, struggling to get back up, to run.

"I thought that this one should be an exception," Lancir said from behind him. "There's something... I swear I've seen him before."

Someone behind Kaspin grabbed him by the hair and pulled his head up, and he felt a cold metal against his throat. Dark stood in front of him, his eyes narrowed. Then he laughed.

"Oh, it's this one!" he said. "I remember the eyes. Yes, this beast slipped his chains and ran off into the woods before you came here. You've never seen him before, Lancir."

The blade shook. "I haven't?" Lancir asked. "But... I was certain of it. I know him."

"You have never seen this beast before," Dark repeated. "Now, beast, where is the girl?"

Kaspin couldn't stop shaking. This was his worst nightmare, and he couldn't have put two words together if he tried. He tried to pull back, and felt the knife slip, felt a warm trickle down his throat.

"Don't kill him yet!" Dark snapped. "He knows where she is!"

"He does speak," Lancir said. "Maybe he needs incentive?"

"Incentive?" Dark laughed. "Perhaps... hold him still. Take away the knife."

The moment the blade was gone, Dark slapped him, hard enough to snap his head to the side. Kaspin tasted blood, and he could barely hear through the ringing in his ears. "Where is she?"

Kaspin didn't answer. Couldn't answer. Couldn't fight back against the blows and kicks. He went limp, closing his eyes and just enduring the beating, the way he'd done so many times in the past. If they got bored, they went away.

It worked. Dimly, through a haze of pain and hammering in his ears, Kaspin heard Dark swear.

"Take the beast and throw it into a cage. Lancir, you're with me. Pelin is back."

KASPIN WOKE WITH A jerk and saw bars. A cage. He was in a cage. He whimpered and moved away from the bars, backing up into the bars behind him. He was caught. He was trapped. He was...

"Easy."

Kaspin turned and saw the cages next to his — there were two on one side, and one on the other, and all three were occupied. On one side, there was a man who was either unconscious or dead. On the other, there were two men, both with red hair, one older than the other. The one closest to him was the older one, and it was he who spoke.

"It's all right. There's no one here but us," he said. He stuck his arm through the bars of his cage. "Give me your hand."

Kaspin stared at the man, who smiled.

"My brother and I are both healers. And the cages are close enough for me to reach you. I took care of some of what they did to you already, but you moved and I couldn't finish. Give me your hand."

Kaspin held his right hand out through the bars, and the older man clasped it. He felt warmth chasing up his arm, easing what pain remained. The older man smiled. "Good. Now, I think I recognize you. You're the one who rescued Aeris."

Kaspin nodded slowly. These must be Aeris' uncles. What did that mean for Drazi? He swallowed and looked around. It wasn't Drazi in the other cage — the man's hair was a mix of dark and gray.

"Where is Aeris?" Aeris' other uncle asked. "You got her away. Is she safe?"

Kaspin frowned and looked around. No one to see him, or hear them. He nodded, then shook his head. Then he shrugged.

"You don't talk?" the older one said. "And... you don't know?" He sighed. "Well, that's better than it could have been, I suppose. They don't have her. If they did, they wouldn't need us anymore." He let go of Kaspin's hand. "That's the worst of it, I think. How do you feel?"

Kaspin swallowed and nodded, still too uncertain of his voice to try answering. Then he examined the bars of the cage. Could he move them, like he'd done before? He rattled the bars, and the younger uncle chuckled.

"I tried that," he said. "The bars are solid. I'm Astur, by the way. This is my brother, Elaias. And that's Frayim, on your other side."

Elaias looked past Kaspin at the cage. "You're a healer, aren't you? I thought I felt that in you. Do you have any training? Can you help him? We can't reach him, and I can feel him fading."

Kaspin nodded, then shifted to the far side of the cage, reaching between bars and taking Frayim's cold hand. He closed his eyes, assessing how badly hurt Frayim was.

Fading was an understatement. Frayim was dying. Kaspin drew his hand back, leaning against the bars. Frayim couldn't die. The

Temple needed him. The High Priest and Rhexa needed him. He was a good man, and he was Rags' friend. Kaspin could save him... if he did something Rags had warned him to never, ever do. He hesitated, then opened his power to the fullest, letting it pour into Frayim,

"What are you doing?" Elaias called from behind him. "No! You'll kill yourself!"

Kaspin heard the cage next to him rattling, heard the shouting. But it didn't matter. Nothing mattered anymore.

Frayim would live.

It didn't matter if he didn't.

ELAIAS ROCKED THE CAGE, trying to get closer to the limp figure in the next cage over. He couldn't reach the young man, couldn't stop that bright light from fading. "Guards!" he shouted again. "Help!"

The door opened, and to his shock, the guard who came in was Lancir. "What are you shouting about?" he demanded. "I... what happened?" He rushed over to the far side of the cage and dropped to his knees. "He wasn't hurt this badly!"

"He opened himself too far," Elaias said. "He's a healer, and he was trying to save Frayim. He opened himself too far."

Lancir looked up, his face gone pale. "He's a *what*?" He touched an out-flung hand, then shook his head. "I'm not enough of a healer for this. I..." He paused. Frowned. Then shouted, "Someone send for my father!"

There was a commotion outside the room, sounds of people running and shouting. Elaias glanced at Astur — they hadn't seen the outside of this place since they'd been brought here, had only seen guards who brought their meals, and who refused to speak to them.

"What is going on?"

The thundering voice was familiar, enough so that Astur moaned softly. Elaias reached across and touched his brother's arm, then sat up straight as their father walked into their prison, followed by the man who'd captured them at the Temple.

"Hello, Fa," Elaias said. "Thought you were dead." He paused, then snorted. "Sorry to see I was wrong."

Elan ignored him, folding his arms over his chest and glaring at Lancir. "Since when do you send for me like a servant?"

"I can't save him, and I think we need him," Lancir answered. "He's a healer, and... what did you say?"

"He opened himself fully, and gave his life to Frayim," Elaias answered. "He's got to be at least a level four to be able to do that."

Elan snorted. "He's an animal. Animals can't be healers." He went to the cage and knelt, touching the boy inside. He frowned, and his frown deepened the longer he stayed on his knees. Finally, he stood up, and the young man in the cage moaned softly.

"He's stable," Elan pronounced. "He'll live long enough to burn. Don't bother me about that again." He didn't look at Elaias or Astur as he left.

"He's your father?" Elaias asked softly. "You know he's our father, too."

Lancir looked at him and nodded. "I heard that, when I got to Terraces," he answered. "I just... he says Gisa's children weren't his. That I'm his only son."

"Well, that's a lie," Astur growled. "What else has he lied to you about, I wonder?"

Lancir shifted from foot to foot, looking first at the cage, then at the door. "I... I don't know."

"Lancir, what's his name?" Elaias asked, gesturing to the cage next to him. "Do you know?"

Lancir shook his head. "He didn't tell me, and Aeris didn't call him by name when I found them."

Elaias nodded. "Can you move him closer to me?"

"So you can heal him?" Lancir hesitated, then went and knelt next to the cage, reaching in and pushing the unconscious man toward the other side of the cage and into Elaias' reach. He rested his hands on the bars. "I know him. I remember him. But... it's an old memory. Or a dream. I don't know." He stood up, glanced at the door, and sighed.

"He's going to take this out of your hide, isn't he?" Astur asked. "I know that look. I've had that look."

"You've also had those bruises. We both have," Elaias added. "Lancir, you don't have to help him. You don't have to stay with him."

Lancir sniffed. "And then what?" he asked. "If I go back, I'll be executed. I know what I did." He turned toward the door. "I betrayed the Firstborn. And the Firstborn doesn't forgive traitors. She executes them—"

"What are you talking about?" Astur blurted.

"I think he means Risha," Elaias answered. "Who is the only traitor I can think of, unless he's also counting Mitok. Those are the only two I think Aria ever killed herself or had executed. The rest of Mitok's raiders either took clemency and were forgiven... ages ago now, or they became Penitents and they're at the Temple." He studied Lancir for a moment. "And you had no idea about any of that, did you?"

"My father—"

"Lied to you, it sounds like. Which isn't surprising. His lies almost killed your older sister, Minna. You've met Minna. You know her and Versi." He waited until Lancir nodded. "Fa told us that her heart was weak, and couldn't be repaired. But Senior Healer repaired it in under an hour. Fa almost killed her to control her. He'll do the same to you." Elaias watched as Lancir paled. "How old are you, Lancir?"

"Twenty-five," Astur answered. "If he told the truth on his paperwork in Terraces. I did his initial intake."

"I didn't lie about my age," Lancir answered. "Why?"

Elaias nodded, looking over at the young man in the cage next to him. "Wondering how old my new youngest brother is," he answered. "And what he's holding over you that's keeping you from running. But you know you have a choice. You've been away from him for... what, three years now? More? You have a life of your own. You have people who care about you. You've lived in Terraces. You've lived in the Palace. You have people who think of you as family, like Karse and Copper." He looked back at Lancir. "You have Dyna, who thinks you hung every star in the sky."

Lancir's face turned pink. "I... if I bring Aeris back, she'll still be mine. He told me I could choose any girl I wanted as a reward. Pelin didn't like that, but Fa told him to abide."

Elaias heard Astur snort, and he shook his head. "You honestly think she'll submit to that? You know her better than that, Lancir. You force her into anything, you'll spend the rest of your very short life waiting for her to kill you."

Lancir's jaw dropped. "What? But she's a healer. Do no harm... Fa said that healers swear to do no harm!"

"You said you weren't enough of a healer to save him," Elaias said. "What does that mean?"

"It means I'm not very strong," Lancir answered. "I can do a little, but I'm not strong enough to waste training on—"

"The same lies he told Treesi, and she's a level four." Astur shifted in his cage. "Lancir, he's lying to you to control you."

"Which means that you haven't been trained to your full potential. Dyna has, by two of the best and strongest healers in Adavar. Senior Healer Jhansri changed the healer's creed, you know." Elaias smiled. "The first part is still do no harm. But now there's a second part — take no damage. Or, if you listen to him, take no shit. He's taught every healer under his guidance how to use our gifts to protect ourselves. And Dyna is a level five healer. She's as strong as her father, and she'll probably be Senior Healer when the time comes."

"Are you trying to scare me?" Lancir demanded. "Because it won't work. Dyna wouldn't hurt me."

"Dyna is the Earthborn Companion," Elaias replied. "And Dyna's father once killed a man without touching him. So yes, I am trying to scare you. Scare you into thinking for yourself." He paused, then held his hand out. "Come here."

"You just told me—"

"I'm not going to hurt you. I want to assess you. I want to see what lies he's telling you." He gestured for Lancir to come closer. "Come on. Come here."

Lancir came closer, like a dog that wasn't sure if it was going to be petted or hit. Elaias didn't move, watching Lancir as he crouched on his heels and took the offered hand. Elaias nodded.

"Let me see," he said, closing his eyes and gently probing the depths of Lancir's healing gift. He snorted. "He told you... what? That you didn't have enough of a gift to train for more than the basics? That learning would be wasted on you?"

"Yes," Lancir answered. "Why?"

"Because it's not true." He squeezed Lancir's hand gently. "Your potential shows you could be at least a four. Which isn't surprising. All of Elan's children are four or higher. He should be proud of you, pushing you to be a healer who saves lives. Not this. Not trying to destroy everything Milon built and everything Aria is working for." He let Lancir's hand go. "He lies to you to control you. Tell him no. Walk away. Help us get out of here, and we'll take care of you."

Lancir shook his head. "I... I can't." He stood up, then looked at the other cage. "See to him. I need to talk to him. I need to know his name. I need to know where I've seen him before." He paused, his brow furrowed slightly. He glanced away, clenching his jaw.

"What?" Astur asked. "You've got that look. The one I used to have before I did something behind his back."

Lancir stared at him, the intense looking falling away. "You did that?"

Astur nodded. "The last time? I smuggled Treesi out of the healing center before he gave her to Mitok as a breeder. It got me thrown out of the healing center." He grinned. "Best thing that ever happened to me."

"What are you thinking?" Elaias asked. "And how can we help?"

"You'd help me?" Lancir asked. "Why?"

"You're my brother," Elaias said. "I liked you before I even knew that. The daughter of my heart thinks you hung every star in the sky. And you're in trouble. Yes, I'll help you. What are you thinking?"

Lancir smiled slightly. "I... he's Water. He has the gills. And he was from here and escaped. Fa said that. That means... he's in the breeding records. And I know where those are. I can get to them." He glanced at the door. "I... I shouldn't be doing this. He'll kill me for defying him. Or worse, he'll let Pelin do it."

"Who is Pelin?" Astur asked. "I'd never seen him before he came to the Temple."

"He's Fa's enforcer," Lancir answered. "He's always been here, I think. He runs things when Fa is away, and he leads the forces against the Penitents. He likes hurting people." He frowned. "I never thought he'd hurt me. But now... I don't know. He was supposed to follow my orders on the way back, but... well, you saw how he didn't. He wasn't supposed to threaten you, or Aeris." He paused, then shook his head. "How you can help?" He nodded toward the other cage. "Take care of him." He paused. "He's... what? Twenty-five? Like me? Knowing that will help me find the right records."

Elaias nodded and reached through the bars, resting his hand on the young man's chest. He closed his eyes and set the healing trance, then tested his healing potential, and examined the markers for his age. Then... he went looking for one more thing...

And there it was. He drew his hand back. "Based on his teeth and his bones, he's probably about that, yes," he said slowly, rubbing his hands together. "And his potential is as strong or stronger than yours. Stronger than mine. He's a natural five, or I'll eat this cage."

Lancir nodded. "I'll see what I can find. Thank you." He looked around. "Do you need anything? Food? Water?"

"Keys?" Astur suggested. Lancir smiled.

"Be careful," Elaias said.

"Thank you." Lancir left, and Astur turned toward Elaias.

"You have got to stop doing that!"

"He doesn't know my tells," Elaias murmured absently. He looked back at the young man. Yes, he could see the resemblance now.

"So... do I get to guess what you weren't saying?" Astur asked, keeping his voice low. "Twins?"

Elaias nodded. "I think so, yes." He took a deep breath and blew it out. "Which means Lancir is half Water."

"He's going to find that out when he finds the breeding records, isn't he?" Astur asked. "Then... what then?"

"Dinnae ken," Elaias answered, tipping his head back against the bars. "It'll like to mang him proper."

"Sounds like he's not the only one manged." Astur sighed, and Elaias felt a warm hand on his arm. "Are you all right?"

"Pure done in," Elaias admitted. "He was pretty gone, and Fa didn't do more than tether him to this side of the grass with a thread and a wish."

Astur blew out a breath. "He had to live to burn, he said. Remember, they were going to burn Frayim?"

"I mind, yes." Elaias rubbed one hand over his face and looked at his younger brother. "We're getting out of here, Astur. We're going home."

Astur smiled. "You keep saying that, Eli. Maybe it'll come true. Now get some sleep. You need it."

ELAIAS SLEPT FITFULLY, and woke when the cage next to him shook. He looked up, and saw mismatched eyes looking back at him.

"How do you feel?" he asked, glancing over to see if Astur was awake. He wasn't, so Elaias kept his voice low. "And what's your name?"

"Kaspin," he answered. "Better. Feel better." He looked down, then his head rose sharply. "Coming!"

Elaias heard the commotion a moment later, and shifted to the back of his cage. "Astur!"

"I'm awake," Astur mumbled. "Where's the fire?"

"Poor choice of words," Elaias muttered. He looked across and saw that Kaspin wasn't the only one awake on that side — Frayim was sitting up.

The door slammed open, and Elan stalked in. He was followed by Pelin and two guards, Between the guards, they dragged a limp body.

"Lancir," Elaias gasped.

"You did this," Elan growled. "You tainted him." He gestured, and the guards dropped Lancir onto the ground. "He is no longer my son. I have no sons—"

"You have four sons. Me, Astur, Kaspin and Lancir," Elan snapped. "And two daughters. Minna and Treesi. And, if you actually cared, you have twelve grandchildren. I have three, Treesi has five, and Astur has four. And you have a woman who still loves you, even though you did everything you could to destroy her. Mam will go into the ground loving you." Elan moved to the front of his cage. "You were an incredible healer, and you sired incredible healers. More than that, you sired the Earthborn Companion. Treesi is the Earthborn Companion to the Firstborn. How can you throw that all away on hate?"

"I have no children," Elan repeated. "Pelin, throw that in with the other animal. They'll burn together."

Chapter Seventeen

Kaspin pressed his back against the bars of the cage, trying to put as much distance as he could between himself and Lancir. The guards had dumped Lancir's body in with him, then left without a word. As soon as they were gone, Elaias reached between the bars.

"Well, they near beat the life out of him, but he'll live," Elaias finally said. "He needs more than I can do right now. I don't think I could heal a skinned knee. Kaspin, could you take over?"

Kaspin stared at him for a moment, then forced himself to speak. "Truth? Brothers?"

Elaias looked at him, and Kaspin could see how tired he was. "Are you my brother? Yes. Is Lancir your brother? Also yes. Is Elan—"

"Dark," Kaspin corrected. "No name. Forgotten. Only Dark."

"Oh," Astur murmured. "I like that. The Mother will never call his name to welcome him home if his name is forgotten."

"I like that, too," Elaias said. "So... is Dark your father? Yes. And I suspect that you and Lancir are twins, but I'm not entirely certain. Alanar or Jehan will be able to tell."

Kaspin nodded. "Said he knew me."

"Do you remember him?" Astur asked.

Kaspin shook his head. "No. No memory. No mother, no brother. Nothing." He shifted closer to Lancir. "Why?" He gestured toward the limp form.

183

"He was going to look in the breeding records. He was trying to find out more information about you. He wanted answers, and Dark must have caught him."

"Or he lost his head when he found out the truth, and he challenged Dark," Astur suggested. Elaias shook his head.

"He didn't strike me as being reckless. He's not you, Astur, to challenge the west wind to a spitting contest, and thinking you'd win. You saw him. He was skeered."

Despite himself, Kaspin smiled. "Talk like Rags," he said.

Elaias chuckled. "Because I'm that tired. Now, can you do for Lancir?"

Kaspin nodded. "Yes." He shifted closer and rested his hand on Lancir's chest. "Elaias? Why him? Why me?"

From behind him, he heard a deep chuckle. "The eternal question," Frayim murmured.

"And one I think I can answer," Elaias said. "You're visibly and undeniably Water, Kaspin. He's not. It would be relatively easy to pass him off as Earth. Except he has the Water lack of body hair."

Kaspin grunted, focusing on Lancir. There was some deep bruising, and a slight fracture in his cheekbone. He set the healing power and nodded. "Not his fault."

Elaias smiled. "No, it isn't. He's been lied to his entire life. Today, he learned the truth, learned his truth. We'll have to see how he lets it settle." He yawned. "How is he?"

"Broken here." Kaspin touched Lancir's cheek. "Do that now. Tired. No more."

"What else is there?" Astur asked.

"Bruised only. Will hurt." Kaspin looked up. "What now?"

Elaias sighed and shook his head. "Dinnae ken. I can't imagine they're not out hunting for Aeris, at the very least." He tipped his head back. "Frayim? Any answers?"

"The Child is safe," Frayim replied. "And she comes to claim what's hers. She will walk through the shadows as did Axia of old."

"Claim what's hers?" Astur asked. "Why do I think that you don't mean us?"

"Because I don't," Frayim answered. "Do I, child of Water?"

"Me," Kaspin said. "Said I was her Water." He felt his face growing warmer, and didn't think he could look up. Until he heard Elaias laugh.

"Oh, we're as good as on the road home," he said. "She's been looking for you for years now. She's not letting you go that easy."

"What was that about walking through shadows?" Astur asked.

"An old tale," Frayim answered. "I don't know all of it. Rags told me once. Kaspin knows it, I'm certain."

"Know," Kaspin agreed. "Can't tell."

"Sounds like the story that Aeris was trying to find," Astur said. "Eli, go to sleep!"

"I will," Elaias said. Then he yawned again. "Now. I'll go to sleep now. Wake me if anything." He laid down on his side, his back to Kaspin.

Kaspin looked down at Lancir again. Brothers. Up until tonight, his brothers had been people who claimed him, who called themselves his brother even though there wasn't a drop of shared blood in them. Now, he had brothers who shared his blood. He wasn't certain how to feel about that.

And Lancir... Aeris had wanted to help him. It had seemed important to her. So he'd help, too. He rested his hand on Lancir's chest again, examining him once more. He was still too tired to do much, so he'd focused on the worst of it, the way Rags had taught him. The break would be mostly repaired by dawn, and once he'd had a chance to rest, he could set more deep healing into the worst of the bruises. And Aeris was coming. Then... then they'd figure out what happened next.

"Frayim?" He looked back at the other cage. "Aeris is coming?"

"The Child is close," Frayim answered. "But the fires are closer. Past that, I cannot see."

"Well, that's... something. I don't know what, but it's something," Astur said.

"Hush," Kaspin murmured. "Elaias sleeping."

"Yes, hush," Elaias repeated, his voice thick and sleepy. "I'm sleeping."

Kaspin chuckled and leaned against the bars, closing his eyes. Maybe he should get some sleep himself...

Lancir gasped, his arms flailing. He rolled away from Kaspin, coming up against the bars on the other side of the cage. He looked around wildly, stopping and staring when he saw Kaspin. His face went ashen, and he shook his head.

"I... I didn't know," he whispered. "I didn't remember."

Kaspin nodded slowly, trying to think of what to do. What he could do. He looked down, then sighed and repeated what he'd told Elaias, "Not your fault."

"But... I knew you... I *knew*... you... we... I should have remembered!"

"Shhh!" Kaspin hissed. "Elaias sleeping. Needs to sleep."

Lancir pressed his lips together and nodded. He glanced at Elaias, then at Kaspin. "I'm sorry," he whispered. "I hurt you, and... and Aeris was right. I should have let her help me. I should have come with you, helped you escape." Kaspin sniffed, and Lancir scowled at him. "I would have!"

"Too skeerd," Kaspin grumbled. "Dark lied. You believed."

Lancir sighed. "I... yes. I believed the lies. I didn't know better. I didn't know the truth." He paused. "I always thought I was all Earth. That's what he told me. I... he told me my mother died birthing me. The records say different." He closed his eyes and recited, "Born, to mute Water female, male twins. Firstborn, tainted male.

Secondborn, no signs of taint. May be worth harvesting." He opened his eyes. "You're older than I am."

Kaspin nodded, his mind racing. He had no memory of his mother... or did he? That sensation of being held. Maybe he did remember something. "Mother?"

"I don't know. I found notes that they took me when I started to walk, but I didn't get far enough into the records to find out what happened to her," Lancir answered. "He caught me before I could find anything else." He shifted and folded his legs. "Did you heal me?"

Kaspin nodded. "Some. Elaias done in."

"Because he healed you?" Lancir looked down at his hands. "I'm glad he did. I'm sorry. I... I don't even know your name!"

Kaspin chuckled. "Kaspin," he answered. "Will heal more after sleep." A thought occurred to him, and he frowned. "Village burned. You?"

"Village?" Lancir frowned. "I... Oh, the Penitent village in the chasm? I knew about it. I'd never been there. Why?"

"Burned. All dead."

Lancir's eyes widened. "No. I was chasing you and Aeris. Pelin did that. I heard him laughing about it, but I didn't know where he meant." He paused. "Was that your home?"

Kaspin nodded, and tried to remember the word that Aeris had used. "Doptive father. Burned. Family killed."

"Doptive? What's...?" Lancir's eyes widened. "Adoptive. You mean adoptive. Oh, no. Oh, Kaspin. I'm sorry. I..." He looked down, then snorted with laughter. "This is ridiculous. I'm going to be apologizing to everyone forever! I'm an idiot! I saw what the world was like when I was away from him. I should have stayed in Terraces. Or at the Palace. I never should have come back here."

"Why?" Kaspin asked. "Come back why?"

Lancir sighed. "I don't know." He scowled, then shrugged. "What did you say? I was skeered? That's it. I was scared. I didn't know I could walk away. I didn't think I had that choice." He ran his fingers through his hair. "If I hadn't come back... but I did. So there's no point in thinking about what might have been if I didn't come back."

Kaspin tipped his head back against the bars, trying to put words together. "You stay there, Aeris stay there. Never find me." He looked back at Lancir to see him frown. "Happens because happens."

"Happens because happens?" Lancir repeated. "What kind of answer is that?"

"Things happen for a reason," Frayim said, his warm voice making Kaspin jump. "That's what the Waterborn means."

"The... the Waterborn?" Lancir's jaw dropped. "You... that's why she couldn't find her Water? And why the visions said you weren't where you were supposed to be?"

"Visions?" Kaspin looked at Frayim, who nodded.

"The Twiceborn and his son both sought you in visions," Frayim answered. "And they were told that you weren't where they expected you to be, and they'd find you in the last place they looked."

Kaspin snorted. "Sense. If find, why look more?" He closed his eyes. "They come?" He wasn't sure why he asked again. Maybe he just needed the reassurance.

"They're coming," Frayim replied. "But I cannot see past the fires." He sighed. "Sleep, Kaspin. It will come when it comes."

"I'll watch, if you want to sleep," Lancir offered. "Not that there's much to watch for."

Kaspin shook his head. "Hard. Fear. In cage, nowhere to run. Easy to hurt."

"Lancir, you lived here," Astur called. "You never saw any of this?"

"I wasn't raised here," Lancir answered. "I lived south of here. The story I told, about being raised by people who weren't mine, and who treated me like their slave? That was all true. I didn't know I was anything else until Dark came and claimed me maybe five years ago. He said I was ready to serve. That's when I came here. I wasn't here more than a year, though. But that's when I learned about the breeding stable, and the records. I wasn't ever allowed to see them, though. The stable isn't even here. There's another village, north of here. That's where, but I wasn't allowed to go there. Which... I understand why now." He shifted over to sit next to Kaspin. "Go to sleep," he said. "I'll keep watch. I won't let anyone hurt you."

Kaspin met his eyes. He'd decided to help Lancir because Aeris had wanted to help him, but he wasn't sure when he'd decided to trust him. "Why?"

Lancir licked his top lip, frowning slightly. "I don't understand," he said. "Why... what?"

Kaspin gestured. "Why..." He paused, trying to think of words. "Why are you...with us?"

"Oh," Lancir murmured. "I thought you were like the Airborn Del, and you couldn't talk more than a few words. And... why have I changed sides? Why am I helping you?"

Kaspin nodded. "Yes. Why?"

Lancir planted his elbows on his knees and leaned forward, lowering his head. He took a deep breath, then looked up. "Because you're real. What I thought was real was a lie. My entire life, up until I woke up in this cage, that was a lie. You, Elaias, Astur. Frayim. Aeris. You're all real." He smiled slightly. "Dyna is real. I want a real life, not a lie. I want a family, not an army." He looked at Kaspin. "Is that a good enough answer?"

"It's a fine answer," Elaias called. "Now, some of us are trying to sleep."

Kaspin looked at Lancir, and they both started laughing. Lancir poked Kaspin in the shoulder. "Go to sleep. I'll watch."

Kaspin nodded and laid down, pillowing his head on his arm and closing his eyes. It was hard to relax, hard to let go of the fear that someone was going to hurt him. Then Lancir started humming softly.

Kaspin was asleep before he could remember where he'd heard that melody.

AERIS SAT ON A FALLEN log and stared into the fire as the sky grew lighter overhead and the camp came to life around her. She'd been unable to sleep, unable to settle, so she'd slipped out of bed in the dark and dressed, coming out to find Karse building the fire. Now she sipped the cup of tea he'd made for her and tried not to scream her frustration and fear.

"You're awake early."

Aeris looked up. "I couldn't sleep, Mama. I've been keeping Uncle Karse company."

Aria sat down next to her. "I understand. Are you feeling up to going? If you haven't slept, you're not going to be as alert as you could be. No one will fault you for staying behind with me and your father—"

"I'll fault me," Aeris said. "And Fa isn't going?"

"Your father is wise enough to know that he is no longer a young warrior, and that he had already come far too close to dying because of it..."

Aeris twisted to face her mother. "What?"

Aria took Aeris' hands. "I hadn't yet had a chance to tell you. When you were taken, we tried to stop them. Your father had just gotten back to the Temple, and we heard the commotion. When he tried to get to you, one of the raiders shot him. We were lucky that Alanar was there — it was a near thing."

Aeris stared at her mother. The words didn't make sense, for all that she understood what Aria had said. The idea of her father dying...

Aria squeezed her hands. "He's fine, my dove."

"It's all my fault," Aeris murmured. "People keep telling me it's not, but... if it weren't for me, none of this would be happening!"

"You're too close."

"Fa!" Aeris turned as Aven sat down on her other side. He put his arm around her and hugged her.

"You're too close," he repeated. "Too close to see clearly. You're the smallest pebble following the avalanche. The first stone? That was the Usurper. Pretty much all of what we've had to face came from his one choice." He hugged her again. "Little bird, little fish, this isn't any of it your fault. These people have been trying to use you since before you were born. And they were grown adults then. Most of them, anyway. And the ones who weren't never had the chance to learn better."

"Like Lancir," Aeris said.

"Like Lancir," Aven agreed. "You can't take the weight of their deeds on your shoulders. You're not strong enough. None of us are strong enough." He sighed. "The most we can say is that we should have known this was happening before it got to this point. And that's on us — on your mother and me and the rest of the circle. If anything, it's our fault for not being vigilant enough, and you're paying the price of that failure."

"And we're doing something about that failure today," Aria added. "I do wish you'd reconsider—"

"I'm going, Mama," Aeris said.

Aria nodded. "I was certain that would be your answer. Give me your left hand."

Aeris held her hand out, and gasped when her mother started to buckle her wrist crossbow around Aeris' wrist. "Mama!"

"I've taught you how to use this," Aria said. "I always knew it would be yours someday. Wear it well, my dove."

Aeris ran her fingers over the weapon. "I'll bring it back."

"See that you do. Along with your Water and your uncles." Aria hugged her tightly. "Now, you'll be with Tierce, and Gannet will be with you."

"And Dyna will be with Othi and Del and the archers," Aeris said. "Drazi will be with Karse. And Copper and Tiras will be here."

"I heard my name?" Tiras stepped over the log on Aven's other side. They yawned, then leaned down to kiss Aeris. "Everyone is still asleep, but we need to wake them up. You should go," they added. "Get ready. The moment is close."

Aven sat up straight. "What have you seen?"

Tiras yawned again. "Fire. Fire that doesn't drive back the shadows. Fire that makes the shadows stronger." They rubbed one hand over their face. "And that's why I'm staying here. Because I'm not seeing the now anymore."

Aven nodded. He hugged Aeris once more, then got up and left the fire, shouting at the top of his voice. Tiras watched him go, then took his place next to Aeris.

"He doesn't bellow like Uncle Captain," they mused. "Has he not learned how?"

"He's never needed to," Aria said. She reached out and ran her fingers through Aeris' short hair. "Before I forget again, Tiras, thank you for taking care of Aeris. This is much neater. And it will grow back."

Tiras blushed. "I'll always take care of Aeris. And it had to match."

"Had to match?" Aeris frowned. "Had to match what?"

Tiras pursed their lips together. "I... I'm not sure how much I should say?" they said slowly. "Or if I should have said that much. But I did see one thing past the fires. Us, standing on the beach at the harbor. I'm not sure when, but your hair was short. So I made it match what I saw, because... well, if it matches, then we'll all come through it. Right?"

"Did you see Kaspin?" Aeris asked. Tiras shook their head.

"No. I'm not sure where he was. If he was with us. That's not clear yet. Gan's finally awake."

Aeris looked over her shoulder and saw that Gannet had come out of the tent. "How did you know?"

Tiras looked startled. "I... I heard him," they said. Then they smiled. "And I hear you. Aeri, I hear you!" They pounced on Aeris, laughing. "You can tell me what's happening. And I can tell Mama Aria... I... oh." They blushed furiously. "I'm sorry. I should have asked..."

"Darling, of course you may," Aria said, smiling. "I want you to stay with me all day. And Aeris, please do keep Tiras informed?"

"Yes, Mama," both of them answered as one.

THE DOOR SLAMMED OPEN, and Kaspin jerked awake, feeling sleep-heavy, staring as the room filled with men, some of them carrying long poles. Lancir shifted next to him, his shoulder pressing into Kaspin's. He moaned as Elan came in, followed by Pelin.

"It's time," Elan announced. "Take them to the purification fields. I want them in place by the time the sun rises." He turned to Pelin. "Once that's done, you have your orders."

Chapter Eighteen

Aeris circled over the abandoned buildings once more, then flew down to land near Karse and Othi.

"They've run for it, it looks like, But they haven't been gone long," Karse said. "The embers are still hot in the firepits."

"They didn't go west," Gannet said, coming to join them. "We'd have seen them if they had. Where else could they have gone? Into the mountains?"

"They went somewhere. That's all I know," Karse said. "Tiercel and his boys are scouting up high, and Del and Drazi and their team are checking for trails to the east." He looked up when a shrill whistle pierced the air. "And that's Del."

Aeris and Gannet fell in behind him as he headed toward the whistle, seeing others coming to join them from around the ramshackle houses and barns. Dyna trotted up to Aeris' side.

"All the buildings are empty," she said. "It's almost spooky."

"Did you find anything?" Aeris asked.

In answer, Dyna held up a sickle that matched the one hanging from Aeris' belt. "Fa Owyn found it in one of the outbuildings," she said. "It was in a pile of things that looked as if they were trash, so I think they might have just thrown it away."

"Which makes no sense," Gannet grumbled. "Why throw away a good tool?"

"If you think it's tainted by who owned it?" Aeris answered. "When someone is really ill with something contagious, you have to sterilize anything they've been in contact with. If it can't be cleaned properly, it's burned." She stopped walking. "Like... like what they did... what Dark did to Rags. They *burned* him." She sprinted ahead to Karse. "Uncle? I need to go aloft. I need to see if there's smoke—"

"I heard you. And it marches along the same path as what they tried to do to Frayim back before you were born. Let's see what Del has to say, then you and Gan can go up and see what you can see."

Del was pacing back and forth when they reached him. He pointed, then started to sign, "*A lot of people and carts took this track. They weren't even trying to hide their trail.*"

Drazi frowned slightly as he watched Del's hands, then looked at the others. "What did he say?"

Karse grinned. "You'll learn. He said they didn't hide their trail."

"Oh, they never do," Drazi replied. "They don't have to. There's no one out here to challenge them, except for us. And... well, now there's not us anymore." He frowned slightly, then looked at Karse. "There's you."

"You're part of us now, lad," Karse said. "So... they're that arrogant? I'll wager they won't expect the largest part of our force will be coming from the air. Aeris, you and Gan get in the air. Tell Tiercel that they've gone east, and be careful up there. Stay in the clouds if you can. We'll follow. And have someone pace us and keep an eye out for guards and ambush. Arrogant don't mean stupid."

Aeris nodded. She stayed on the ground long enough to kiss Dyna, then launched herself into the air. The moments while she was still close to the ground were nerve-wracking — an archer undercover would have made an easy target of her or Gannet. But nothing happened, and she quickly joined the flock of armed warriors circling among the clouds.

"East!" she shouted to Tiercel, flying alongside him. "And watch for smoke!"

Tiercel pointed, and when Aeris looked, she saw the slender spiral of smoke rising in the distance.

"It just started!" Tiercel shouted. "Is that where we're going?"

Aeris nodded, her heart in her throat. She looked at Tiercel. He gestured, and the flock headed east.

"Let's go!"

They flew east, toward the smoke, and Aeris studied the ground beneath them. Another village, off to the north. She couldn't see much else because of the trees, but as they flew further, the trees seemed to thin, and what did grow looked sickly. She glanced to her right, where Gannet kept pace with her, and saw the puzzled expression on his face. He'd noticed it, too.

"There!" Tiercel shouted. "I see a trail!"

Aeris nodded. She could see the trail below them, leading almost due east toward the rising smoke. As they followed, she noticed that the trail seemed to be sloping downward.

"A valley!" she called.

"Stay high!" Tiercel called. "Out of range! We'll circle, and then head back and wait for the walkers."

Aeris nodded, beating her wings to gain height as she soared through one of the smoke plumes. She started to circle, looking down. She could see the light of the fire below, but nothing else — the valley was thick with shadows.

"I can't see anything!"

"Neither can I," Tiercel called. "So we can't be sure it's safe to go lower. This is it, though. Let's go back." He gestured, and two of the other fliers started to circle. Aeris took another pass over the valley, then flew back toward the west to meet Karse and his guards.

"Report!" Karse snapped the moment Aeris' feet were on the ground.

"We've found the source of the smoke," Aeris said. "At your best pace... an hour? Maybe. It's a valley, and it's... it's strange. From the air, we can't see the ground. We can barely see the fires. The shadows are too dark."

"Shadow Valley?" Drazi gasped. "That... they're in Shadow Valley? They've gone there?"

"You know the place, son?" Karse asked.

"That's where it happened!" Drazi answered. "The story. *Axia and the Shadow*. That's where it happened. A place where the sun never shines, where it's dark as midnight even at midday. That's where the Shadow waits. Rags told us."

"It's a real place?" Aeris asked. "You've been there?"

"No," Drazi answered. "No one goes there. Rags, he showed us on his map. Warned us never to go there. People who go there don't come back." He looked around. "We're going there?"

"That's where they've taken Kaspin and the others," Aeris said. "We're going."

"But before we go, we need a plan," Karse said. "They have hostages. We need to get them out safely."

"Distract them?" Tiercel offered. "Draw them off, and me and my men can get in and get them out."

"Get them out how?" Karse asked. "Can you fly while you carry a man?"

Tiercel frowned. "I... I haven't tried. Not with someone not Air. It might take two of us to each person. We can make carry slings. We do that with the very old, and invalids."

Karse nodded. "Right. So us on the ground raise a ruckus, and draw them off, and you get them out? That's a start of a plan."

"And it could all go wrong very quickly," Aeris said. "If they think they're under attack, what's to stop them from setting the fires and killing the hostages before we're in place?" She frowned. "The Shadow, he wanted Axia, didn't he?"

"Yes," Drazi answered. "Why?"

"Because... I just had a fuckheaded idea."

Karse groaned. "You are your father's daughter to your fingertips, girl. Tell me, so I know why your parents are going to take turns murdering me."

KASPIN HEARD CHAINS clattering and clashing, could hear Lancir grunting behind him as he struggled and cursed, could hear Elaias and Astur loudly promising that the Firstborn would come for them.

Kaspin had fought, too, but it had done nothing but given the men an excuse. Now everything hurt, and his wrists were torn and bloody from the sharp edges of the manacles. He could smell the oil they'd thrown on the wood piled knee-high around the post where he and Lancir had been chained back-to-back, but there was nothing he could do to save himself or anyone else. He couldn't move, couldn't get free, and there was no point in fighting anymore. Elaias and Astur were wrong. No one was going to find them — Kaspin had been all through these hills for years, first as a feral runaway, then as one of Rags' fighters. But he'd never been here before. He'd avoided it as a runaway, following some vague instinct to keep his distance. Then, after Rags had claimed him, he'd learned why. The trail had been steep, leading down into an area so dark that torches had to be lit alongside the path to light the way. There was another, empty stake on the far side of the bonfire. For Aeris, Kaspin guessed. Outside the stakes, there were torches ringing the clearing, and beyond the torches, there were only shadows.

Lancir fell still. "Kaspin?"

Kaspin turned his head slightly. "Lancir?"

"I'm sorry," Lancir said. "If I'd listened to Aeris, we'd be safe by now."

Kaspin snorted and shook his head. "Not safe. Never safe." He dared to look up, seeing Dark stalking across the clearing. He looked away, tipping his head back, trying to catch a glimpse of sky... and saw something circling overhead, partially veiled by clouds.

"Lancir," he whispered. "Up."

"Up? I... I can't see," Lancir answered. "What is it?"

"Help." Kaspin tugged against the chains again, then looked out into the clearing. He couldn't see past the ring of torches, couldn't tell if there was movement out there. Then he heard a howl from out of the darkness, and he *knew* that voice.

Drazi was alive, and he was somewhere out in the shadows.

Dark heard the howl, too. "A celebratory hunt!" he called. "Once we've cleansed the world of this lot!"

A ragged cheer went up, and Lancir took advantage of the noise to ask, "That wasn't a wolf, was it? Karse has a wolf, and the howl was good, but it wasn't a wolf."

Kaspin turned his head slightly. "Drazi. Brother." He frowned. "Adoptive?"

He heard Lancir laugh. "You got it." Chains clanked. "If we had more time, we could work on you talking."

"Promise?"

Lancir laughed again. "I promise. If we survive this, and I survive what comes after, I'll work with you."

Kaspin looked down the row of stakes. Frayim was chained to the stake between this one and the one where Elaias and Astur were chained. The Seer was still and silent, his head bowed, his eyes closed. What was he seeing now, Kaspin wondered?

"Frayim?" he called.

Frayim raised his head and looked at Kaspin. "I heard the young wolf," he answered. "The old wolf is with him. They hunt in the dark, and the shadowhawks circle. The time is now."

"Prattling again?" Dark scoffed as he came closer. He stopped at the bonfire, pausing long enough to light a torch that he carried toward them. "Spare us your blasphemies and your lies. We are the true children of the Mother, and once the world is cleansed of animals and degenerates like you, there will be peace."

"You are no such thing, and you never were."

Kaspin jerked, tugging on the chains when he heard Aeris' raised voice. He couldn't see her, but he could see a light, coming closer.

"You are not the true children of the Mother," Aeris continued, her voice growing closer. Dark turned and started toward the sound, and Kaspin surged forward against the chains.

"No!"

Behind him, he heard a flurry of movement, then a strangled word from Lancir, "Gan?"

"Hush!" The voice was unfamiliar, and Kaspin couldn't turn far enough to see who was behind him. "She's got them distracted. Let's get you out of this. You're in for a thumping, Lancir."

"I deserve a thumping," Lancir said. "Gan... I'm sorry. I'm an idiot—"

"Agreed," Gan said quickly, cutting him off. "But this isn't the place to discuss it. And... there. Head for the trees."

"Not leaving without my brothers," Lancir said. "I'll guard."

"Go guard Frayim. If everything goes wrong, he'll be the first target." He paused. "Second target. But Aeris can go up. Take my crossbow. It's on the ground over there." A moment later, the largest Airborn Kaspin had ever seen came around to face him, and Kaspin felt a shiver of... something. The Airborn seemed to feel it, too. He grinned. "You're Kaspin. You're ours. I'm Gannet."

Kaspin recognized the name, and understood what he was feeling. "Air Companion."

"Yeah. Let's get you out of here." He started doing something to the manacle on Kaspin's left wrist. Kaspin looked out across the clearing, and saw Aeris coming into the light. She held her torch high, and her wings were spread wide.

"I am Aeris. I am the Child you've been waiting for," she announced. "I am the daughter of all four tribes. And you're wrong. You're not the true children of the Mother. You deny her dreams, and make war on her children." She tipped her head to the side. "The Mother's dreams made all of us, Dark. We are all kin in her love. Who are you to say otherwise? And how dare you?"

"We are the Mother's Chosen!" Dark proclaimed, but Kaspin could see the men around him shifting uneasily. The manacle fell away from Kaspin's wrist, and Gannet moved around him to start working on his right wrist. Kaspin looked to his left, saw that Astur and Elaias were already gone, and that a girl was working on Frayim's chains. Lancir was standing in front of Frayim with a crossbow held ready.

"You aren't," Aeris said, drawing Kaspin's attention. "She said so. She does not know your names. You especially." She pointed at Dark. "Your name has already been forgotten. We know you only as Dark. When you die, you will be lost forever. No one will ever welcome you home, and no one will mourn you. Is that what you want? Is that what any of you want?"

"She.... She said so?" someone stammered. "How... how do you know?"

"I've seen her," Aeris answered. "And my Fire speaks with Her, and has since they were a child." She gestured toward Dark. "Can you say the same? Have you seen the Mother? Have you spoken with Her? Has She told you that this is what She wants? Have any of you seen Her? Spoken to Her?" For a moment, all Kaspin could hear were the torch flames crackling and the moaning of the wind. Aeris snorted, her derision very clear. "I didn't think so."

"How dare you claim to have spoken to the Mother! You are an animal!" Dark shouted.

"I am the Child," Aeris shouted back. "You all decided that, not I. You and your people have wanted me even before I was born. One of you is even responsible for me being born. My mother told me that — that she and my father were not going to make a child, but the woman who led you before did something to make me happen. Your people *made* me." She shifted her torch from one hand to the other. "You've been waiting and hoping and watching for the Child for how many years? Well, here I am. I am everything you wanted. I am the culmination of every bit of Wanderer lore for generations. But now that I'm here, you don't want me. You are rejecting your greatest dream, because I don't look the way you think I should. I am all of the tribes in equal measure, and that includes the tribes you fear." She sniffed. "Coward."

"Fuck," Gannet whispered as the manacle he'd removed from Kaspin's right wrist slipped from his hand and fell loose with a clatter. Aeris swore and took flight as Dark turned. He went still for a moment, staring at the stakes.

"No!" Dark shouted. "No, I will not be robbed of their deaths! Bring me Gisa's bastards!" Then he threw his torch.

"No!" Kaspin shouted. He kicked at the kindling surrounding his legs, stumbling and almost falling as he scrambled out on top of the pile and dove into the way of the flying torch, knocking it away from the pyre. Gannet caught him before he fell, and he shook off the Air's hand. "You go! And her!"

"Dyna."

"I can't get this lock!" Dyna sounded panicked. "Gan, help me!"

"Lancir, shoot anyone that comes close," Gannet called. "Kaspin, you get clear. You're not armed."

"Not leaving," Kaspin growled. He moved to stand at Lancir's shoulder, out of the way. Gannet joined Dyna, and Kaspin could hear them swearing as they worked behind him. In front of them, Dark and his followers were lighting torches. None of them were coming close. That, he knew, would change.

"Can shoot?" he asked Lancir.

"I was a Palace guard," Lancir answered. "Of course I can shoot. Karse wouldn't have let me out as an escort if I couldn't." He glanced back at Kaspin. "You're not armed. You should get out. Aeris needs you."

"Not leaving." Kaspin stooped and picked up two long lengths of wood. They'd serve as clubs, at least for a few minutes. It would hopefully be long enough for the others to get away. He glanced back and nearly dropped his clubs.

Aeris was behind him.

"What?" he sputtered. "Go! Go safe!" She stepped up next to him and held out his sickles. He stared for a moment, then dropped the clubs and took them, shaking the blades open. "Now go."

"I might be needed," Aeris answered, raising her left hand, which boasted the smallest crossbow Kaspin had ever seen. "I'm better at picking locks than they are."

"Locks?" Kaspin sniffed. "Really?"

She glared at him. "I couldn't reach and I didn't have my tools."

"You two stop it," Lancir snapped. "They're not doing anything. Why aren't they doing anything?"

It was, Kaspin thought, the worst timed question ever, as the gathered men all drew back their arms to throw their torches all at once. He heard a shout, and a rain of arrows fell from above, striking down a number of them men, whose torches fell useless to the ground. But not all the arrows found targets, and torches landed in oil-soaked kindling.

Chapter Nineteen

The fires started in four places. Maybe five. Kaspin didn't stop to count. He kicked burning kindling away from his feet and backed up, trying to move the kindling away from Frayim, to give them some room. The smoke was already making him cough, and he could feel his skin prickling from the heat of the growing fire. "Aeris, go!"

"Aeris, I need help!" Dyna called. "I'm not going to get this in time!"

"I've got it," Aeris said in a calm voice. "Get back to Karse. The flock will cover you. Gan, once we get these off him, I want you to take him up and get him out of here." She started coughing.

Another rain of arrows distracted Kaspin, as Dark's men screamed and fell and ran for the shadows. There was more screaming coming from the dark, and he glanced at Lancir, who was coughing.

"That's where we heard the howl," Lancir murmured. "There must be men waiting. Aeris? We can't stay much longer!"

"Just a moment... got it!" Aeris stepped back, bumping into Kaspin. He heard a grunt and felt the rush of air as Gannet took off. Smoke billowed around them, obscuring Kaspin's vision.

"Go!" Kaspin gasped as a wave of coughing took him. "Go with Gannet."

"We're done here!" Lancir added. "Get airborne, and we'll follow you." He raised the crossbow and fired, and another man fell. "Aeris, go!"

"You don't know where you're going!" Aeris said. "Come on. This way." She herded them away from the fire, with all three of them coughing and trying to get away from the smoke. The flames were growing behind them, and Kaspin looked back to see the stake where he and Lancir had been chained was completely engulfed. He looked around again. There was no one moving in the clearing. Nothing but bodies. Kaspin frowned as he realized something.

"Dark gone?" Kaspin asked. He couldn't see any sign of Dark among the fallen men. There were no more screams coming from the darkness. All that he could hear was the cracking of the fire behind him.

Lancir coughed and lowered the crossbow, starting to reload. "I don't see him."

"If he ran off, Karse's men or the flock will find him," Aeris said. She rested her hand on Kaspin's arm and he gave in to his need to touch her, taking both sickles in one hand so he could put his arm around her. She leaned into his side and sighed when he kissed the top of her head, then coughed again and straightened. "We're not safe yet. We need to get back to Karse. That way—"

As he turned to follow her, Kaspin saw movement, too rapid to be the smoke. He dodged between it and Aeris, shouting, "Fly!" Aeris took to the air, and Kaspin heard a small snap as she fired her little crossbow at Dark as he barreled into Kaspin, driving him down to the ground. Kaspin landed hard, the air leaving his lungs explosively as something dug into his back just as Dark landed on his chest. The man looked mad — his face streaked with blood and ash, his clothing torn. He howled like a beast and went for Kaspin's throat with hands like claws. There was another snap, and Dark jerked as the bolt hit him. It didn't stop him.

"Don't let him touch you!" Lancir shouted. "He has to make skin contact to use his healing gifts. Don't let him!"

Kaspin grabbed one flailing hand, keeping the cloth of Dark's sleeve between their skin. Dark was that poor a healer that he needed skin contact? That was something that Kaspin had never needed. He focused his power into his other hand and punched Dark in the chest. Skin parted, bone crumbled, and Dark screamed as Kaspin's fingers closed around his heart.

"No more," Kaspin growled. Then he pulled. Dark screamed again, the sound turning into a gargle that stopped abruptly as the man went limp. Kaspin shoved the body off of him and slowly got to his feet. He looked down at his hand, at the heart that didn't look as if it were poisoned and hateful. It looked... normal. Kaspin shuddered and threw it into the fire, then crouched and closed his eyes. He felt sick.

He'd just murdered his father.

He'd had no choice. He knew that. Dark was going to kill him. But... he'd just murdered his *father*. Maybe he really was an animal, the monster that he'd been called since the moment he could understand.

But his brothers were safe.

Aeris was safe.

That was what mattered.

"Kaspin?"

He looked up. "Elaias?"

"Are you..." Elaias frowned slightly and looked at the body. "He didn't hurt you, did he?"

"No." Kaspin looked past him, to the men and women standing and staring. For a moment, he wanted to turn and run. But if he ran, he'd be running from Aeris, from Gannet and Dyna. From the brothers he'd never known.

"Hey," one of the men said. He came forward slowly, his hands open and wide. "Hey, it's over. It's all right. You don't have to run. You're safe. No one's going to hurt you. And don't no one blame you for what you had to do." He smiled. "I'm Owyn. And we've been waiting for you a long time, Kaspin."

"Aeris said. Two years."

Owyn nodded. "It's good to finally meet you. Now, can I help you throw that onto the fire, or are we leaving it for the shadowhawks and wolves?" He looked down at body and snorted. "My man is going to love training you."

The abrupt change in topic made Kaspin's head hurt. "What?"

"My man is a healer. A powerful one. He killed someone once without even touching them. Stopped their heart cold." Owyn walked over to the body. "He's going to like this. But he's bloodthirsty like that. Don't be surprised if he asks you how you did it. Come on. I'll get his feet."

"I'll help." Another man came forward. "I'm Karse—"

"Don't hurt Lancir!" Kaspin blurted. Karse looked startled.

"Hurt him? Never. He's one of my boys. He just caught a case of stupid is all. Eli says it's treatable." Karse grinned as Kaspin stared at him. "Oh, you've already had a day. And we're not helping, are we? It's fine, son. I've already heard an earful from Eli and Astur about why he did what he did, and how he tried to help you all. So don't you worry. He'll have to make it up to the Firstborn, so I expect he'll be on latrine duty or mucking out stables until he's forty, but no one's going to hurt him." He frowned. "Except I think the Companions are going to thump him a little. And they can explain that to you."

Kaspin looked at Owyn, who just nodded. "It's all right," he said. "Really. I know it's a lot. Believe me, I understand where your head is right now. Let's get this done so we can go. There are folks waiting to meet you." He looked past Kaspin. "Seen Del yet?"

"Not yet, but I heard what sounded like him and Othi and Drazi and their lot having a grand time over that way." Karse gestured. "Wait... here they come."

"Kas!"

Kaspin turned, seeing first the shock of bright gold hair as Drazi came toward him at speed. "Drazi!" he gasped. Then he yelped as Drazi barreled into him. They wrestled for a moment, and Drazi ended up face down on the ground, as usual. He laughed.

"Yield!" he called, and rolled over as Kaspin let him go. He sat up, letting Kaspin help him to his feet. "You made it through! You're alive! I thought I wasn't going to see you again this side of the grass!" He hugged Kaspin tightly. "And... he's dead? Dark is dead?" Kaspin nodded. Drazi took a deep breath and let it out. "They can rest easy, then. Rags and the others. It wasn't for nothing." Then he coughed and pointed. "Wait... he's one of *them*!"

Kaspin turned and saw Lancir standing with Elaias and Astur. "Helped us."

"He did?" Drazi sounded skeptical.

"Drazi..." Kaspin paused, putting words together. "He is my brother. Same mother."

Drazi's brows shot up. "No! Really? How'd you find that out?"

"Healers. And records."

"Excuse me?"

Drazi turned and grinned. "Othi, this is Kaspin, my brother. Kas, you'll like Othi. But don't try to look him in the eye until you've got something to stand on. You'll break your neck."

The biggest man Kaspin had ever seen chuckled as he came closer. "I can sit, if you want to look me in the eye. And I knew this was Kaspin. I saw the drawings. It's good to meet you, cousin."

"Cousin?" Kaspin looked up. "Oh. Water. Same..." he frowned. What had Aeris called it? "Same... canoe?"

Othi grinned. "Not sure yet. But you said there were records?" Othi seemed almost indecently eager. "We've been looking for anything that might give closure to people back on the Deep. We've been looking for this for twenty years now."

Kaspin nodded and turned. "Lancir knows. Lancir!"

"Yes?" Lancir came trotting over. "What is it? Karse wants to get us moving out of here."

"Records?" Othi repeated. "There are records?"

Lancir nodded. "There are breeding records. He... Dark was very complete about that. I'll show you where." He looked around. "Once we get out of here. I agree with Karse. We need to leave. I... this place feels like it's growing darker."

"Now that you mention it, it does." Owyn looked up. "Not as many of the flock up high. And it looks like Tierce is coming in."

Kaspin looked up to see one man flying down to meet them. "Where's Aeris?"

"We'll ask Tiercel," Owyn said. "I'm sure she's fine."

The Air warrior landed a good distance from the fire, and walked toward them.

"It's a good thing that's burning," he said as he reached them. "You can't see anything from above anymore. Did you clear all of them out?"

"The ones here, and as many as ran into the woods, yeah," Karse answered. "Any get past us?"

"We've seen nothing on the trails out of the valley," Tiercel said. "So I sent the flock back to that village where we started. They took Frayim in a carry sling, and Aeris and Gannet went with them." He looked around and smiled when he saw Kaspin. "You would be Kaspin? Aeris told me to tell you especially that she's fine, and that she'll see you soon."

"Thank you," Kaspin replied. Tiercel nodded, then took off, and Karse started shouting orders.

"Kaspin? A word?" Elaias called. "Lancir? You, too."

"Talk as we go," Karse said. "We're moving out. Take torches — it's dark as the bottom of a barrel until we get about halfway out."

They started walking, picking a careful path through the dark and shadows. Somehow, the torch Kaspin carried didn't seem to do anything to drive back the gloom at all. If anything, the light made it worse.

"You wanted to talk?" Lancir prompted Elaias.

Elaias nodded. "Astur and I were talking," he said. "And... the hill people, they don't like us. They know we're Gisa's sons, because of the hair. Which means they know who our father was. Even though he denied it, they all know. And they don't trust us because of it. They don't trust Treesi, which is why this went on as long as it did — none of them would talk to her." He paused, then nodded. "Neither of you know who your father is. Not for certain."

Kaspin looked at Lancir, who looked confused as he stammered, "But... the breeding records..."

"Neither of you know who your father is," Elaias repeated, his voice a little harder. "What Kaspin told Drazi? That you share the same mother? That's the truth. And that's your story. The people who know better... well, they won't care. But you're going to be a healer of some talent, and I fully expect you to be part of Aeris' Circle, the way Alanar is. And Kaspin is Aeris' Water. She's already going to have a time of it bringing the hill people out of ignorance. Don't give them an excuse to turn from her... or you. You are your mother's sons. That's all anyone needs to know."

"Deny you?" Kaspin asked. He frowned. "You deny us?"

"No!" Astur gasped. "No, we are not denying you! We know you're our brothers. But this way... you won't have anyone hating you because of him."

Behind them, Kaspin heard Drazi's braying laugh. "Are you dim?" he demanded. "We all already knew. The hill folk, they know.

Him being Water, there's only one way he got here. He came out of Dark's breeding stables, the same as about half a dozen other kids in Sanctuary."

Elaias stopped and turned. His face looked like chalk under the flickering torchlight. "There... there were more? We had more family up here, being treated like animals?"

"Did you know?" Lancir asked Kaspin, nudging him gently. "That you... we had other brothers and sisters?"

Kaspin shook his head. "No. Never told. Never guessed." He shivered. "All dead? Drazi?"

Drazi nodded. "They killed everyone. And when our brothers and I got there, Dark's man killed them, too." He stopped. "Wait... did you get him?"

Lancir's breath caught. "Pelin. Dark said he had his orders. And... I never saw him again. He wasn't here." He moaned softly. "It's not over. *It's not over*! Not unless we find Pelin!"

"Easy, Lance," Karse said gently. "Easy. Where would they have sent him? What orders? Do you know?"

Lancir shook his head, then closed his eyes and tucked his chin. "I,., the barns. The breeding stables. The records. If I was trying to cover my tracks, I'd destroy them first."

"And you know where those are? Once we get out of here, you can show us?" Karse whistled, sharp and shrill. "Pick up the pace!"

The group started moving faster, and soon Kaspin was trotting alongside Drazi, a ground-eating pace that the pair of them could keep up for miles. The trees around them grew lighter, the air clearer, until they crested a hill and the ground leveled out, showing Dark's abandoned base in the distance.

"Right, take a moment," Karse shouted. "There's some that need it." He grinned as he came over to clap Kaspin on the back. "I could make a guard out of you in a heartbeat, lad. But you're meant for more than that. Still, once we're back at the Palace, I want you to train with the Guard. Lance can tell you about it." He walked away. "Eli! You dying yet?"

"I'm considering it," Elaias wheezed. He stood not far away, bent at the waist, with his hands on his knees. Astur was stretched out on the ground, arms and legs spread wide. Kaspin walked over to them.

"Elaias?" he asked. Elaias looked up at him and grinned.

"Not a guard or a fighter, Kaspin. Keeping pace with you lot... that's done me in."

"But you did it," Lancir said from behind Kaspin. "That's impressive for someone with no training."

Elaias laughed and straightened. "You've lived in Terraces, Lancir. It's the stairs. Now... oh. Kaspin, turn around."

Kaspin turned to see Aeris had come up behind him. There were people behind her; but he didn't notice who they were. Didn't care who they were. He took a step toward her, and she ran into his arms, throwing her arms around his neck. He wrapped his arms around her and held on as tight as he dared.

"You're safe," she whispered. "You're safe."

He nodded. He could say the same about her, but she'd been considerably safer than he'd been over most of the past day, so he understood her worry. He started to let her go, then gasped as she grabbed him and kissed him, hard enough that time seemed to stop, and it started to get harder to breathe.

"Aeri, you're both going to pass out."

Aeris started giggling, swaying slightly as she released Kaspin. "I should properly introduce you," she said. "To Dyna and Gannet. I don't think earlier really counted."

"I think it did," Gannet said. He came closer and held out one big hand as Aeris stepped back. Kaspin took the offered hand, and was pulled into a tight embrace that caught him off guard. He tensed, and Gannet let him go immediately. "Sorry!" he said, his face turning red. "I... I shouldn't push. But we've been waiting for you for so long. I just... you need to get to know us."

"Kaspin, this is Dyna," Aeris said. Kaspin turned and bowed to the pretty girl who reminded him of a bird.

"Healer?" he asked. "Lancir's healer?"

She smiled. "Healer, yes. Lancir's healer? I'm not so sure."

"Not his fault," Kaspin said. "Lied to. Helped us." He glanced over at Lancir, who was standing with Elaias and Astur. He was watching them, his face sad. "Lancir brother. Twins." He paused. "Dark father," he added. He paused, then decided he needed to tell her. Tell them. "Killed him."

"You killed Dark?" Aeris said. Then she blinked. "We'd sort of guessed that he sired you. Honestly, with your healing? It had to be him. And Lancir is your twin?"

Kaspin nodded. "Killed him. Killed Dark." The swirl of emotions rushed to the surface again. "Killed my father."

"You didn't kill your father," Aeris said. "Rags was your father."

Kaspin frowned. "Difference?"

"Rags was the one who wanted you. Who loved you and treated you like his own," Aeris said, taking his hands. "What you told me about Rags? That he taught you to speak and to read? And he took you in and tamed you and taught you to be a person? That's what a father does. Being a father doesn't mean blood. It means love. And Dark didn't have that." She looked past him. "You said he tried to help you?"

"Dark denied him. Me. All of us." Kaspin waved vaguely toward Elaias, Astur and Lancir. "Said no children."

"See?" Gannet said. "Take the man at his word. He said it himself. He wasn't your father."

Something shifted and settled. It would take time before the hurt eased, but what they said helped. "Forgive Lancir?" he asked. "Karse said yes."

"Probably. We might thump him a little," Gannet said with a grin. "We told him that if he hurt Dyna, we'd thump him."

"And I agreed to it," Lancir called. "You all are loud. I heard most of that." He came over and bowed to Aeris. "I'll submit to the thumping. I made... so many mistakes. And then... then I'm leaving the Palace. For a few years, anyway."

"Why?" Dyna gasped. "I..."

"Training," Lancir answered. "Elaias says I have it in me to be a healer. A good healer, like you and Kaspin. He wants to train me himself. So I'll be staying at the Temple, at the healing center they're building there. Once I'm... once I'm worth something, I'll come back." He smiled. "Maybe you'll have forgiven me by then." He turned before Dyna could say anything. "Captain? If you want the breeding records and the stables, they're this way."

Karse nodded. "Gannet, go aloft and tell Tiercel we need sweep patrols to find that Pelin and his men. Then head back to camp and tell the Firstborn we'll be back soon, and to be on alert." Gannet nodded and took to the air, and Karse whistled loudly. "Right. Let's go! Lancir, take the lead!"

Chapter Twenty

The place looked like a normal village, like any of the hill villages that Aeris had visited on her Progress. But there were no people in the common areas. No children playing. No chickens scratching in front of the houses or near the well. No animals of any kind. Lancir pointed to each building in turn and told them what was inside. The caretaker's house. The breeding records. The stud stables. And the breeders. There were other buildings, but Aeris didn't remember what Lancir said.

Breeders.

Karse was swearing softly as he singled out the five women among the guard. "We don't have enough women," he said. "We can't send a man into that building. We *can't*."

"Aeris and I can go," Dyna said. "And... Aeris, take off your jacket. Let your tattoo show."

Aeris nodded and reached up to start unfastening the buttons behind her neck. Underneath the jacket, she wore a light leather vest that left her arms bare — basic armor for an Airborn archer. Del joined them, carrying his own jacket. He wore a similar vest, and his tattoo stood out against his pale skin. His falling stars dangled from his belt, but he'd taken off the wrist sheaths where he wore his throwing spikes.

"Are you coming with us?" Dyna asked. "I'm not sure that's wise."

"*I'll be at the door with Othi,*" Del signed. "*Use Water signs, if you can. It might help.*"

Aeris nodded and followed Dyna to what appeared to be a barn, where the guards were waiting. The barn's double doors were locked shut, but Lancir came toward them, carrying a heavy ring of keys.

"You'll need these," he said. "They should open anything in there. We've already unlocked the other doors that needed unlocking, so we shouldn't need them."

Aeris took the keys and waited until Lancir had gone before unlocking the doors and opening them wide. Dyna joined her, and they walked inside together.

There were cages along each wall, but only half of them were occupied. Dyna gestured once; Aeris nodded and went left, while Dyna went right. The guards followed them — three with Dyna, two with Aeris.

The girl in the first cage couldn't have been more than ten. She crouched at the back of the cage, watching Aeris with wild, wary eyes the color of new leaves. Aeris crouched and signed, "*Can you speak?*"

"I... yes."

"My name is Aeris. We've come to get you out of here. You're safe now. No one is going to hurt you again." She unlocked the cage and opened it. "You can come out."

"But..." The girl cringed back into the cage, and Aeris' heart broke. "Out? Safe?"

"Truly?" the woman in the next cage whispered. "But..."

"He's dead. The one who's been doing this, the one behind it. We call him Dark, so his name will be forgotten for his crimes against the Mother. He's dead, and he will never hurt you again. We're here to take you home to the Deep."

"I don't know how to swim," the girl whispered. Aeris held her hand out.

"We'll teach you. What's your name?"

The girl stared at the offered hand as if it was going to bite her. "No one asks names. Not here. We don't have names."

"I'm asking. Do you have one?"

The girl nodded. "It's secret. My... my mother said it was secret, so I'd know when the Mother called me. It doesn't have to be secret anymore?"

"No, sweetheart. What may I call you?"

"Asta." The girl looked puzzled. "You're not Water. But you know the signs. My mother said the signs were only for Water."

"I'm part Water," Aeris said. She tipped her chin up. "See? I have gills, just like you."

"And wings. Are... are you the Child?"

"They said I was," Aeris answered. "They stole me from my parents when I was a baby because they said I was, but my parents stole me back. Then they tried again, and that's how we found you. But I don't think they really were looking for any child. It was just an excuse to hate other people." She smiled and offered her hand again. "Coming?"

A small hand slipped into hers, and Aeris stood up and led Asta out of the cage. They moved on to the next cage, where the woman was standing at the bars. She looked to be of an age with Aeris' parents.

"Your tattoo says Neera's canoe," she said. "I don't remember a Neera who was Clan Mother of any canoe. The only Neera I remember was my age. Who are you?"

"Aeris, daughter of Aven, of Neera's canoe. Neera is daughter of Jisa, daughter of Arana, of the line of Abin. My father is Aven, son of Aleia—"

The woman looked startled. "I... I remember Jisa. And Aleia. She was Companion before the Firstborn fell. I remember when she came back to the canoes with her Earthborn man and her son. They didn't stay, though. Then... the Neera who is Clan Mother is my friend Neera?"

"Yes, and my father Aven is the Waterborn Companions. My mother is the Firstborn, and I am her Heir." Aeris smiled and unlocked the cage. "Come out. I'm sure my grandmother and my aunt will be happy to welcome you all home." She nodded toward the door. "There are a pair of Water warriors just outside the door. My uncle, and one of my mother's Companions." Aeris looked at the door. "Del? Stand where people can see you?"

Del stepped into the doorway and started signing, "*I am the Air Companion of the Firstborn. My name is Del.*"

"He's not Water. How is he a Water Warrior? How does he know Water signs?" the woman asked.

"He had a Water tutor when he was young, who taught him because he doesn't speak. And all of my mother's Companions were welcomed into the canoes." Aeris answered. The woman nodded. Then she gasped, and Aeris looked back to see that Othi had stepped into view.

"You... you're Jisa's son," the woman whispered. "I remember you. Othi."

"Tella?" Othi said. "I... I thought you went north!"

"My canoe did. And... I may be the last of my canoe left." She closed her eyes and shook her head. "I haven't seen the Deep in so long."

Othi nodded. "We'll get you home, Tella. Come out into the light." He held his hand out. Tella looked at Aeris, who nodded.

"Go on. I'll bring the others out."

Tella hesitated, then followed Othi out of the barn. Aeris looked down at Asta. "Do you want to go with her, or stay with me?"

"I can stay?" Asta asked. Her hand in Aeris' shook a little, and she pressed a little closer to her side.

"You can stay." Aeris held up the keys. "Do you want to open the locks?"

Asta's eyes widened, and she smiled. "I want to open *all* the locks! No more locks!" She took the keys from Aeris and went to the next cage, unlocking the lock and flinging the door wide. The fact that there was no one in that cage didn't seem to matter. Asta was serious in her intent to open every lock in existence. Aeris followed, gently assuring the women who ventured timidly from the cages that it was true. That they were going home. That no one was going to hurt them again. That they were free. Dyna joined her as they led the women toward the doors. She looked troubled.

"What is it?" Aeris asked.

"There are so few of them," Dyna answered. "How many were we too late for?"

"We'll find out," Aeris answered. "There are records, and all of their names will be remembered. We'll make sure their canoes know. We'll make sure their names return to the Mother."

"How?" one of the women asked. "They took the dead and burned them. The Mother won't know them—"

"The High Priest found something in the Temple records, a ritual for the Mother's children who die far from home," Aeris answered. "There's a way, and we've remembered all those that we knew their names. All the ones who vanished from the Deep, from Terraces, or from Jasper Inlet have been remembered and sent home to the Mother. We'll do what's necessary, once we get back to the Deep." She walked out into the sun and tipped her head back, looking up to see high clouds like lacy ribbons strewn across the sky, like the ones that Tiras occasionally braided into their hair. It reminded her that she'd promised to keep Tiras informed. She wasn't sure that they'd hear her, but she hadn't even tried.

"*Tiras,*" she thought. "*If you can hear me, I'm sorry. I forgot to tell you what was happening. We're safe. We found them. Uncle Tierce is on his way back with Gannet, and they're bringing Frayim. We found survivors, and they kept breeding records. We'll be bringing those with us. And we'll be bringing back nine Water women and a child. They'll all need careful handling.*" She sighed and looked around. "Come with me," she said aloud. "I'll introduce you to my mother's Captain of the Guard." She held her hand out to Asta, and they started walking.

"Are there more locks to open?" Asta asked.

"I'm not sure," Aeris answered. "If we find more, you can open them."

Asta jingled the keys in her other hand, looking around. "The sky is pretty. I've only seen outside when the door was open. Are those clouds? My mother told me about clouds. And... who is that?" She pointed at Karse and Lancir, who were coming toward them.

"The older man is Karse, who is Captain of the Palace Guard. I call him Uncle Captain," Aeris said. "And the young man with him is Lancir. He's a guard, too. And they're going to help take care of you. Neither of them will hurt you."

"Aeris?" Lancir called as he stopped. "I... I don't want to intrude, but you need to come. I... Kaspin is... he's in the stud stables. And he's stopped talking. Elaias and Astur are keeping an eye on him, and I told them I'd come get you."

"Asta, will you come with me?" Dyna asked. "We'll see what we can find to eat." She smiled at the other women. "I'm sure you're all hungry. My father will be able to find something for you to eat, and I'll examine you while he cooks."

"You're a healer?" one of the women asked.

"Level five," Dyna answered. "Asta? Are you coming?"

Asta nodded and let go of Aeris' hand; Dyna led her and the women toward the rest of the guards. Karse ran his fingers through his short hair.

"There's no one in the stud stables," he said. "Looks like it's been empty for years. But something in there has Kaspin spooked."

"I'll go see what it is." Aeris looked around. "How soon can we leave?"

"Soon. We've found wagons, and we're loading the records to take back with us. There should be room for the women in the wagons, too, so they don't have to walk." He paused. "She's got green eyes. That little one. Reminds me of Treesi's eyes."

Aeris nodded. "And like Kaspin."

Lancir coughed. "Wait... you think..." He turned to watch the women walking away. "A little sister?"

"We'll ask Dyna to check," Aeris said. "Now, where's Kaspin?"

The stud stable was very similar to the one where Aeris and Dyna had found the women, except that this building wasn't as well maintained. Aeris could see that the doors were tilted on their hinges. Elaias and Astur were standing in the doorway, but she couldn't see Kaspin.

"Was this even locked?" she asked.

"No," Lancir answered. "And even if it had been, there's a huge hole in the back wall. This place... the Captain is right. It hasn't been used in years. They were letting it fall apart."

Aeris frowned. "Then what were they doing with the boys?" she asked softly.

"I think you know the answer to that," Karse answered, his voice just as quiet. "Drazi said something about possible younger siblings, other Water kids. I wonder... I'm going to go talk to him. Lance, you stay here."

"Yes, sir," Lancir said. He dragged one of the tilted doors a little further open, and Aeris saw Kaspin. He was crouching about halfway down the row of cages, his hands pressed together in front of him so that his fingers were pressed to his lips. He was staring intently at something that Aeris couldn't see.

"He hasn't moved," Astur said, keeping his voice pitched low. "I'm not sure he's even blinked. He won't answer us."

Aeris nodded. "Dyna might need help. She was going to examine the women we found. There are nine of them, and a little girl who may be your sister."

Elaias coughed. "Why do you think that?"

"Her eyes. She has green eyes. Dyna is going to check, but I'm sure she'll appreciate some help."

Elaias nodded. "Astur, you stay. I may be back. If they recognize me as his, they won't want me anywhere near them." He patted his brother on the shoulder, then walked toward the larger group of people. Aeris went further in and knelt next to Kaspin, close enough that her shoulder brushed his ribs, and her left wing rested against his back. Then she tried to see what it was that he was seeing. The cage he was staring at didn't seem to be any different from any of the others....

"Was mine," Kaspin murmured. "Never fixed." He lowered his hands and pointed to a wide gap in the bars. "See? Bars loose there." He turned toward Aeris. "Come. Show you." He stood up and held his hand out to Aeris. "Come see."

Aeris rose and took his hand, letting him bring her into the open cage. "Was this locked?"

"No locks. No need." Kaspin looked around. "Don't use. Haven't used. Years, maybe. I was last, maybe." He sighed. "Boys in Sanctuary saved. Not escape."

"Oh," Aeris murmured. "We were wondering. What do you want to show me?"

Kaspin smiled slightly and knelt, pointing at a knot in the wood. "This." He carefully pried the knot out of the wood, showing the hole. Aeris had to crouch low to see out — it pointed away from the rest of the village, toward the woods.

"Only way to see out," Kaspin said. "Storm broke wall. Broke ceiling. Loosened bars. Too small to move then. Got bigger. Got stronger. Moved the bars. Took back the sky."

Aeris looked up. "How old were you when the storm came?"

Kaspin frowned slightly, then looked at the wall and touched a spot that wouldn't even have come to Aeris' hip. "That tall."

"I remember that storm," Lancir said from outside the cage. "We would have been about four. It was a bad storm, and it went on for days. I was terrified of thunder for years because of it."

"You're twenty-five. That means... oh. The Mother's Fury," Aeris said. "We call that storm The Mother's Fury. It happened when Ri... when the woman who came before Dark almost killed my father, when she tried to break the cycle of the change."

Lancir arched a brow. "That caused the storm?" he asked. He sounded skeptical.

"That caused the storm. And when Fa Owyn drowned, and was dead for almost a minute, that's when the Smoking Mountain erupted and Forge was buried." Aeris sat down and folded her legs. "When Grandfa Milon almost died, the ground shook. That happened... twice? I think? Fa Owyn would know." She looked up and around. "Kaspin, let's get out of here. It's not good for you in here."

"Wanted to see." Kaspin got up and dusted off his trousers. "This... made me."

"Only partly," Lancir said. "But I think Rags made you more than this did. This... this made you a survivor. Rags made you a good man."

Kaspin looked at Lancir and smiled. "You a good man. Mostly."

"I'm trying to be," Lancir said. "And that's nothing to do with whoever our father was, and everything to do with Karse and Leesam." He grinned. "I haven't told you about him. Lee was my commander in Terraces. He's a good man, and I like him a lot. He's the one who trained me, and between the two of them, they made me start being more than... than Dark's puppet." He looked around.

"Should we burn this place down, do you think? So it doesn't fall in on itself and possibly hurt someone?"

"We'll talk to Karse. If we burn it down, then someone has to stay and make sure it doesn't spread." Aeris got to her feet. "Kaspin, I want you to meet someone. Her name is Asta."

Kaspin nodded. "Where?"

"She's with Dyna right now." Aeris took his hand and led him toward the door. "She's... maybe about ten? She was with the other women—"

Kaspin stopped in his tracks. "Breeder? That young?"

"Mother of us all, I hope not," Lancir murmured. "She didn't seem to be afraid of men. Just of strangers. And she warmed up to Aeris and Dyna quick. I think we got to her in time." He paused. "You going to tell him or do I get to?"

"What?" Kaspin asked.

"She has green eyes," Aeris said. "Like yours. And like your older sister Treesi. Elaias is going to check, but you might have a little sister." She frowned and turned around. "Where's Astur?"

"There," Lancir pointed. "And... wait. That's Frayim! Didn't... wasn't he on his way back to the camp?" He looked at the others. "Something is wrong."

Aeris nodded, looking up. "I...I don't see Gannet." She started toward the group, and before she'd taken two steps she was running. Owyn stopped her near the edge of the group.

"Aeri, there's trouble."

"Frayim is here. The flock was supposed to take him back to camp, and Gannet was going with them. But Frayim is here. Where's Gannet? What's wrong?" She looked past Owyn. "Where's Uncle Tierce? What's happening?"

Warmth at her back, and Kaspin said a single word from behind her. "Pelin."

Owyn blinked. "You're quick. Yeah. The camp's been overrun. And... Keliar said Gannet went down. He said Tierce ordered them to get Frayim out of range, but... they don't know what happened, except they saw Tiercel fall. It... it don't look good."

"And Frayim didn't see anything? There was no warning?" Aeris demanded. "You didn't hear anything from Mama or Fa or Tiras?"

"Aeri," Owyn's voice was stern. "You are not going to lose your head and start yelling at people. That's your mother's trick, and it took forever for her to grow out of it. Don't you start."

Aeris swallowed, fighting back her temper. She took a deep breath and tried to act like her grandmother. "I can't just react. I need to think. To plan. Like Granna taught us. I need to think like the War Leader."

"Or come up with something fuckheaded. That usually worked for us." Owyn looked around. "Karse is sending Frayim and the women back to the other village with the female guards and about half the flock. As for the rest of us..." He paused, took a deep breath, then grinned. "Well, it's been a minute since I last helped save the world. I hope I haven't forgotten how."

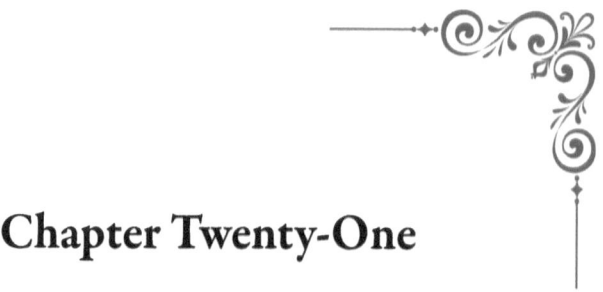

Chapter Twenty-One

The records and the women were split between two wagons, and accompanied by half of the Air warriors, the five women guards, Elaias, Astur and Frayim.

"We won't do any good in a fight, but we can take care of things here. Send someone to fetch us when you win," Elaias told Aeris before he left. "And tell Dyna to keep her head down."

"I will," Aeris replied. "Keep both eyes on Asta, will you? I don't want her running off."

"We'll take care of her," Astur said. He looked over his shoulder and grinned. "We've got almost the same name."

"You go bond with her over that," Elaias said. "I'll be with you in a moment." He waited until Astur had gone over to climb into the wagon with Asta, then turned his back to them. "Tell Othi that he's not to feel guilty about putting Treesi first. I know he wants to be in both places."

"I'll tell him. And I'll tell Dyna to be careful. Any other messages?"

"You be careful yourself, Aeris," Elaias said. He kissed her on the forehead, then went to climb up into the other wagon. A moment later, they started rolling. Aeris watched as they moved down the trail, then went back to the others. Drazi was crouching at the center of the group of guards, drawing in the dust. Crouching across from him, scowling furiously, was Kaspin.

"That's it," Drazi said. "That's the camp." He started pointing with his stick. "Tent. Tent. Tent. Kitchen setup. Horses over here. Stream there." He grinned. "All right, Kas. Go."

Kaspin grinned, then cocked his head to the side. "Guards?" he asked, looking up.

"Four guards, and my son Copper leading them," Karse answered. "Aven, Treesi and Aria all fight, but I'm not going to count them as fighters. Weapons... well, you've seen what my guard carry."

Kaspin nodded and went back to studying the map. Aeris made her way around to Karse's side. "What is he doing?"

"Drazi said this is how they plan their raids," Karse answered. "From what Drazi says, your Water is as good as your father at planning. Maybe as good as the War Leader."

"Hostages," Kaspin said. "How many?"

"Not guards, I guess you mean?" Karse asked. "Four. The Firstborn, two of her Companions, and one of Aeris'."

Kaspin looked up. "Who?"

"Tiras," Aeris answered. "And... do we count Gannet as a hostage? And Uncle Tierce?"

"We count them as unknowns," Karse said. "They might be hostages. They might have got away. They—" He grimaced and stopped talking.

"They might be dead," Aeris said. She touched the pockets in her jacket. "No. Gannet's alive, at least."

"No gem?" Owyn asked.

"Nothing in my pockets but air. And I want it to stay that way." Aeris looked down at the map. "Kaspin, what do you think?"

Kaspin frowned. "Lance, how many? Pelin. How many?"

"Pelin's men? Standard squad of thirteen." Lancir walked over to stand by Drazi. "But those thirteen were the worst ones Dark had. They need to be hit fast and hard."

"Keliar, what did you see when you flew in?" Karse asked one of the Air scouts who remained.

"Not a lot. They're shooting anything in the sky," Keliar said. "They were expecting us, and they were ready. There's not a lot of cover there, so we can't fly reconnaissance — there's no cloud cover." He frowned and closed his eyes. "You said four guards? I think I saw four men in livery on the ground and not moving. Maybe dead. I think dead.. One of the tents was down. And...people kneeling. I hadn't realized that's what it was, but there were people kneeling." He gestured to Drazi. "May I?" Drazi handed him the stick, and Keliar drew three small circles in the dirt. "There. None of them were the Firstborn."

Kaspin nodded. He shifted, sitting down in the dust and resting one elbow on his knee, looking at the map with half-lidded eyes. Every so often, he'd shake his head, as if mentally dismissing something.

"We have advantages they don't," Owyn said. "If I get close enough, I can hear Aven, Aria and Tiras."

"And Tiras can hear me," Aeris added.

"When did that happen?" Owyn demanded. "They didn't tell me!"

"Right before we left. They hear me, and they hear Gannet." Aeris looked down at the map. "I wonder..."

"What?" Kaspin asked.

"We need a diversion..."

Kaspin stood up so quickly that Aeris had to jump backward to keep from being knocked over. Her wings flared for balance, and people scrambled away from her. "No!"

"No?" Aeris folded her arms over her chest. "You don't even know what I'm suggesting!"

"Like before!" Kaspin said. "Go alone. No!"

"Do you have another idea?" she asked. "What other diversion do we have that won't make them kill everyone right off?"

Kaspin scowled, then looked at the map scrawled in the dust. He cocked his head slowly to the side, then held his hand out to Keliar, who handed him the stick. He slowly walked around the map, and every so often, he scratched a mark outside the perimeter.

"Drazi," he said without looking up. "Check?"

"That's about right," Drazi answered slowly.

"About right for..." Lancir started to ask. Then he coughed. "Sentry positions. You... you just marked out the positions that our squads station sentries. How...?"

"We killed enough of them," Drazi answered. "And they never changed the patterns. Ever."

Kaspin grinned. "Hunters get hunted." He pointed with the stick. "Come this way?" he asked.

"That's the approach, yeah," Karse answered. "You've got a plan?"

Kaspin nodded. "Drazi there, with one. Me here, with one." He gestured a wide circle all around the camp. "Back to start. Eight down. Five and Pelin left."

"Better odds, but there's still hostages," Lancir murmured. "At that point... it might be worth it to send Aeris in." He held his hand out and took the stick from Kaspin. "Archers here and here." He marked the places. "And... when they're all looking this way, we can get people in from the rear of the camp and get anyone in the tents out."

"The same plan we used in the valley," Karse said. "Right. Who's on the initial team? Drazi? Kaspin? Who are you taking?"

"Who can move quiet and don't have an issue with knifing someone in the back?" Drazi asked.

"Del," Owyn, Othi and Karse all answered at the same time. Del just smiled.

"It's always the quiet ones, isn't it?" Drazi said. "You'll be with me, then."

"Lance?" Kaspin asked. Lancir shook his head.

"I'm no good out in the woods like that," he said. "If there's a tree root, I'll find it and trip on it." He looked over his shoulder at Karse. "Captain? Who would you send?"

Karse turned and looked around at the group surrounding the map, and Aeris noticed his gaze kept going back to Dyna.

"So..." he finally drawled. "Dyna, what do you think?"

"I think I might be the best option we have," Dyna admitted. "Fa Del taught me knives. And I can move quietly. If Tiras were here, they'd be better, but they're not here."

"And we don't have time," Karse said. "Let's get moving. No chatter once we leave. When we're in place, Kaspin and Drazi, you take your people and get to work."

AS THEY CAME UP TO the halfway point, Kaspin was admitting to himself that Karse was right — Dyna flowed through the trees like water, and made less noise than he did. She killed silently and efficiently, and he wondered how much of that was knife skill, and how much was her healing abilities. He didn't think it mattered, but if it was healing, he'd have to learn that trick. He waved her to a stop and ducked into a stand of trees. Drazi and Del should be along shortly, and they'd continue on around the other side of the camp.

Dyna pressed close to his side and whispered softly, "How do we know they're all right?"

Kaspin smiled and whispered, "I call." He howled, imitating the sound of a wolf calling for their pack. Almost immediately, his call was answered, but not by Drazi. A wolf limped out of the underbrush. Kaspin stiffened, but Dyna gasped and moved past him, dropping to her knees next to the wolf, who started to wash her face.

"Oh, Howl," Kaspin heard her say. "Poor baby. Who hurt you?"

"Dyna?" Kaspin whispered. She looked up and gestured him closer.

"This is Howl," she said as Kaspin knelt next to her. "Karse raised him from a puppy. Howl, this is Kaspin."

The wolf looked at him, and Kaspin held his hand out to the gray muzzle. "Old, old man," he murmured, and Howl licked his palm. As the wolf touched him, Kaspin felt the wave of pain. He glanced at Dyna. "Healing?"

Dyna nodded. "It looks as if someone shot him, but it only grazed him. He'll be fine. And he's lived around healers his entire life. He knows we'll make him feel better."

Kaspin nodded, then looked up at the sound of another howl. The wolf next to him snorted, and Kaspin fought back a laugh at the wolfish criticism. Drazi never could manage a convincing howl. Dyna arched a brow at him, and he shook his head. A moment later, Drazi and Del appeared. Howl raised his head as Del came closer, and his tail thumped the ground.

"All clear on our side," Drazi said. "Who is this?"

"Howl," Kaspin answered. "Dyna, tell him go."

"Howl, go find Karse," Dyna said. Howl got up and shook himself all over, then trotted off into the brush. Dyna got up and dusted off her knees, then started gesturing. Del responded with more gestures, then touched Drazi's arm and pointed.

"Right, I guess we're going," Drazi said. "See you back at the start. Keep your head down."

Del gestured, and he and Drazi moved off. Kaspin touched Dyna's arm. "We go," he said.

She nodded and smiled up at him. "Shall we?"

Kaspin saw four places where there had been a struggle, but there were no bodies apparent — Drazi had always been good at hiding his spoor. As they started the final part of their prowl, Dyna touched his arm and tugged him back under cover; a heartbeat later, a man broke through the brush and stalked past them.

"Agar!" he growled. "Where are you?"

Kaspin shook his head and swore silently, then glanced at Dyna. She nodded, gesturing to the left, then the right. Her meaning was clear, he thought — flank the guard, take him down. Kaspin nodded and they both moved — him to the right, her to the left. He thought he'd understood... until she stumbled out into the guard's path. Kaspin's mouth went dry and the man laughed aloud and grabbed Dyna's arm, hard enough that she winced.

"Well, look at what I found," he crowed. "Pretty thing. Be nice, and I...." Kaspin never had a chance to move to Dyna's defense, and the guard never finished his sentence. He just dropped like a stone.

"Dyna!" Kaspin growled. She smiled at him.

"Seemed like the quietest way to get rid of him," she answered, her voice barely audible. "We're too close to the camp to risk a fight. Let's go. You can yell at me later." She started through the trees, and he followed, his emotions growing hotter by the minute. By the time they reached the meeting place and saw the others, he felt as if he was going to explode.

"Good work," Karse said as they came closer. Howl, Kaspin noticed, was pressed against Karse's leg. "And... what's wrong, Kaspin?"

Kaspin growled and turned to Dyna, who was grinning insolently. "Reckless," he snapped. "Reckless. Stupid..." He scowled, angry and frightened because in a heartbeat, she could have been hurt or killed and he hadn't been close enough to stop it. He couldn't think of another word to express how reckless she'd actually been.

No, he could.

"*Fuckheaded!*"

"Kaspin!" Drazi gasped. "Rags would wash your mouth out!"

Aeris walked toward him, with Owyn right behind her. She looked up at him and her brow furrowed. She touched his chest, her hand solid against him. Then she turned to Dyna. "What did you do?"

"We ran into a guard that shouldn't have been there," Dyna answered. "And it was too close to the camp. They would have heard a fight. So I stepped in front of him, let him touch me, and stopped his heart."

"Arm," Kaspin growled. Aeris looked up at him again, then went to Dyna and held her hand out. Dyna rolled her eyes and pushed the sleeve of her coat up, revealing the small, round bruises just starting to darken on her skin.

"Dyna!" Owyn brushed past Kaspin and took Dyna's hand from Aeris. He studied her skin for a moment, then sighed and shook his head. "Dyna, could you have done for the guard another way?"

"No—"

"Yes," Kaspin growled. "Done it before."

Owyn looked at Kaspin, then back at Dyna. "Right. He's got more experience on this than you do, Dyna. And your other fathers are going to lose their collective minds when they find out you put yourself at risk like this." He held up his hand as Dyna started to protest. "You did not think this through. If he'd moved faster than you thought, if he'd knocked you over the head, what then? If he'd stabbed first and asked questions later?" He let Dyna go and folded his arms. "That was an unnecessary risk."

"It worked!" Dyna protested. "And the worst that happened was a few bruises. They'll heal."

"You didn't tell Kaspin what you were doing, did you?" Aeris asked. "You just did it." She frowned. "Dyna, were you showing off? Now?"

"I was not!" Dyna protested. "There... there wasn't time—"

"Make time," Kaspin growled. "Stupid makes dead." He shook his head and turned, walking away, back down the track, back toward Dark's village. When he was far enough that he couldn't hear the others, he stopped and sat down with his back to a tree, closing his eyes and trying to make sense of what he was feeling. His guts were churning, and he didn't understand why. It wasn't as if he and Drazi hadn't taken equally stupid risks, and Rags had taken it out of both of them. But he'd never gotten this angry. And Kaspin had never gotten this angry before when someone in his squad took an unnecessary risk. What was different?

He heard the footstep, and knew it was Aeris without turning. Then he heard another, and turned to see that Aeris wasn't alone — Dyna was with her. He tipped his head back.

"Sorry," he mumbled. "Too much."

"It wasn't," Dyna said. She came around him and sat down on his right, pressing against his shoulder. Aeris sat on his left and did the same, leaning into him. "I didn't think it all the way through, and I didn't warn you. And you were my commander on that, and I know better." She sniffed. "Stupid makes dead. You're right. And Fa Owyn and Aeris were right, too. I was showing off and I took a very unnecessary risk. We could have taken him out together without making a fuss. I'm sorry."

"Can't risk," Kaspin said, not looking up. "Not you. Not either." He looked at Dyna, then turned to Aeris. "Special."

Dyna took his hand. "You're just as special, you know." She ran her thumb over his knuckles, her touch making his skin feel unusually warm. When Aeris took his other hand, he realized that her touch felt the same.

"Oh," he murmured. "Companion." He squeezed both of their hands. "Special."

"The Companion bond," Aeris said.

Kaspin nodded. "Why so much. Afraid because special."

Dyna frowned slightly, then smiled. "You reacted so strongly because of the Companion bond. I put myself at risk and you were afraid I'd get hurt."

"Did get hurt," Kaspin pointed out.

"It's just a bruise," Dyna sniffed. "It's nothing."

"Could be something," Kaspin said. "Poison claws."

"Poison claws?" Aeris repeated. "What are those?"

"Drazi explain better. Lancir explain better." Kaspin grimaced. "Not words."

"Then let's go find them. This sounds like something we need to know before we go in," Dyna said. She hesitated, then let Kaspin's hand go and wrapped her arms around him. "I'm sorry I scared you."

Kaspin put his arm around her shoulders and hugged her, then kissed the top of her head. "Not again."

"I won't do it again," Dyna agreed. She let him go and stood up. "Let's go. We need to get the others."

"Go back, and we'll meet you there in a moment," Aeris said. Dyna smiled and ran off, and Aeris shifted, swinging one leg over Kaspin's so that she was straddling his legs. She rested her hands on his chest. "Thank you," she said. "Dyna...she's very good at what she does. She always has been. So she's... she shows off. Especially when she wants to impress someone."

Kaspin was having a hard time finding words. Or letters. Or anything that didn't involve parts in close proximity to the woman sitting in his lap. He covered Aeris' hands with his own and tipped his head back to look up at her. She smiled and leaned down to kiss him.

No words necessary.

WHEN AERIS AND KASPIN returned to the others, they were standing around a recreation of the map that Drazi had made back in the village. Karse looked up and watched as they approached.

"You good?" he asked Kaspin. "Got your head on straight? I'm going to need you."

"Ready," Kaspin answered. Aeris squeezed his hand, and Dyna moved over to stand by his other side.

"Good. Now, you, Drazi and Lancir all know their methods better than any of us." Karse gestured to the map. "How would you do this?"

Kaspin looked down at the map, then back at Drazi. "Four and Pelin now."

"And they've split the hostages," Drazi added. "Unless there are some not marked here? Where's the Air scout?"

"Here," Keliar called, and came through the group.

"The kneeling ones. Men or women or both?" Drazi pointed to the three circles. "And you said one of the tents was down? Which was it?"

"Yes. That one. Not sure if it was knocked over or destroyed, but that's not important." Keliar frowned. "The hostages are men. I think. I saw tattoos on the one in the middle—"

"Fa," Aeris said. "That's my father."

"The other two... I'm fairly certain they were men. No wings, so not the Firstborn. I can't be more specific than that."

"Which means that Aria and Treesi are there?" Othi pointed. "In one of the tents?"

"And probably under guard," Karse said. "If they're not, then they're secured somehow. Otherwise, Aria would have torn the tent to shreds already. We just don't know which one, and we only get one chance."

Kaspin nodded, trying to come up with a plan that didn't involve diversions and putting people he cared about in danger.

"Need a better look," he muttered.

"How about eyes on the inside?" Aeris asked. "Owyn, you said you can hear Tiras? Are we close enough?"

"You can hear people?" Drazi said. "Without talking?"

"It's a Smoke Dancer thing. It's called heart visions, and Tiras and I can both do it. We might be close enough," Owyn said. "And they can hear you, so call them. Ask them what they see."

Aeris nodded and looked distant. Almost immediately, Owyn swayed and had to be steadied by Del.

"Yeah," he stammered, shaking his head. "Yeah...I hear them. Poor kid is terrified. And loud. Right. Yeah. The three kneeling are Tiras, Aven and Copper. Copper is hurt, and Aven is trying to take care of him without anyone noticing. Aria and Treesi are in that tent." He pointed at the map. "They see all four of Pelin's guards, and they don't see Pelin right now. Aeris, ask about Tiercel and Gannet." A pause, then Owyn grimaced. "They can't see Tiercel. Gannet... Tiras, hold it together... Gannet is staked out on the ground in front of them. They... fuck..."

"What?" Aeris asked. "What have they done to Gannet?"

Owyn looked at her. "Tiras says Pelin has been pulling out Gannet's feathers to make him scream."

Aeris went pale, and Dyna moaned softly. Kaspin shifted, putting an arm around each of them.

"Feathers grow back?" he asked.

Aeris looked up at him. "Maybe? Pulling the feathers out... that damages the shaft and the skin. And it hurts. Kaspin, they're torturing him!"

"It's like getting cut," Keliar added. "Over and over. If his wings are damaged too much, he'll never fly again."

Kaspin shuddered and looked at Drazi. "Plan?"

Drazi nodded. "Right. Del, you and me will go around to where we're at the back of the tent where the Firstborn is. We'll get in from that side and get her and the other woman out." He frowned. "Owyn, come with us. We need to know that all the guards are out where your Tiras can see them."

"Then how will we know when you're clear so we can go after the others?" Karse asked. "Owyn can't be in two places at once, and we can't wait for him to get back around here."

"Archers," Kaspin suggested. He stepped forward and crouched, poking holes with his finger. "Here, here, here, here. Firstborn safe. Signal. Drop the guards."

"For archers, we have Dyna, Keliar, Lancir and me," Aeris said. "Which means none of us can afford to miss a shot."

"What about the rest of us?" Othi asked.

"Backup." Karse answered. "Rush the camp once the archers put the guards down, take out any loose ends." He looked around. "Right. Poke holes in it."

"Kaspin said something about poison claws," Aeris said. "And that Lancir or Drazi could explain."

"They're... well, they're just what they sound like," Lancir said. "Small ones are like rings that fit over your fingertips. Larger ones are gloves with talons attached. I don't know what poison they use, but it works fast. Pelin likes them. A lot."

"Forewarned," Karse said. "We know to watch for them and to stay out of reach." He paused. "Do we need the distraction still?"

"We might want to keep that plan close to hand, in case we need it," Owyn said. "Much as I hate to say it. That's our everything is fucked plan, though. Kaspin, you stay close to Aeris."

"Yes, sir."

Karse nodded and looked around. "Right. It's not much of a plan, but it's what we got. Drazi, take your team and move out. Good luck. Dyna, Keliar, you go with Drazi and take position where he tells you. Othi, you're with Dyna. Lancir, I'll be with you. Kaspin, you're with Aeris." He divided the remaining guards up among the archers, then sighed. "Everyone comes back. That's an order."

"When clear, Drazi howl," Kaspin said. "Signal."

"Got it," Drazi said. He held out one clenched fist. "See you on this side of the grass, my brother."

"Or not at all," Kaspin said, knocking his fist against Drazi's. Drazi grinned, gathered up his team, and vanished into the woods.

"Kaspin, let's get into position," Karse said. "Move out."

Chapter Twenty-Two

Aven shifted slightly, trying to ease the pain in his hip. He didn't think anyone noticed — the guard wasn't close enough. Then he heard Tiras whimper softly next to him and forced himself to stay still. The attackers had told them that if any of them moved, the guard would kill Tiras first. Which, Aven had to admit, made sense. Copper was too badly injured to stop them, and Aven wasn't going to be able to move fast enough to stop the guard before they struck.

In his current position, Aven could just barely see Tiras out of the corner of his eye — they were pale, their face streaked with tears and blood. Aven wondered what they were seeing — if they were seeing things that weren't there, or the horror that was right in front of them. The attackers had shot Gannet out of the sky, then staked him out on the ground and amused themselves by pulling out his feathers. Now Gannet lay quiet and still, his wings bare and bleeding. Aven could feel the pain rolling off of him, but there wasn't anything he could do about it.

Nor could he do anything for Copper. He'd been trying to heal the worst of the damage, but the guard had noticed that Aven was close enough to touch Copper, and had forced them apart. Now Copper was failing, and it was only a matter of time before the young guard collapsed from pain and blood loss.

As if thinking it made it so, Copper moaned softly, slumped, and tipped to the side like a falling tree. As Copper sprawled in the dust, Tiras burst into tears.

"Lost me a bet," the guard said, and Aven heard his footsteps coming closer. "I thought the little one was going to go first."

"Leave them be," Aven called. "They're a child. Let them be."

"No changing the stakes," the guard said. He laughed, and Tiras moaned. Aven turned, and saw the blade against Tiras' throat. He tried to force his body to move the way he needed it to, dimly hearing a wolf howling in the distance...

And felt the sharp rush of air as a quarrel flew over his head and pierced the guard's chest. The blade fell as the guard did, leaving only a red welt on Tiras' skin.

"WHEN YOU SHOOT, GO up," Kaspin murmured, watching the camp from their hiding place. "I go in, you go up."

"If I go up, they'll shoot," Aeris protested. "Keliar said they're shooting anything in the air. I'll stay here and reload." She frowned and raised the large crossbow Karse had given her. "What... Copper!"

Kaspin watched as one of the three kneeling hostages collapsed. The guard laughed, and they could clearly hear him as he walked up behind the prisoners.

"Lost me a bet. I thought the little one was going to go first."

"Leave them be." Aeris's father said. He sounded desperate. "They're a child. Let them be."

"No changing the stakes," the guard said, drawing his knife and holding it to Tiras' throat. Aeris raised the crossbow.

"Hold," Kaspin growled.

"He'll kill Tiras!"

"Hold!"

Then they heard it — Drazi's imperfect howl. Aeris fired, and the guard fell. She lowered the crossbow to reload, but Kaspin didn't wait; he burst from their hiding place, his sickles open and ready.

One of the other guards had only been wounded, and he came toward Kaspin with his blade bared... and fell before he ever got close, a second quarrel in his chest. Kaspin glanced back to see Aeris lowering her bow once more. She smiled at him, and bent to reload. Kaspin turned and dropped to his knees next to Gannet. He cut the ropes that held Gannet down, rested his hand on the small of Gannet's back, and realized that he had no idea what he was doing. He could block the pain, but he didn't know anything about healing wings or feathers, or about the anatomy of an Airborn.

"Do you know how to lend your power to another healer?"

Kaspin looked up to see the tattooed Water had joined him. Past him, Kaspin could see Owyn holding Tiras, and Dyna kneeling next to the unconscious man. With Dyna were a red-haired woman who looked like Astur, and an Airborn woman who could only be the Firstborn. Kaspin forced his attention back to the man.

"Aeris' father?" he asked.

The man smiled. "My name is Aven. I know you're Kaspin. And I know you're a healer. Do you know how to link your power with another healer?"

Kaspin frowned. "I... no."

"Then listen to me." Aven held his hand out. "Take my hand and relax. Open yourself to your power the way you would if you were the one doing the healing, but don't do anything. Let me take the lead. Understand?"

"No," Kaspin answered. "But no time." He rested his hand on Aven's and closed his eyes, opening himself up to his healing. He felt it draining away, the way it would if he was actually healing someone, and wondered if this was something he could learn to do himself.

"You're doing just fine," Aven said. "We'll have Gannet feeling better soon."

"Feathers come back?" Kaspin fought the urge to open his eyes. If he opened his eyes, it might break whatever he was doing. "Fly again?"

"I'll do my best to make sure he does," Aven said. "It will take time. Feathers don't grow fast. You can open your eyes."

Kaspin blinked and looked at Gannet. His color was better, and his wings looked better. They were still bare, but the skin didn't look as raw, and the pain that had been clear in his face was gone. Kaspin smiled and reached out to brush his pale hair back.

"Good," he said. "Thank you."

Aven smiled. "You're very good. You'll be better. I'm looking forward to seeing that." He turned. "Owyn, bring Tiras over here. You can watch Gannet until he wakes up."

"Will he be all right?" Tiras asked. They got up and wobbled slightly. "I... you're you. I...you're Kaspin."

Kaspin slowly got to his feet. "I am."

"We've been waiting for you." Tiras came closer. They looked small and fragile, terrified of everything. Aeris said that they weren't, that they were a dirty fighter, but right now, Kaspin was having trouble believing it. He held his hand out, and Tiras stared at him with wide eyes before taking it. Kaspin pulled him into a gently hug, feeling them shivering.

"Safe now," Kaspin said. "Promise."

Tiras drew back and smiled slightly. "Thank you for taking care of Gannet."

Kaspin smiled. "Like him," he said. "Aeris?"

"Where is she?" Aven asked. He stood up slowly, wincing, and Kaspin turned toward him. Aven shook his head. "No, don't worry about me. It's an old injury. Aeris was where?"

"There." Kaspin turned and pointed. He frowned, realizing someone else was missing. He raised his voice. "Lancir!"

"Lancir is here?" Tiras gasped. "But—"

"Lancir turned," Kaspin said, looking from side to side. Karse was kneeling next to the guard Dyna had healed, who Kaspin guessed was his son. Drazi was with the Firstborn. Where was Lancir? Or Aeris? "Helped us. Brother," Kaspin added. "Same mother."

Aven coughed. "He's part Water. And I never once noticed." He nodded. "There they are. Tiras, stay with Gannet. We'll move him into the tent to recover once we get the tents cleared. I need to go help see to our people. But first I need to see my daughter. Kaspin, come with me."

Tiras nodded and sat down, taking Gannet's hand. Aven gestured for Kaspin to walk with him.

"Sir?" Kaspin said slowly. "I...know nothing. About Water."

"Raised out here? I'd be surprised if you did," Aven said. "I imagine you know as little about living Water as I did about living on the land when I first became a Companion. You'll learn. I'll help, and Othi will help. We'll find your canoe, and you'll learn." He paused. "You know about cheese, I hope?"

Kaspin grinned. "No cheese."

Aven laughed. "Oh, good. I learned that the hard way." He stopped and held his hand out. "Aria, come meet Kaspin."

Kaspin turned, saw the Firstborn coming toward him, and dropped to his knees hard enough that his teeth clicked together. Above him, he heard a sharp intake of breath, and two people walked into his view. One of them was Aeris, and she sounded shocked when she asked, "Mama, what did you say?"

"I haven't said anything yet!" Aria protested. "Kaspin, please. That's unnecessary. Stand up and let me look at you."

Kaspin stood up slowly, keeping his eyes downcast. He wasn't expecting the gentle touch under his chin, raising his face so that he was looking directly at the Firstborn. From everything Rags had told him, Aria the Blesséd Mother was ten feet tall, her wingspan wide enough to touch opposite walls of the house where they had lived. But the woman in front of him didn't even come up to his chin, and her golden eyes were kind.

"Rhexa was right," she said. "You do have beautiful eyes. Welcome, Kaspin."

Kaspin looked down again, then bit his lip. "Blesséd Mother?" he whispered. "Forgive Lancir? Don't..." He stopped. He had no idea what she might be planning to do to his brother, and was afraid to even guess.

"Mama, Lancir and Kaspin are twins," Aeris said. "Uncle Eli confirmed it."

"Lancir helped us," Kaspin added. "Turned. Almost killed."

"Is that so?" Aria raised her chin slightly. "Lancir? Attend."

Kaspin looked up and saw Lancir and Karse coming closer.

"Firstborn, I'll vouch for him," Karse said. "We found them chained to stakes for burning when we went in. That Dark bastard was going to kill all of his boys and Frayim."

"Denied us," Kaspin said. "Not his."

"He said that," Lancir agreed. "Said he had no children. And honestly, I'd rather be fatherless than be his get." He stepped closer to Kaspin, then took a deep breath. "I was stupid, Firstborn. Stupid and scared, and I should have trusted you. Trusted Karse, and trusted that the world outside that valley was real and everything he told me was a lie. I know better now. And... and I have it in me to be a healer, Elaias says. So that's what I'm going to do." He looked back at Karse. "And... speaking as a healer-to-be, we should get the wounded off the ground. Gannet especially, although Copper needs a bed, too. Permission to go?"

Aria started to laugh. "Aeris? Your thoughts?"

"Lancir risked his life to save Frayim, our family, and my Water," Aeris answered. "And I consider him part of my circle. I'm inclined to say his punishment should be training with Grandfa, but Uncle Eli wants to take on his training."

Lancir coughed. "Part... *really*?"

"Means what?" Kaspin asked.

"It means that we all know very well that Dyna thinks Lancir hung every star in the sky, and that they'll probably pair when she's old enough," Aria answered. "Agreed. Go help the healers, Lancir. I'll speak to Elaias about the conditions of your parole."

Lancir bowed. "Thank you, Firstborn."

Karse nodded, then turned. "Right! I need hands to get those tents back in shape, and we need to get the wounded off the ground," he bellowed as he walked away.

Lancir turned to follow, and stopped when Kaspin called his name. "What?"

Kaspin looked around. "Pelin?"

Lancir blinked. "Fuck," he breathed. "Captain? How... how many dead? How many enemy dead? Kaspin and Drazi and Del and Dyna took out nine in the woods. How many here? Did we get him?"

"Good question," Karse said as he came back. "Let's get an answer."

"If you mean the one in command," Aven said, "I'm not entirely certain he was here when you attacked."

"He wasn't here?" Karse asked. "Fuck..."

"Do you think he went back to the village?" Lancir asked. "The women and the healers and Frayim."

Karse nodded and turned, whistling. "Drazi! I need you! Lance, you with the healers or you with me?"

"With you, Captain," Lancir answered.

"Captain, what are you planning?" Aria asked.

"I'm taking a small team back to that village, and bringing back the healers, Frayim, and the women we rescued. If we find that Pelin, we'll make sure he's the Mother's problem."

Aria nodded. "Proceed. Kaspin, will you go, or will you stay?"

Kaspin frowned and looked around. "Stay. Need healer here."

Karse patted him on the shoulder and walked away, once more shouting. Kaspin looked over at Gannet and Tiras.

"Time to work."

THE FALLEN TENT WAS set back up, repairs were made, and Karse's son was brought to one tent that Aven and Treesi declared was their temporary healing center. Gannet was brought to a second tent and laid face down on a wide bed.

"Air don't like being on our backs," Aeris told Kaspin. He nodded and saved the information for later. For now, his focus was on helping the other healers with seeing to Copper and the Air warriors who'd help take the camp. Dyna, Treesi and Aven. Aeris stayed with Tiras and Gannet, and when Kaspin passed the tent, he could have sworn he heard Tiras crying. But when he looked in, Aeris shooed him away.

"Tiras hurt?" he asked when he went back to helping Aven.

"Tiras has had a very bad fright," Aven said. "Up until we came east, their experience of being a Companion has been the sweet of it. This is their first experience with how hard it can be, and how it can hurt." He gestured to himself. "Companions have their scars. Tiras' scars are still bleeding. Now, Aeris is a very good mind healer. She'll be able to help them."

"Mind healing?" Kaspin considered the idea. Rags had talked about healing heart wounds, and how it was different from regular healing. "Hard to learn?"

"Talk to Treesi about it," Aven said, smiling. "Later. I think we're done here, and you need a rest. Go back to the Heir's tent and take a nap. No more healing for you today."

"But—"

"No," Aven said, his voice firm. "You've done more than your share, Kaspin, and I'm grateful for it. But as well-trained as you are, you're still not fully trained. I don't want you to push too far."

Kaspin sighed. "Yes, sir."

"Go rest," Aven said. He looked around. "Dyna, go with him. Gannet will be waking up soon, and he'll feel better if you all are with him."

Kaspin waited until Dyna joined him before leaving the tent. She took his arm as they walked.

"Aven is right," she said. "We've none of us had to deal with anything like what they did when they became Companions. We've never had anyone try to kill us, or even raise their voices at us. I think the worst thing that ever happened was Tiras breaking Gannet's nose."

"Really?" Kaspin shook his head. "Why?"

"Gannet had some odd ideas when he first came to us. It's nothing. He's learned better."

"Oh. Aeris said. Old-fashioned?" Kaspin shrugged. "What means?"

"His flock thinks that if you're Air and you don't have wings, you're not as good." Dyna stopped when Kaspin growled. "What?"

"Rags was Air. No wings."

"Oh," Dyna breathed. "Oh, I'm sorry. Kaspin, I'm part Air. When we get to the Temple, you'll meet my father. He lost his wings and his sight when he was a child, and part of his flock didn't want him. So we don't hold to that at all in the Palace. And Gannet... well, he said the wrong thing around Tiras, and Tiras broke his nose."

Kaspin started walking again, thinking about tiny Tiras and Gannet, who was as tall as Kaspin himself. "Stood on a box?"

Dyna burst out laughing. "A bench, actually!" She muffled her giggles in one hand as she scratched her fingernails on the tent canvas, then held the tent flap open.

Aeris was sitting on one of the two beds, her back against the low headboard. Tiras was asleep with their head in her lap, and she was idly combing her fingers through their hair. Gannet was on the other bed, still asleep.

"How thon?" Kaspin asked, sitting down on the floor.

"Thon?"

"Another hill word," Dyna said. "Combination word. That one. Thon."

"For ootwith," Kaspin added.

Aeris looked down at Tiras. "They're still badly shaken. They didn't tell Owyn what the guards were planning. If any of the hostages moved, they were going to kill Tiras first. So when Copper collapsed... well, that's what we saw." She closed her eyes and sighed. "How is Copper?"

"He'll be fine," Dyna answered. She curled up on the foot of the bed. "I can't wait to go home. This... how did our parents do this? How did they live like this?"

"No choice?" Kaspin asked. He leaned his shoulder against the side of the bed. "Peace through pain." Aeris started running her fingers through his hair, and he sighed and leaned into her touch. "Not over," he murmured.

"What do you mean?" Dyna asked. "Dark is dead. Pelin is as good as dead, once Uncle Captain catches him. It's over."

"Others." Kaspin tipped his head back and looked up at her. "Other people. Think the same. Start over." He grimaced and yawned. "Disease."

"As much as I hate to say it, you're right," Aeris said. "Dark wasn't the only one who thought I was the Child. He's just the one who tried to act on it. Which means someone else might try, and there will be more problems. If not for us, then for our children." She fell silent, and Kaspin listened to the wind and the birds outside the tent, to Tiras' soft breathing, and to Gannet's slightly muffled snoring.

Distantly, he heard raised voices, calling welcome. The others must be back. He should go and see his brothers. He should...

Gannet wailed, jolting Kaspin out of a half-doze. He rolled onto his knees to see the big Air on all fours on the other bed, his tattered wings spread wide. Aeris tumbled off the bed, and Tiras followed her.

"Gannet!" Aeris reached out to touch his bare shoulder. "Gannet, we're here—"

"Don't touch me!" Gannet shrieked, pushing away Aeris' hands and scuttling away from their voice. "Don't touch me!"

"Gan!" Tiras shouted. "It's over! You're safe!"

Kaspin jumped up and ran around the bed, blocking Gannet from falling off the far side. He watched Aeris, trying to take his cues from her as to what to do. She nodded, slowly coming around the bed to join him.

"Gan?" Tiras sounded close to crying again as they raised their voice to be heard over Gannet's panicked cries. "Gan, it's over." They got onto the bed and crawled closer. "Gan, it's me. It's us. We're all here."

"Gannet," Kaspin added, raising his voice. "Wake up!"

Gannet shuddered, then curled up on the bed and started sobbing. Kaspin heard one word — wings. Aeris sat down on the bed and gently drew Gannet into her arms.

"It's over. Your wings will heal," she murmured. "You're not going to lose them, Gan. You'll be fine."

Gannet shook his head and whispered something Kaspin didn't hear. Tiras, however, did.

"Your feathers are so going to come back," they said. "Right? Kaspin?"

"Aven say yes," Kaspin answered. "Take time." He hesitated, then rested his hand on the small of Gannet's back. "Want see you fly."

To his surprise, that got a wet-sounding laugh. "You saw me."

"Didn't," Kaspin protested. "Shadows. Dark." He cocked his head to the side and let his power flow, examining the structure of the wings. The way the feathers that remained sat, and the places where there should be feathers. "Will grow," he said. "Will fly." He paused, then added, "Just...look like mites."

Aeris gasped as Gannet sat up. "I do *not* have mites!" he protested, his eyes wide. Then he blinked. "I..."

"Awake now?" Kaspin asked.

"I..." Gannet looked around. "Oh. I..." He blew out explosively and sat down. "Fuck."

"That's an insult, you know," Aeris said. "To tell an Airborn they have mites? That's very insulting."

Kaspin nodded. "Rags said it. Very bad. Very angry." He sat down next to Gannet. "Feathers come back."

Gannet nodded, pulling a blanket up over his legs. "It's going to itch. It's going to itch so much."

"So, we'll scratch it for you," Dyna said, crawling onto the bed to press against his side. She reached out and straightened his gem. "Aeris, where's the Water gem?"

"At the Temple with the Diadem," Aeris answered. "Kaspin will have to wait until we get back." She looked at the tent flap. "You can come in now."

The flap opened, and Del came inside. He gestured gracefully for a moment.

"We'll come out soon, Fa," Aeris said. "Thank you." She turned to Kaspin. "Del says that there's food ready, and that the others are back. Everyone we left at the village is fine, and they're taking people out to search for the Air warriors that were shot down." She paused. "And there was no sign of Pelin anywhere."

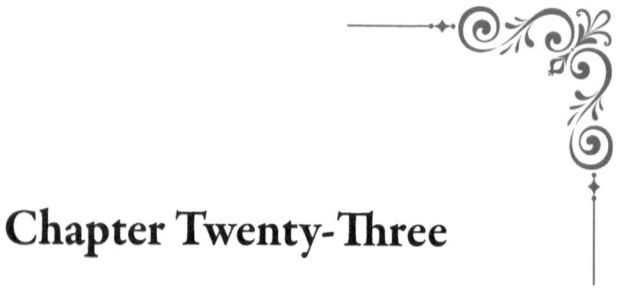

Chapter Twenty-Three

The High Priest and Rhexa were already waiting for them as the wagons and carts rolled up to the Temple. Before they had even stopped moving, Frayim had jumped down and run to them; Kaspin tried not to look – it felt intrusive to watch their reunion. He focused on helping Gannet down from the cart. Gannet was healing, and he was steadier, but after almost falling from his horse on the first day, he'd opted to ride in a cart. Kaspin had decided to keep him company. It was better than falling off a horse himself.

"Firstborn." An Air warrior Kaspin hadn't seen before landed near the Temple and came toward them. He looked around, then looked up. "Aria? Where is the rest of the flock?"

"Ionith." Aria embraced him. "Walk with me."

Ionith's wings flared. "Where's my brother?"

Aria hesitated, then sighed. "The camp was overrun while the flock was away, and they flew into an ambush. Tiercel was one of several to fall. We found him, and Keliar formed an honor flight to take him back to the mountains," Aria said. "They'll wait for you, he said. But you'll need to come soon to be invested."

"Invested." Ionith closed his eyes and shook his head. "I never wanted to lead the flock. Tierce was always meant for it. I... what am I going to tell Liona?"

"Do you want me to come?" Aria asked. "I can come to the mountains for a few days—"

"You've got the rest of the world to worry about," Ionith answered. "I'll take the flock home, and we'll see him taken care of. Keliar can tell me what happened." He stepped back, bowed, then flew off.

"Come inside," Rhexa called. Kaspin led Gannet toward the Temple, and watched as Rhexa's eyes widened when she saw them. "Oh, Gannet."

"I'm fine, Auntie."

Rhexa folded her arms over her chest. "Really? Gannet, you look like you're going to fall over. And Kaspin. It's good to see you." She looked past him, then frowned. "Araglar?"

"Dead," Kaspin answered. "All dead. Drazi and I only left."

Rhexa closed her eyes. "I'm so sorry, Kaspin," she said. "Come inside. Aeris and Tiras have already gone in. Dyna is over there with her father, and you'll meet Alanar later. For now, you all need a long rest and a good meal. Let's get you taken care of." She winced as Gannet walked past her. "Gannet, your poor wings!"

"The feathers will grow back, Aven says," Gannet answered. "I'll fly again."

"Good. I... what's he doing here?"

Kaspin looked where she was pointing. "Lancir helped us," he said. "Saved Frayim. Saved Eli and Astur and me. Forgiven."

Rhexa sniffed and turned, walking toward the Temple. Kaspin growled softly.

"Easy," Gannet said, resting his hand on Kaspin's shoulder. "She was there when he helped them kidnap Aeris. She's still angry. She'll come around. Let Owyn handle it."

Kaspin nodded and offered Gannet his arm. "Inside."

The Temple was cool and dark, and Aeris and Tiras were waiting inside. Tiras was smiling from ear to ear and bouncing slightly on their toes. It was a welcome change from how solemn they'd been.

"I'll go get Dyna," they said, and ran off.

"Oh?" Gannet grinned. "We doing this now?"

"I'm tired of waiting, and I have it," Aeris answered, holding up a pouch. "I came in to get it. Inside or outside?"

"What?" Kaspin asked. "Gannet needs sitting."

"I'm fine," Gannet said. "And outside, so everyone can see." He slung his arm over Kaspin's shoulders and led him back out into the late afternoon sunshine. Tiras was there with Dyna, and a small crowd gathered around them as Aeris led Kaspin and Gannet to join them. Aeris turned to face Kaspin and opened the pouch, tipping a pendant out into her palm. The stone was the same size and shape as the ones worn by Tiras, Dyna and Gannet, but it was a deep, pure blue.

"Kaspin," Aeris said, her voice solemn. "This is yours. It's been waiting for you for far too long." She held the pendant up by the cord. "Your place is with us, as my Water. Your place is by my side, as Abin stood by Axia."

Kaspin stepped forward and knelt, looking up at Aeris. She lowered the cord over his head and adjusted it so that the stone sat at the hollow of his throat. It felt good. It felt right, and he caught her hand and pressed a kiss into her palm. She blushed. Then she laughed as Tiras pounced on Kaspin, knocking him over.

"It looks good on you," Lancir said as he helped Kaspin to his feet. "It looks right. I'm proud of you." He looked around. "And... I'm making people uncomfortable. So I'm going to go down to the healing center tents. Elaias said I could stay there. I'll see you before you leave."

"No," Kaspin protested. "Stay." But Lancir shook his head and walked away. Kaspin started to follow, but Elaias caught up with him before he got far.

"Don't worry about Lancir," he said. "I'll take care of him. Although... I hadn't realized that Rhe... that he might have trouble here. It might be better to send him on to Terraces and have him learn from the Senior Healer. Less... friction. I'll talk with him. See what he wants." He looked around. "Treesi, where's Asta? I was going to bring her to meet Lachin and Mannit."

"Trista took her down to the tents already," Treesi answered. She hugged Kaspin and ran her fingers over the stone. "This looks good on you."

"Thank you." Kaspin touched the warm weight of it and smiled, then put his arm around Tiras' shoulders. "Feels good."

"I remember that feeling," Treesi agreed. "Steward has asked everyone to come inside. I think he wants to thank the Mother for bringing Frayim and Aeris back. Everyone else has gone ahead, so I came to get you both."

"In a moment. Trees, maybe you could talk to Rhexa?" Elaias asked. "She's not inclined to forgive Lancir, which will make him staying here awkward."

Treesi nodded. "I'll see what I can do. Now, we should—"

Whatever they should do was cut off by a high-pitched scream. Kaspin recognized Asta's voice. "Treesi, go Temple!" he shouted, as he pulled his sickles out and shook them open, running toward Asta, who was running toward them.

"He's here!" she screamed. "The scary man is here!"

"Scary man?" Kaspin repeated. Then he realized who she meant. "Pelin."

"In the tent." Asta pointed. "Kaspin, he hurt Lancir!"

Kaspin went cold. "Claws?"

"Yes."

"Asta, go to Frayim, inside Temple." Kaspin said. "I get Lance." Kaspin started toward the tents, moving quickly. He heard footsteps behind him and looked back to see Elaias.

"No one else is out here, and we don't have time to wait," Elaias said. "I heard Asta. How much time do we have?"

"Not much," Kaspin answered. "Fast poison."

Elaias nodded. "Lead the way."

Kaspin started to run toward the tent. As he got close, Pelin stepped out, pushing a woman in front of him.

"Trista!" Elaias shouted. "Let her go!"

"Where's the Child?" Pelin called back. "You want all of these brats? Give me the Child."

Kaspin growled and called, "Let her go. Walk away."

"I don't deal with animals," Pelin sneered. "Or traitors. I told him not to raise the whelp up as a person. Told him it would turn out sour." He pulled Trista back into the tent. "Bring me the Child!"

Kaspin turned, and nearly ran into Aeris as she landed behind him.

"There are three children in that tent, and Trista, Elaias' wife. Everyone else is in the Temple. Is anyone hurt in there?" she asked.

"Lancir in tent. Poisoned. You. Up high." He looked up. "Stay safe."

"Kaspin, my sister is in there," Aeris snapped. "I'm not staying safe."

Kaspin shook his head. "Crossbow," he said. "I draw out. You drop."

Aeris shook her head. "Turn it around," she said. "I'll draw him out. He wants me, not you. I'll draw him out. You drop him." She pointed. "Go around the side of the tent and wait. I'll draw him out. You come up behind him. We don't have time to argue. Now go."

Kaspin nodded and headed for the side of the tent, ducking out of sight just as Aeris shouted, "Pelin!"

The tent flap opened and Pelin came out, pushing Trista in front of him. "Come here," he called. "Come closer."

"Send the children out first," Aeris said. "And let my uncle take them and his wife." She held her arms wide. "I'm not going anywhere. I'm also not getting any closer until the children are safe. So if you want to wait until my father gets here with a crossbow...."

Pelin scowled, then stepped back, shouting into the tent. Lachin and Mannit appeared, each of them holding onto one of Yana's hands. They stopped outside the tent, looking frightened.

"Lach, come here," Elaias called.

Lachin didn't move, staring at the man holding his mother hostage. "Mama?"

"Go on, Lach," Trista called, her voice shaking. "Go to your father."

Lachin nodded and started walking again, leading the other two children up the gentle slope to Elaias, who picked up Yana and backed slowly away.

"Come here, Child," Pelin called. "You come here, and I'll let her go."

Kaspin watched as Aeris started down the slope, moving slowly, her wings spread wide as if she was trying to keep her balance. Pelin took a step toward her. Another, and Kaspin slipped around the tent and ran at him, sickles held crossed in front of him. He slashed down, smelling blood as the blades cut into Pelin's back; Pelin howled and let Trista go, whirling to face his attacker. Kaspin slashed again, then darted away. His chest hurt. Why did his chest hurt?

He looked down to see the four slashes across the front of his shirt, and the blood that was starting to well up in the wounds.

AERIS WATCHED IN HORROR as Kaspin crumpled to the ground. If she panicked, they were both going to die. She couldn't give in to her first instinct, which was to run to him. Or run away, her second instinct. Instead, she folded her arms over her chest, using her thumb to arm the wrist crossbow she hadn't yet returned to her mother.

"Useless cur," Pelin scoffed, and spat on Kaspin. "You'll see, Child. Once you understand, you'll see. They're all animals."

"I'm part Water," Aeris said. "And I'm part Air. You know that. The Child is all four tribes in equal parts. Isn't that your lore? Doesn't that mean I'm an animal, too?"

"The Child is Axia reborn," Pelin snapped. "And now we'll do everything over. We'll do it right. No more animal tribes. Only the true children of the Mother. Only us."

"And yet, I'm still part of the animal tribes." Aeris shifted, and managed to get a quarrel on the string. Had he noticed? She didn't think so.

"We'll find a way to rid you of the wings," Pelin said. "And in the mountains, we don't have to worry about water. Once the wings are gone, you'll make it all better. You'll do that, because that's what you were born to do. You are Axia come again, and you were born to change the world."

Aeris moved closer. "And if I say no?" she asked. "If I tell you that you're wrong? That there's nothing wrong with Air, or Water?"

Pelin sniffed. "Then you're not the right one," he said. "You're a mistake, just like all the other mistakes. If you're not going to destroy the tainted tribes, you're no good to me." He stepped closer to Aeris, close enough that she could smell dirt and sweat. "But I think you're the right one. You come with me and we'll end all of this."

"Yes," Aeris said. "We will." She raised her arm and fired, and the dart caught Pelin in the throat. He coughed, staggering back a step, sputtering and wheezing. Aeris stepped back and put another quarrel to the string, then fired again.

This one found a home in Pelin's eye, and he dropped like a stone.

"Elaias!" Aeris shouted. "Fa! We need healers!"

KASPIN WAS THIRSTY. He couldn't remember ever being this thirsty, and he wanted salt water more than anything. He licked his lips, and heard a familiar voice.

"Kaspin?"

Someone held his head up, and put a cup to his lips. Kaspin could smell the salt water, and he let them pour it into his mouth, swallowing gratefully.

"He's waking up."

Same voice. Girl's voice. Who?

Oh. Dyna.

If Dyna was there, then...

"Aeris?" He blinked heavy eyelids and looked up. Stone ceiling. Where was he? He coughed and tried to turn his head.

"Easy." A tall, pale man moved into view. "We haven't met. I'm Alanar. And I'm told you have a story to tell me, once you're feeling up to it." He rested his hand on Kaspin's chest and cocked his head to the side. "No lasting damage from the poison."

"What?" Kaspin croaked. "Story?"

Alanar smiled. "I'm told you ripped someone's heart out? I want to hear this. When you're feeling better. For now." He rose and stepped away from the bed as the door opened. Aeris came inside, with Tiras and Gannet right behind her.

"Wait," Kaspin said. "Lancir?"

"It took us a little longer to get to him, so he was a little worse off than you," Alanar answered. "He'll be fine. He's recovering in the next room, and I'll go and let him know you're awake." He left the room, closing the door behind him.

"Want to sit up?" Dyna asked.

"Yes."

It took Dyna and Gannet to help him get into a sitting position, supported by cushions and pillows. Aeris sat down on his left, and Dyna on his right. He put his arms around them both and sighed.

"I'm sorry," he said.

"It's not your fault," Aeris replied. She leaned into him and sighed. "It's not over."

"Not?" Kaspin looked around. "What?"

"We've been talking, while we waited for you to wake up," Gannet said. "And Pelin said that they'd start over. They didn't get what they wanted with Aeris, so they were going to start over. So none of this is over. We've just... postponed things until someone else starts again."

"Unless we stop them," Aeris said.

"Stop how?" Kaspin asked. "Kill?"

"No!" Tiras shook their head emphatically. "No, no killing. Not anymore. We need to show them. Show them that Air and Water aren't animals. That the child of all four tribes is a woman and that's all. That we're all children of the Mother. We need to go out there and shine that light in the darkest places, so the shadows don't have a place to hide."

Kaspin frowned. "Go to the hills?"

Aeris nodded. "Go out there and show them that they're wrong. It won't be easy. It'll be dangerous. But... I can't think of another way to stop this, and I'm tired of people trying to use parts of me to destroy the other parts. I'm tired of being someone's excuse to hate. So I'm going to show them." She looked around the bed. "We're going to show them."

"Firstborn says what?" Kaspin asked.

"She hates the idea," Gannet said. "But she also can't disagree. So... we'll be staying here while you recover, and while supplies and Owyn's Traveler wagon are brought from the Palace. Then we'll head east, and we'll get started."

"Lancir?"

"Won't be coming with us when we go," Dyna said. "His choice. He's afraid that someone will recognize him, and that just being with us will destroy what we're trying to do. So he's staying here to train."

Kaspin nodded and closed his eyes, taking a deep breath. It would mean putting off learning who he was when he was in the deep, but this was more important. He nodded. "How long?"

"We'll be done when we're done," Aeris answered. "Or not at all."

Epilogue

The early morning sun made the Palace shine in the distance, and Aeris smiled. A few hours more, and they'd be home. She looked at the man riding to her right.

"Are you ready to see the sea?"

Kaspin looked skeptical, and it took him a moment before he spoke. "I'm not sure I believe you," he said slowly. "That you can't see the other side."

"You'll see," Gannet said as he rode up next on Kaspin's other side. His wings had finally filled in, and the feathers were shiny and bright in the sun. "You not only can't see the other side, I don't think anyone has been to the other side."

Kaspin snorted. "You're teasing."

"I'm not," Gannet laughed. "You'll see."

"And we should go," Aeris said. She looked at the sky. "It's getting late, and we'll need to stop soon. I'd rather it be a final stop than a break." She looked back at the wagon behind them. "Lance?"

"Everyone is still napping," Lancir called. "Are we stopping or going?"

"Going."

ARIA WAS IN HER OFFICE with Danir when she heard someone shouting.

"Is that Copper?" Danir turned in his chair. "What's wrong?"

Aria stood up as the door opened and Copper burst in. "You have to come down to the Salon," he panted. "You have to come right now."

"Copper, what is it?" Aria demanded. "What's wrong?"

"Nothing. Nothing's wrong." Copper grinned. "Come on." He grabbed her hand and tugged her along with him like he was one of the children. He refused to answer questions, refused to let go, and when Aria tried to dig in her heels, he turned and picked her up.

"You're coming with me right now!" he insisted.

"Fine! Put me down and I'll walk, if it's that important."

Copper put her onto her feet and laughed. "Trust me. When we get there, you'll be angry at me that I didn't rush you more."

"You know, I let you get away with things your father never could have. What's so..." Aria stopped. She studied him for a moment. "Copper, I have never seen you this... giddy. Not even at your wedding. What is it?"

He grinned. "Salon. Now."

Aria laughed and took his hand. "Fine. Salon. I needed to stop working anyway. I... Aven?"

Aven was coming toward them, with Asta leading him. He looked at Aria. "Let me guess. Salon, now?"

"Salon, now," Aria agreed. "And Copper won't tell me why."

"Neither will Asta." Aven took Aria's other hand. "Shall we?"

There seemed to be more people than usual in the halls, servants running back and forth carrying bundles and boxes. As they reached the Salon, Aria heard laughter.

Familiar laughter.

"Aeris?" Aven breathed. Asta darted ahead of them and pulled open the door, and Aria saw her oldest daughter for the first time in two years. She turned and smiled.

"Mama!" Aeris ran into her arms and hugged her tightly. "I've missed you!"

"We've missed you, my dove," Aria murmured. She surrendered Aeris to Aven's embrace, looking around to see that her daughter's Companions had come closer. Gannet had his arm around Tiras, who seemed somehow more grounded. Gannet's wings looked healthy and strong once more. Dyna stood behind them, with Lancir at her side. Then Kaspin came closer. He smiled shyly at her, and looked down at the bundle in his arms.

"Aeris!" Aria gasped. "Is that..."

Aeris laughed and went to Kaspin, taking the bundle from him. She came back, and put the sleeping baby into Aria's arms. "This is Varian," Aeris said. "Your grandson. He's three months old."

"Grandson," Aven repeated. "Aeris..."

"We would have come sooner, but the snows came early, and so did he," Kaspin said. "We stayed at the Temple."

Aven blinked. "You've been practicing," he said. He looked past Kaspin at Dyna, who had come out from behind Tiras. "And you're next? How does Owyn feel about being a grandfather?"

"I don't think he's noticed, to be honest," Dyna answered. "And before you ask, I asked Lexi to send the cutter to Terraces for Fa Allie and for the Senior Healer and Aleia. Depending on the tides, they'll be here late tonight or tomorrow."

"They will be overjoyed to see you. All of you," Aria said. She couldn't take her eyes off the tiny, sleeping face. His hair was dark, his skin the same olive as Aven's, and the soft, gray down of his baby wings was just visible. "Aeris, he's perfect. He's beautiful."

"Mama," Aeris said slowly. "It's... not just good news that we've brought."

Aria looked up. "What?"

Aeris gestured toward the rear of the Salon. Aria saw Del, Owyn, and Treesi there, with two people Aria could only see from the back. Asta went to join them, and the smaller figure turned.

"That's Rhexa," Aven said. "What is she...oh..." His face paled as he realized who the other person was, and what it had to mean. "Frayim. Rhexa and Frayim are here." He looked at Aeris. "When?"

"After the first snow," Dyna answered. "The day Varian was born. He went in his sleep. I... I think he waited to meet the baby."

"The pass down from the Temple was snowed in until right before we left," Tiras added. "So this is the soonest you'd have found out in any case." They looked toward the group, then back at Aven. "I'm sorry. He was your uncle, wasn't he?"

Aven nodded. "Yes. And... oh, is that why Owyn hasn't noticed?"

"He saw Aunt Rhexa first," Dyna answered. "He saw her face, and he knew." She looked back toward the group. "He'll notice once he's had a chance to let the news settle."

"What's going to happen at the Temple now?" Aria asked. "Come and sit."

They moved over to a collection of chairs, and Aria sat down with Aven by her side, while Aeris and her Companions took the other seats. Aria heard movement, and looked up to see Frayim had come to join them. He bowed his head, but said nothing, tucking his hands behind his back.

"When we left the Temple, the priests and the Penitents were choosing a new High Priest. I expect you'll get a messenger in a week or two," Tiras answered. "And... this isn't a vision, but it wouldn't surprise me if the new High Priest was Astur."

"Astur?" Aven repeated. "That's... I didn't realize he'd taken that course."

"Very much so," Aeris said.

"Astur followed his heart and took his vows as a priest not long after you left the Temple, Blesséd Mother," Frayim said. "He told us that he wanted to follow Iantir's example. And he is right. There is still much healing to be done, and it would be a good thing to have the High Priest be a healer as well — putting the world back together needs a healer's touch. Steward approved of him very much."

Aria nodded. "It makes sense. And... Aeris, did you do what you set out to do?"

Aeris leaned into Kaspin's side, sighing as he put his arm around her shoulders. "I think we did," she said. "There were so many who wanted to know that we weren't all that different, no matter if we had feathers or fins, or were healers or dreamers. They wanted to hear that the Mother really did dream us all. I think we found every little village, steading and encampment in the mountains. We met with Wanderers and hill folk and Wingless Air. We healed their sick and talked to them. Listened to them. That was the biggest part of it — the listening. A lot of them, that's all they wanted. They wanted to be heard, and they wanted their fears acknowledged. They wanted to know that they weren't abandoned. They're so alone out there, and even before the Temple fell, there wasn't much contact. We've changed that." She stopped and yawned. "Excuse me!"

"It's been a long day," Tiras said. "So much of this was born in ignorance and forgotten stories. Forgotten connections. Forgotten dreams. So we've set up paths of communication between the hill folk and the Temple, and Astur will make sure that the Temple keeps talking with them and listening to them. I think there's a firm foundation to build on now, because we're all talking again. And we have so many stories for Del — lore that none of us had ever heard before. I wrote them all down, and we're making sure everyone has copies, and making sure that everyone, no matter how far back in the hills they are, can read them. We've arranged for teachers from the Temple, and books from Terraces. And we've updated all the maps, so everyone is on there. There's no way someone is going to get lost and forgotten now."

"That's amazing," Aria said. "You've done so much."

Aeris rested her head on Kaspin's shoulder. "We have. There's more to do, but it's for the Temple to do, now. It was time for us to come home."

"Because your work is done," Frayim said. "The Child has changed the world. Just as the prophecies said."

"Just not the way some of them thought you would," Aven said. "Which is a good thing. Aria, let me hold him."

Aria passed the baby to Aven, then folded her hands in her lap. "Are you going to stay?"

Aeris smiled. "It's time for us to settle. We would have been back before Varian was born, but like Kas said, the snow came early and so did he."

"How early?" Aven asked.

"Three weeks," Dyna answered. "Fa Elaias attended, and everything was fine." She looked over at Aeris and smiled, reaching over to take her hand.

"Fa, I can feel you trying to restrain yourself," Aeris added. "Yes, he has gills."

Aven laughed. "I didn't want to seem too eager."

"You're a new grandfa," Owyn said, coming up behind Aven. "You're allowed." He leaned on the back of the chair and looked down at the baby. "Oh, he looks like he'll be a handful. I bet..." He straightened and looked at Dyna, and his voice trailed off. "I...oh."

"Autumn," Dyna answered. "And we are staying. So you won't miss anything."

Owyn smiled. "And I heard you say that you sent for Allie. He's going to be giddy." He looked over his shoulder. "If no one's told you yet, Auntie Rhexa and Frayim are going to stay, Aria. Rhexa doesn't want to go back to Terraces. She said there are too many memories there."

"Aunt Rhexa and Frayim are more than welcome," Aria said. She looked up as someone knocked on the Salon door.

"I heard a little bird flew home?" Karse called as he came into the Salon. Afansa followed him, and Aeris got up and went to hug both of them. Then she looked past them.

"Where's Uncle Trey? And Howl?"

"Out on the training ground," Karse answered. "Copper finally managed to convince Trey that he can still teach. And it's warm out there, so Howl is with him, sunning his old bones. They're both going to be happy to see their Aeri girl." He looked past them and grinned. "So... Mama Aeri?"

Aeris smiled. "His name is Varian, and Fa might let you admire him."

"I might bite," Aven added. Karse laughed and went over to stand with Owyn.

"I'm having the Heir's suite prepared," Afansa said. "Do you have anything to take up? Luggage?"

"We traveled light," Lancir said. "Nothing that couldn't fit into the wagon. So not much. I can help—"

"You can stay right where you are," Afansa said. "You've had a long road, and it's time you rest."

"We actually have one more thing to do before we settle in," Aeris said. "Fa... Kaspin needs you. And Uncle Othi, if he's here?"

"Needs me?" Aven looked up. "I... oh." He smiled. "I'm honored."

Kaspin blushed slightly. "Now?"

Aven nodded. "Aria, would you take the baby? And someone send for Othi?"

AERIS TOOK A DEEP BREATH and let the sea air settle into her lungs. She shifted Varian in her arms and smiled. The sea was calling her.

"How long does it take?" Lancir asked. "To change? I never asked."

"It takes as long as it takes," Aria answered. She walked up to stand next to Aeris. "You're not dressed to join them, my dove."

"Because this is Kaspin's time," Aeris answered. "I'll swim later. And we have to introduce Varian to the sea. But Kaspin needs this." She looked up the beach, and saw them coming down from the Palace. Aven and Othi were acting as Kaspin's escorts, and they'd dressed him as the Water warrior he was, in a kilt and an open vest. All that he was missing was the tattoos, but now that they were home, Othi would no doubt take care of them. Kaspin stopped as he reached them, looked out at the water, then smiled.

"Time?"

"More than time," Aeris said. She shared a long breath with him, then kissed him and stepped out of his way, watching as her father and uncle escorted him down to the water. They waded out into waist-deep water, and Aven turned to say something to Kaspin. Kaspin nodded, and the three of them dove. For several minutes, nothing happened, and the only sound was the waves against the shore.

"What color will he be?" Owyn asked. "Do we know?"

"We'll find out," Treesi answered. "You don't know until they change the first time. We had no idea with any of the children." She smiled and pointed. "Look!"

Out in the harbor, there was a flash of sunlight on blue-green scales as Othi arched up out of the water, then splashed down to disappear. A second figure arched up, sunlight on silver as Aven launched up and out of the water. He fell back, and Aeris bit her lip.

A moment later, Kaspin appeared, soaring out of the water, black scales glittering and catching the light as the water welcomed him home.

"He's beautiful," Dyna murmured. "Black scales. That's rare, isn't it?"

"I think so. And I think that confirms his canoe – there's only one line I can remember that has black scales. We'll find out when they change back." Aeris looked down at Varian's dark curls. Would his scales be blue, like hers? Or black? Or both?

She couldn't wait to find out.

Aria put her arm around Aeris' shoulders. "Welcome home, my dove."

Axia and the Shadow

Worlds begin. Worlds end. Worlds begin again. So it is with worlds.

In the days when the world was young, when the Mother still dwelled in the hidden places between the sea and the stars, her daughter Axia went walking out into the hills that surrounded their home. She did this often, unable to explain to her mother what it was that she sought. She would go in search of something, and come back and tell tales of what she had seen and done. This time, she did not return, and the Mother went in search of her.

For days, the Mother walked, seeking the way that Axia took, until She at last found the trail half-hidden in shadow. That shadow path led into a valley the Mother had never before seen, one obscured by clouds so heavy that the sun did not shine through, and within the valley, all was sere and dead, and the weight of death and decay lay heavy on Her. As She walked, She called Axia's name, and the shadows came to her call.

"Who are you?" they demanded. "We know you not, and you trespass in our lands."

"I am the Mother. I watch over this world, for it is mine. This valley is mine."

"We know you not," the shadows insisted. "And you are not welcome here." The path grew darker, and the Mother could not find Her way. She retreated to the light, and paused to think and to commune with Adavar.

"My world, my beloved," She called. "Our daughter has gone missing, and her path leads into a valley of shadows where they claim to know me not. Do you know this place?"

Beneath her feet, Adavar rumbled. "The shadows have taken root in that place, and they know only their own darkness. If that darkness is allowed to spread, it will consume all that it touches."

"Then I must return to the valley," the Mother said. "And bring Axia home."

At her feet, a stone began to glow with a warm, amber light.

"Take this," Adavar said. "And let it light Your way. It bears my love for both You and for our daughter."

And so the Mother set Her feet on the path once more, and once more the shadows challenged Her. This time, She did not retreat, pressing deeper into the darkness, bringing with her the shining beacon of light and love. Some of the shadows fled from the light, retreating deeper into the darkness and refusing to face the Mother. Others came closer, curious about something they had never before seen. The Mother welcomed them, and they recognized Her, and knew that they had been led astray. Some were ashamed, and fled from Her back to the depths of the shadows, for it was easier to refuse the light than it was to admit they were misled. Others accepted that they were wrong, and learned from it, and so grew wise as they left the shadows behind.

At last, the Mother reached the valley floor, and there She found the heart of the shadows, the darkest of the dark places. The Mother faced the Shadow, and felt the fear radiating from it.

"You are afraid of me," She said. "Why? I will not harm you. I have only come for my daughter."

"I do not fear you!" the Shadow lied. "She has joined me, and will be my Queen. Now go. You have no place in my realm."

"I would hear this from her own lips, and in her own voice," the Mother insisted. "Where is my daughter?"

"Your daughter does not wish to speak to you," the Shadow said. "And she does not wish to see you. She loves you no longer."

"Now that is a lie," the Mother said. "And you lie when you say you do not fear me. Yet I have done nothing to you. Until today, I did not even know you were here. Why then are you afraid?"

"I am not afraid!" the Shadow insisted. "You and she are different, and that I cannot abide!"

"And yet, you want my daughter for your queen?" The Mother moved closer to the Shadow. "She is different."

"When she is my queen, she will become one of the shadows."

Out of the darkness, the Mother heard Axia's voice. "I will not be your queen! I will not fall to the shadows."

"Axia," the Mother called. "I hear you. Come, and we will go home."

"I hear you, Mother, but I cannot find my way."

The Mother held the beacon given to her by Adavar high, letting the light cut through the darkness. The Shadow howled in rage and attacked Her, throwing her to the ground and knocking the beacon away to be swallowed in darkness.

"You are helpless now," the Shadow said. "You are all that I abhor. The darkness will consume you, and this world shall be mine."

"I have done nothing to you!" the Mother protested, feeling the weight of the darkness pressing down on her, pinning her to the ground in despair. "How can you hate someone you do not know?"

"You are not like me, not like us!" the Shadow answered. "You are different, therefore, you are all that I hate and despise. I will not allow you to remain in this world."

Then the Shadow screamed, and the Mother saw Axia, holding Adavar's beacon high overhead. The beacon shone like a star and the shadows fled before it. Axia came closer, and the Mother felt the despair leave her.

"I will not be yours," Axia said, her voice low. "I do not fear the different, and hate has no place in my world." She held out her other hand. "You can have a place in that world," she added. "Leave behind the fear. Come and see the wonders of the world, and learn to love them."

"I will not!" the Shadow cried. "The world outside this valley is strange, and I refuse!"

"Then you will remain here, alone and unloved, until the world ends," Axia said.

"You cannot defeat me. The stronger the light, the sharper the shadows. I exist, and always will."

"You exist," Axia agreed. "Fear and hatred exist in this world now. But love is and always will be stronger." She helped the Mother to her feet, and they left the valley, returning to their meadows.

"Mother," Axia said as they arrived. "In the darkness, I dreamed. I dreamed of people who are like us, but who are not like us. People of air and of water, of the earth and of the fire. They live in the cliffs over the sea, and in the sea, and in the caves overlooking the sea, and all along the ocean's shore. We must go and find them."

"There are no such people, my darling," the Mother answered.

"There are," Axia insisted. "And we must go and find them, for among them are the ones who will stand with me against the shadows. We must go and find them."

The Mother agreed, and together they left behind the hidden places between the seas and the stars.

Worlds begin. Worlds end. Worlds begin again. So it is with worlds.

Also by Elizabeth Schechter

Heir to the Firstborn
Worlds Begin
Written in Water
Forged in Fire
Bones of Earth
Wings of Air
Visions in Smoke
Children of Dreams
Valley of Shadows

Rebel Mage
Counsel of the Wicked
Haven's Fall
Where Home Lies
Rebel Mage: The Complete Series

Swords of Charlemagne
Hidden Things
The Lady and the Sword
Ashes and Light

Table of Stone
Swords of Charlemagne: The Complete Series

Standalone
The Rape of Persephone
Fools Rush In
Her Captive
To Market
Infernal Machine
Chains of Light
The Chronicles of John Zebedee
Snowbound

Watch for more at elizabethschechterwrites.com.

About the Author

Elizabeth Schechter has been called one of the top erotica and alternative sexuality writers in the world. Her writing credits include the award-winning steampunk erotic romance *House of Sable Locks*, the Celtic fantasy *Princes of Air*, and 2021 VIVIAN finalist *Written in Water*.

She was born in New York at some point in the past. She is officially old enough to know better, but refuses to grow up. She lives in Central Florida with her husband and son.

Elizabeth can be found online at http://elizabethschechterwrites.com, or on Facebook at https://www.facebook.com/Elizabeth.A.Schechter. You can also find her on Patreon, at https://www.patreon.com/EASchechter.

Subscribe to Elizabeth's newsletter at https://www.subscribepage.com/k4u7k2

Read more at elizabethschechterwrites.com.